G000152079

The Vera Conundrum

Martin Thompson

Design: Lisa Kirkham

Typeset in Kingfisher

Cover image: head, 1933 circa linocut by Ben Nicholson
© Angela Verren Taunt. All rights reserved, DACS 2022
Courtesy of Kettle's Yard Cambridge

Acknowledgements

The author wishes to thank Jo Browning Wroe and the members of her creative writing group who gave their advice and encouragement. And of course, grateful thanks go to Jenny for her editing skills and support throughout.

Prologue

BEFORE THE UNFORTUNATE INCIDENT had sent him scurrying home to recover, Miles Mallalieu had found himself in an uncharacteristically buoyant mood on that bright early autumn morning.

The daily commute involved a short scooter ride from his flat near London's Oxford Street to the Department of Ancient History, housed in a minor Fitzrovian square. The cool air whistled through his helmet straps, creating a catchy hum which seemed to increase his good humour as he sped through the traffic-thronged streets.

Had his goggles been marginally less smeared, he might have spotted the obstacle a second or two earlier. As the car door swung open directly in his path, Miles was obliged to take avoiding action. Squeezing the brakes hard, he somehow succeeded in bringing the scooter to a halt barely an inch from the young male driver who had been climbing out, oblivious to impending disaster.

The scooter began to totter tipsily before keeling over. To Miles' astonishment, he had remained vertical, legs arched like a rodeo rider whose mount has bolted from under him. His gaze now turned to the weasel-like features of the driver who had tumbled back into the car. As shock gave way to anger, Miles tapped on the window and prepared to berate the youth for his extreme carelessness. Before he could mouth the words, the window rolled down and the fist shot out like a well-oiled piston. A second blow of equal force followed, capped by a torrent of abuse. Miles stood transfixed in disbelief as his assailant, anger now assuaged, sped off down the street.

✦

"How many times must I tell you, it was his fault?"insisted Miles, nursing his jaw.

"Nonsense. You weren't concentrating, as usual," his older sister replied. "You live in cloud cuckoo land, Miles, wherever that is. In your case, somewhere that disappeared under the sand millennia ago. I've never met anyone with so little awareness of the world around him." Elspeth paused to give her brother's injury a cursory examination, cupping his jaw in her bony hand, causing him to flinch.

"That's very painful, I'll have you know."

"It's only superficial," Elspeth replied. "I haven't got time to be your nursemaid. Arnica will soothe it. If it was his fault," she added, "then why on earth did you let him get away with it? Sounds as if you literally turned the other cheek. Typical. I suppose the machine's a complete write-off?"

Miles nodded wearily. The acquisition of the second hand Vespa had been Elspeth's idea, a response to his constant laments about having to leave home on foot at an ungodly hour to deliver his nine o'clock lecture to ungrateful students. It was obvious to him that the experiment would end badly. At the age of 55, or was it 56? Miles had lost count, he considered himself too old for such two-wheeled shenanigans.

"Got to go," said Elspeth. "Can't be late for bridge. Aren't you going away?"

"Wednesday. If I recover," said Miles, without looking up.

Elspeth shrugged. "Yet another jaunt at the taxpayer's expense. Where to this time?"

"Chicago. And how many times do I have to tell you they're not jaunts, they're valuable fora for exchanging ideas," replied Miles indignantly. He was not about to give his sister the satisfaction of admitting he was beginning to tire of dragging himself to these annual parades of inflated egos.

"I hope you're going to get that shabby blazer cleaned before you go. You seem determined to make yourself unappealing. What hope is there of you finding any female selfless or desperate enough to take you on?"

Miles expelled a deep sigh. Were Elspeth and he destined to remain forever locked in this state of low-level warfare? The answer, he decided, was affirmative, unless his sister made any move to find a place of her own. After a messy divorce in her late forties had left her allegedly penniless, six years on, there was no sign of her giving up her rent-free co-occupation of the tiny former tenement flat which Miles had occupied since postgraduate days.

Miles sunk further into the battered leather Chesterfield. "Don't just sit there brooding...ring the Department and tell them you'll be in. A minor mishap's no excuse for letting them down," she added, before turning on her heels.

It was with some relief that he watched Elspeth's tall, spindly frame disappear before rising slowly and shuffling towards the bathroom. He smeared a dollop of Arnica cream on his cheek which did nothing to dull the pain. The sight of his fleshy jowls prompted him to turn away from the mirror with a shudder. There was no doubt that the morning's road rage incident had taken its toll. He would need time to recover his equilibrium before the Chicago conference which, if nothing else, would provide a respite from his sister's constant carping.

He waited until he heard the front door shut before extracting the diminutive replica statuette from its hiding place at the back of his bedroom cupboard. A few minutes in Her presence would provide some badly needed solace. Were Elspeth to stumble upon this ritual, it would simply reinforce her view of her brother's behaviour as bizarre, bordering on the disturbed. How could he explain that he could talk to this idol without fear of being judged?

Placing the Venus-like figure with burgeoning belly on the rug, Miles sank slowly to his knees, never a pain-free manoeuvre. Eyes squeezed shut, he launched into a short eulogy of his own devising, extolling the virtues of the ancient Phoenician goddess of fertility, and humbly requesting her support in his struggle to cope with the vicissitudes of daily life. Reaching into a drawer, he extracted a Bounty Bar which he placed before the statuette as a votive offering. Astarte, he had decided, had a sweet tooth which must be indulged.

CHAPTER ONE

Chicago blues

"Are you with the exterminators?"

"I beg your pardon?" replied Miles, edging uneasily away from the only other occupant of the hotel lift. Had he stumbled on a convention of freelance assassins?

The burly questioner in a shiny suit pointed proudly to his badge. "Exterminators of America, eradicating pests of all shapes and sizes. It's our yearly jamboree."

"I'm with the ancient historians... our annual symposium..." muttered Miles, fumbling to retrieve his conference badge from his pocket. He had no wish to be mistaken for a rodent killer.

"Let's hope we don't get mixed up!" the man guffawed.

Miles managed a half smile. Much to his relief, a staccato ping announced their arrival at ground level.

"Ancient historian, you say? No offence intended but you sure look the part!" added the rat catcher with a broad grin before vanishing into the throng of guests crowding around the arriving lift. Having waited for the lift hall to empty, Miles made his way warily towards the centre of the vast glass-domed lobby to ponder his next move. He was already regretting his decision to make a token appearance at the pre-conference reception.

He spotted a group of all-too-familiar faces gathered at the bar in a corner of the lobby. Taking a deep breath, Miles manoeuvred his way into the raucous crowd of fellow delegates. As ever, the American voices were the shrillest while the Scandinavians boomed away, laughing heartily at their own witticisms. Towering above them all was a bearded, Viking-like figure. Miles pressed on towards the bar. He would need to fortify himself before having to face Lars Christiansen's inevitable probing as to the progress of his much-delayed magnum opus.

As ever on these occasions, Lars was encircled by a bevy of younger academics, hanging on to his every word. And as ever, his attention was chiefly reserved for the females among them, his eyes bright with the prospect of sexual conquest. Miles observed this scene disapprovingly. He had always prided himself on remaining above such tawdry conference carryings-on. Yet, as he was forced to admit, in all the years he had been attending these events, he had not once been presented with such an opportunity.

Ignoring a beckoning gesture from Lars, Miles decided on a temporary retreat. He was feeling queasy after a turbulent flight and his jaw was still aching. Finding an unpopulated corner of the lobby, he lowered himself into an armchair. Had he taken more interest in his surroundings, he would have acknowledged the nod of greeting from the elderly pianist tinkering away at a white piano nearby. His expression of mild disdain seemed to imply that anyone who has nothing better to do than listen to his Muzak should regard themselves as a social failure.

"Can I get you anything, sir?" A waiter had appeared, startling Miles out of his reverie. He ordered a vodka Martini, strictly for restorative purposes. The first sip induced an instant lightening of mood. By the fourth sip, Miles was feeling positively ebullient. He was about to reconsider joining his colleagues when his attention was aroused by a raised female voice cutting across the mellifluous piano chords. Miles was able to make out a woman, possibly in her early forties, with wavy shoulder-length hair. Although partly obscured by the fronds of a large potted palm, he could see that she was talking animatedly into a mobile phone, her expression etched with fury.

As the diatribe, in a language Miles recognised as Slavic, grew more intense, he found himself gripped. There was a something strangely compelling about this fiery woman. Was she a fellow delegate? Could she possibly be an exterminator? Miles permitted himself a smile at this unlikely prospect. As she stabbed at her phone to end the call, he caught her gaze. Averting his eyes, he stared into his empty cocktail glass with feigned nonchalance.

"Kids! They suck the blood. Why do we have them?" the woman exclaimed, before hurling herself into the vacant chair beside Miles. "If she wants to mess up her life, who am I to stop her?" she added, breaking off to glance towards him. "You don't mind if I sit here?" Her English was fluent but heavily accented.

Miles could only release a nervous grunt as she settled back and begun prising off her high heels. "If she doesn't kill me, these shoes will. What is that you are drinking?" the woman asked while massaging her exposed feet. "Whatever it is, I need one badly."

"It's a Martini. Strong stuff," replied Miles with a nervous laugh.

Vera snapped her fingers. The waiter appeared without delay and hovered unctuously. "We will have two more of the same.... You really don't mind me disturbing you?" asked Vera turning to Miles. "I just needed to talk to someone...normal." She tossed her phone on the low table and stretched out her legs while peering at Miles' conference badge. "Dr Miles Mall.. al..ieu." Vera savoured the syllables. "Do you have children, Miles?"

He shook his head. "And you are?" he asked hesitantly.

Miles' myopia forced him to squint nervously at her lapel badge which read 'Dr Vera Petrovna. University of St Petersburg.'

"You must call me Vera. We are both delegates. Of course! Mallalieu...I have made the connection now. It's strange we have never met. Your early work on the Phoenicians was very influential in its day."

Miles felt his face flame. "That's kind of you to say so. These days I feel I am quietly fading into oblivion."

"You are a modest man, I like that," replied Vera. "Maybe you know my work on Cycladic burial practices?"

"Perhaps so," he replied. In truth, he had no memory of ever having encountered it.

"You are very generous too." The waiter had reappeared and Miles found himself insisting on signing for both drinks. "This will get my daughter out of my head. Za zdorovie! Cheers," added Vera, gulping down her cocktail as if it were lemonade.

Having been coerced into clinking glasses, a custom Miles normally resisted, droplets spattered his shirt front. He was about to dab them off discreetly with his sleeve when Vera delved in her bag. As she leant forward to proffer a tissue, Miles could not help but notice the absence of a wedding ring. She raised her glass to clink once again. This time Miles responded with greater enthusiasm. He was beginning to relish this sparky encounter.

"Are you and I going to be anti-social?" asked Vera, indicating the small cluster of fellow delegates lingering by the bar on the far side of the lobby.

"Yes I rather think we are," replied Miles beaming as he settled back into the armchair.

"That's good. Because I want to get to know all about you," said Vera, planting her hand gently on his forearm. Miles felt the last drop of tension drain from his body. The Chicago trip had already yielded unexpected fruits. If only Elspeth could see him now.

✦

Miles had awoken to find a narrow shaft of sunlight boring through a chink in the heavy curtains. He groped for his glasses, cursing himself for neglecting to ask for a wake-up call. His skull felt as if it had been trampled on by an elephant and his throat was as dry as papyrus. How had he come to be in this state? He could recall accepting Vera's offer of a fourth Martini but beyond that, his memory was a void.

He fingered the collar of his flannel pyjamas. He had no recollection of changing into them. Discombobulated, he hauled himself out of bed and pulled back the curtains. The sharp Midwestern sunlight seared into his eyes. Turning away from the glare, his gaze fell on the clothes he had worn the day before which, to his surprise, had been neatly folded on the armchair.

This was equally puzzling. He knew for certain he would never have gone to such lengths whatever state he had been in. He was far more likely to have fallen asleep fully dressed. It was only then that he spotted the folded note propped up on the sideboard. He picked it up gingerly and retrieved his glasses. The writing was flowery yet precise. A woman's hand beyond doubt. He studied it as if it were an ancient manuscript. 'You collapsed on me. Let's speak when you wake up. V x'

Before he could absorb this find, the phone by the bed began trilling. Miles hurried to answer it. He was confronted not as he had hoped with Vera's voice but with the conference organiser's southern drawl. "How are you this morning, Dr Mallalieu? Are you on track to deliver your paper? Just checking as we hadn't seen you at breakfast."

"Yes, yes of course," replied Miles curtly, only too aware that there would be little chance to review the rehashed lecture on Phoenician trade patterns he was due to deliver in less than ninety minutes. He replaced the phone and fingered Vera's note. She would undoubtedly be there for his paper. Afterwards, they would find a quiet corner to talk. Where could he take her to dinner?

❖

Battling the legacy of jet lag and alcohol, Miles stumbled his way through to his conclusion as if on auto-pilot. The lukewarm applause he received confirmed his lacklustre performance.

The truth was his mind was elsewhere. At several points, he had looked up from his notes to scan the rows of semi-attentive faces. The fact that there was no apparent sign of Vera Petrovna was both perplexing and disappointing. As he gathered together his notes at the end, eager young academics hovered around the lectern, anxious to buttonhole him to promote their own half-baked theses. Miles gave them polite but scant attention before sliding away to the lobby. Having found a house phone, he asked to be put through to Dr Petrovna's room.

"I'm sorry sir but there is no one of that name currently registered as a guest."

The operator was adamant. Further enquiries at the reception desk revealed that Vera had checked out at nine that morning. There was no further note, nothing to explain her unscheduled departure. Slumping disconsolately in a chair, Miles stared vacantly at the departing guests trailing oversized suitcases. Had she been embarrassed about what may or may not have taken place in his bedroom the previous evening and had been reluctant to face him? Would that be reason for her to leave a conference that had barely started. It was all rather strange and dispiriting.

Distraction came in the form of the smell of bacon seeping out of the nearby breakfast room. There had been no time to eat before giving his paper and Miles realised he was ravenous. As he ladled generous quantities of maple syrup onto his blueberry pancakes topped with crispy bacon, he came to the reluctant conclusion that all further thoughts of Vera Petrovna would have to be abandoned.

CHAPTER TWO

Metropolitan matters

"Welcome back. It's good to see you, Miles. Chin chin." They clinked glasses before tucking into the rich, dark minestrone soup into which Miles had ladled quantities of grated parmesan. The prospect of Elspeth cooking supper had failed to materialise and, on his second night home, Marian appeared only too pleased to join him at La Giaconda, the shabby but reliable Italian off Gower Street which they had patronised over the years. Twice-divorced, Marian had been a member of the non-academic staff since Miles' arrival at the Department as a postdoctoral student twenty five years earlier. He had come to think of Marian as an 'old sock' friend in whom he could confide although, on this occasion, he failed to make any mention of his encounter with Vera Petrovna.

Marian's current role as PA to the Director placed her in a powerful position. There was little that took place within the Department without her knowledge. She had worked for a succession of long-serving academics who had been elevated to the top post despite lacking any semblance of management skills. Inevitably, each would become dependent on her. The current incumbent, Tony Barstow, known to his few admirers as 'Wunderkind', was no exception. He had quickly learnt to appreciate the value of Marian's role as guardian of the inner sanctum, willing to cover for his unexplained absences between two and four on Tuesdays and Thursdays.

"I was going to call you anyway. We have to talk shop." Marian glanced nervously around the restaurant which was a favourite haunt of older faculty members. The coast seemed clear. "Tony wants to see you first thing in the morning and you'll need to think about how you are going to play it."

Miles had never warmed to this ambitious younger man whose dubious PhD he had supervised. "What does he want to see me about?" The summons filled him with disquiet.

"You don't need me to remind you that you haven't published anything for at least three years."

"There have been articles, quite a few actually," replied Miles defensively.

"They don't count, and you know it. We've got to get some more weighty publications out there to give us brownie points." Marian placed her hand on his sleeve. "Tony's going to put a thumbscrew on you to finish the book."

Miles' knees began shaking. He guessed that she knew full well that the long-delayed definitive work on Phoenician penetration of the Western Mediterranean was far from complete. Greeks from Asia Minor and Carthaginians had established colonies on Corsica long before the arrival of the Romans. Yet what of those most ubiquitous of seafarers and traders, the Phoenicians? For the past twenty or more years, Miles had been searching for evidence that they had established flourishing settlements on the island. Fellow scholars of early Mediterranean history were uniformly dismissive of such a concept. Yet Miles knew that if he could be proved right, the entire history of the Mediterranean Basin would have to be revised. The truth was he was stuck, in desperate need of new material evidence. He stared past Marian at the faded mural of rustic life. He had never liked its leering figures tending their flocks of skeletal goats, and now both man and beast seemed to taunt him.

"Are you listening, Miles?" asked Marian. "You know what this means? The Vice Chancellor will use our lousy publishing record as an excuse to cut our budget to the bone. Not that he needs any excuse. We're a soft touch. They're trying to close us down Miles and you're a major part of the problem. At least that's what Tony thinks." Marian took a large swig of Montepulciano. "There. I've said it. Sorry to be the messenger of doom."

Their spaghetti vongole arrived to break the moment and, as was his habit, Marco, the proprietor, made suggestive play with the black pepper grinder. Marian responded with her customary stage wink. Miles retained an unspoken awkwardness about his friend's penchant for tightly-fitting tops with a low cleavage. No doubt he was a prude, he told himself, but it seemed to him to send out the wrong signals.

Once Marco had departed, Marian's expression darkened. "You're just going to have to lie to Tony. Tell him it's nearly finished – a few months at the most. Don't give him the ammunition he's looking for."

"What do you mean, ammunition?" Miles began twirling spaghetti on his fork.

"To get rid of you."

"He couldn't do that." Miles could feel the sweat forming on his brow.

"We can't be too sure about that. Don't say I haven't warned you." Marian tapped her upper lip twice as if to indicate to Miles that he should attend to his mouth.

"Haven't you got anything cheerier to tell me?" asked Miles, dabbing his lip.

"I hate to spoil your meal but there's something else you need to know," Marian continued.

"I'm not sure I can take any more bad news tonight. Can't it wait?" asked Miles.

"No I'm afraid it can't." Marian refilled their glasses. "It's not only your publication rate, it's your teaching. There've been complaints from students. You don't officially know yet, but you've been marked near the bottom of the scale for lecturing skills and general attentiveness. Apparently you never answer students' emails."

"I do reply, eventually. I've been having trouble with my laptop."

"Miles, that's no excuse and you know it." Marian sighed. A look of concern spread over her face. "You're going to have to seem surprised when Tony brings all this up and have your answers ready. Do you want to rehearse them with me?"

"I need some air," said Miles, shaking his head. He was feeling distinctly bilious. Pushing away the pasta, he rose from his chair. Marian signalled to the attentive Marco and explained that the food was delicious as ever, but that Dr Mallalieu was not feeling well and they would have to cut short their meal. Having settled the bill, she helped Miles to negotiate the narrow stairs leading up to the street.

It was drizzling heavily as they emerged and Marian linked arms to enable Miles to share her umbrella. Further conversation was postponed until they reached the corner of Southampton Row. She turned to face him as they waited for the lights to change. "Feeling better?" Miles nodded. He reminded himself that Marian was a true friend, perhaps his only one. "What are you going to say to Tony?"

"I haven't a clue, Marian. I haven't a clue."

"OK, here's a suggestion to take the sting out of his tail," she said as they walked on, avoiding clashes with oncoming umbrellas. "There's this Chinese postdoc. You know who I mean. Chunhua, she's the one complaining most about you. As it happens, her dad is a Hong Kong property billionaire and they've got him marked out as a potential benefactor. Complicates things a bit as you can imagine."

"That girl?" said Miles. "They should never have offered her a place. Her English is atrocious and her first degree is highly dubious."

"That's beside the point Miles, and you know it. Why don't you email her first thing in the morning and offer her a one-to-one? Apologise for not getting back to her. You've been away after all. You might just get her to withdraw her complaint."

The crowds were beginning to thicken. Miles clutched at Marian's arm as they steered their way through a swarm of bright-eyed young faces. "I shouldn't be telling you this," Marian continued "but it's not only the size of her father's bank balance that Tony's interested in. I came across them in his office one evening. I'd had to pop back for my mobile. He was showing her some ancient manuscript. The body language was a dead giveaway. If I'd arrived five minutes later, things might have gone further."

"How did the girl react?" asked Miles who had long suspected that Tony took advantage of his position.

"She looked highly embarrassed. She's probably terrified that her father will get to hear about it. This could be your only leverage, if you see what I mean."

"Are you really suggesting I would stoop so low?" asked Miles, smiling at the absurd prospect of his becoming a blackmailer.

They had reached the entrance to her mansion block off Drury Lane. "Do you want to come up for a night cap? I'm afraid I rather put you through it," said Marian.

"Thank you but no. I need to catch up with some sleep."

"Well don't forget to set your alarm. The Wunderkind wants to see you at ten sharp. And Miles, be prepared for his tricks."

Having pecked him on the cheek, Marian vanished inside. He stared after her before turning wearily towards home.

✦

"How was your meal?"

Elspeth was curled up in her usual feline position in a corner of the Chesterfield devouring the latest Joanna Trollope. She was, in her own parlance, a night bird.

"Fine. Don't let me disturb your reading." Miles scurried towards the bathroom, anxious to avoid further interrogation.

"What's the gossip from the Department then?" Elspeth called out, undeterred. "I imagine Marian was her usual indiscreet self."

"If you must know, things are not looking good," said Miles, about to shut the bathroom door.

"Are they going to close you down? Survival of the fittest and all that. They'd have to find something else for you to do. Can't have you hanging round the flat all day."

"I don't want to do anything else," said Miles crossly. "Now if you'll forgive me, I've got an early start."

Miles began to brush his teeth in a desultory way. If only Elspeth was a different person, he reflected. He would be able to unburden himself from time to time. It would only seem fair. She was more than willing to dump her emotional detritus on him. He would particularly like to have brought up the subject of Vera Petrovna, her kindness and her vanishing act, but for the second time that evening he felt inhibited about mentioning her.

✦

Miles slept fitfully, still under the influence of jet lag. He was woken by the dreary cooing of pigeons perched on his bedroom window ledge. Having opened the curtains, the change in the weather had the effect of marginally raising his spirits. The endless rain had given way to a brilliant early autumn morning. He began to feel almost bullish about his forthcoming encounter with Tony Barstow. He would go on the offensive. Marian would be proud of him.

Having set off on foot, Miles rewarded himself with a double expresso and almond croissant at Dino's sandwich bar en route. Suitably energised, he strode purposefully up the Department steps and paused to check his post. As usual, his pigeon hole was overflowing. A cursory sifting of its contents revealed that there was nothing that could not wait.

"Ah Miles. Can I have a wee word?" Gavin Armstrong stood at the foot of the staircase blocking Miles' progress.

"I'm due to see Tony in ten minutes. Can't it wait?" said Miles, trying to avoid his gaze.

Gavin was a broad shouldered Scot with piercing eyes, a ginger beard and unreformed Trotskyite views. Miles had no wish to be dragged into the dialectical quick sands which were Gavin's natural habitat.

"That's exactly why I need to speak to you," replied Gavin without giving way.

"Very well," said Miles, allowing himself to be steered into a quiet corner of the entrance hall.

"I just wanted you to know that we are all with you." Gavin's eyes were ablaze.

"How do you mean?" asked Miles.

"In your struggle against Barstow. Remember Miles, united we stand!" With that exhortation, Gavin darted away up the stairs, pausing to call out: "You're our knight in shining armour!"

Miles was far from certain that the support of Gavin and his cabal would improve his chances of escaping retribution. What, he wondered, had Marian been putting about? He must try and have a word with her before seeing Tony.

✦

As it happened, Marian was conspicuously absent from her station outside the door of Tony's office. The door was ajar and Miles knocked twice. There being no response, he decided to announce his presence via a pointed clearing of his throat.

"Ah Miles," said Tony, finally looking up from his mahogany desk which, as colleagues liked to jest, was as over-sized as his ego. There were none of the customary pleasantries and Miles awaited the expected onslaught. He could not help but notice that Tony's expression was strained and his normally baby-smooth features framed with an arc of stubble. Far from taking the offensive, Tony remained oddly silent. Miles was left to find a seat and gaze out of the window at the canopy of plane trees. Perhaps he going to have an easy ride after all? Yet Marian had warned him to stay on his guard and he would heed her words. Tony's demeanour suddenly darkened and he seemed to Miles to be on the verge of tears. Finally, Tony rose from behind the desk and began to mumble incoherently. Straining to catch his words, Miles thought he overheard:

"Things are not looking good for me," and "I need your advice."

"Would you like me to get you a glass of water?" was all Miles could think to say.

The Director shook his head feebly and eventually shuffled back to sit behind his desk. He showed no signs of regaining his composure. Instead, he began pounding the leather surface, sending his pen and diary flying. Miles felt ill-equipped to handle this unravelling situation. Could this be the prelude to a nervous breakdown? Miles recalled two former directors who had resigned citing unspecified health issues. He peered through the open door but there was still no sign of Marian. Should he engage Tony in general conversation to take his mind off whatever was disturbing him? Some gesture of support for a fellow human in distress seemed appropriate.

Had Tony received news of the impending closure of the Department? While Miles was struggling with this uncomfortable thought, Tony slowly opened the top drawer of his desk and extracted a hand-written letter which he slid towards Miles. A rapid scan of its contents revealed it to be from Tony's wife's solicitor informing him that she was suing for divorce and would be seeking custody of their child.

"I'm very sorry indeed, Tony," said Miles lamely. It was then that the Director began to sob. Spotting a box of Kleenex on the far side of the desk. Miles reached over and, extracting some tissues, created a crumpled pile by Tony's elbow.

"I'll be upstairs...just a phone call away. Perhaps you should take the rest of the day off?" Miles added, backing towards the door. As he passed through the still empty outer office, the sobs became a low moan of despair.

✦

After seeking refuge in his cubby hole of an office, Miles attempted to dissect the encounter with Tony. It had been an immeasurable relief to have escaped confrontation but he had been left in uneasy limbo. He needed to discuss the implications with Marian but there was no answer from her extension. Perhaps she had a dental appointment? He found it strange that she had given no hint of her boss's personal problems over dinner the previous evening. Despite Elspeth's opinion of her as a gossip, Marian may have erred on the side of discretion.

Miles switched on his veteran desktop computer. Having gazed abstractedly at the blue bar as it crept along at snail's pace, he discovered his inbox was awash with unopened emails. He began to work through them, his cursor poised on the delete icon. One missive inviting him to make contact with young Russian women seeking husbands in the West caught his eye but was summarily deleted. Inevitably, his thoughts turned to Vera. Her unexplained disappearance still rankled.

He sent a slew of holding replies to the most persistent correspondents and then checked his diary which was mercifully empty for the remainder of the day. Miles knew he should seize the moment to continue drafting his book but despite several recent attempts, he was unable to settle into the task beyond re-shaping his last sentence, only to return it to its original form.

Having crept down the main stairs and managing to avoid Gavin, Miles paused on the outer steps. Ahead lay the square and its well-tended public gardens dotted with students and office workers basking in what the forecasters had predicted would be the last gasps of an Indian summer. A decision was reached. He would allow himself the luxury of sitting without purpose until he felt sufficiently revitalised to return to his desk. The benches within sight were all occupied and Miles was forced to hover in mid-path until a vacancy appeared. Finally, a young couple disengaged from their glue-like embrace and as they wandered away, turned to give him a sympathetic smile as he took their place.

Feeling strangely uneasy without something to read, Miles fixed his gaze on the pigeons that strutted between the benches, willing morsels to tumble from over-filled baguettes. He closed his eyes and allowed his breathing to slow. He was distracted by a deep-throated cough. He looked up to see a heavily-bearded vagrant pushing a supermarket trolley laden with newspapers towards him, searching in vain for a seat as occupants of benches scrambled pointedly to spread themselves out. Before Miles could react, the vagrant had squeezed in beside him. Miles shuffled his bulk to create more space but despite this, their thighs were jammed together. The acrid odour seeping from his neighbour's soiled gabardine raincoat was overpowering. He fumbled for his handkerchief and to camouflage the urge to retch, made a great play of blowing his nose. By now, the benches around them had emptied and they were alone. Miles was about to make his escape when a large bottle of cider was extracted from the cart and waved in his face. He politely brushed the bottle away.

"You don't recognize me, do you?" The voice had a North Atlantic burr.

"I'm sorry. Should I?" Miles burbled. "I've no memory for faces, I'm afraid."

"I'll give you a clue...Mesopotamian ziggurats."

"Crosswords aren't my forte," said Miles, stifling the rising bile.

"My paper. You were the only one to endorse its conclusions."

"What paper?" asked Miles.

"Oh come on Miles, you remember."

Miles bristled with alarm at the mention of his name. There was indeed something unnervingly familiar about the timbre of the man's voice. His thoughts were dragged back to a conference in Ankara in 2005 or thereabouts. He recalled there had been this American who had held forth each night in the hotel bar. In those days, Miles was open to joining such brandy-fuelled sessions where new collaborations were often formed away from the formal hustings. Could this derelict creature be the same academic who had attracted a regular crowd with his anecdotes and stories? Miles recalled that he had been destined for a senior post in a leading Ivy League university. He had read subsequently that there had been a scandal, an accusation of plagiarism, a prison sentence for drunken driving. Now here he was sleeping rough on the streets of London. What on earth was his name?

"OK, let me jog your memory. It's me, Doug...Doug Allardyce," said the vagrant, belching a plume of dog breath in Miles' direction.

"Ah yes of course, Doug. It's nice to er... see you again," replied Miles, aware of the lack of conviction in his voice. "Now if you'll forgive me, I must be..."He raised himself from the bench.

"Hey, don't you wanna know why I'm here?"asked Doug. Miles shook his head. "I'll tell you why. I can watch you all come and go, you slaves to the Great Machine. It gives me a real kick. And besides, I've got nowhere else to go. Hey Miles, any chance you could offer me a floor for the night?"

Miles felt his cheeks colouring. It would be hard to imagine Elspeth's reaction were he to turn up with this evil-smelling former academic with his trolleyful of detritus. Should he not act the Good Samaritan though? How could it be that

Allardyce had sunk so low? There but for the grace of God etc.. Miles began to back away nonetheless, extending his right arm in a hesitant wave.

"I was only kidding...about the bed. I just wanted to see your face if I asked," chuckled Doug. "You in some kind of trouble by any chance? Being on the road gives you a sixth sense about people. Not in love are you, Miles? Don't let the bastards get you down. You don't want to end up like me."

✦

Miles was chewing over the encounter when he almost collided with a young Chinese woman as he turned the corner of the street. Her appearance was familiar despite the fact that she was walking head bowed, studying her smart phone. Miles was about to let her pass when it struck him that this would be an opportunity to follow Marian's advice. He turned to pursue her, and having caught up with her, tapped her lightly on the shoulder.

"Dr Mallalieu!"

"I'm sorry to startle you. I've been meaning to have a word." The young woman smiled vacantly.

"I'm afraid I've been rather slow to answer emails lately. Computer troubles, you know. Perhaps you have time for a coffee?" Miles added reticently.

She shook her head. "I'm on my way to meet a friend. I'm a little late already. Another day maybe?" Despite her reassuring expression, Miles was aware that she was keen to conclude the encounter.

"No matter. I was simply going to say...how are things going...with your work I mean?'"

"Fine, thank you, Dr Mallalieu. It's kind of you to ask. I always found your comments very helpful."

"Really?" replied Miles, trying to suppress his sense of relief. "And my lectures?" he ventured. "How do you find those? Some people say I mumble..."

She smiled reassuringly. "They were always very inspiring."

"Do you not plan to continue attending them this term? May I ask, is it because of...?"

"I'm not sure I follow you, Dr Mallalieu."

"I was told you had made a complaint about my teaching." There. He had blurted it out.

"Perhaps you don't remember me, Joy Lan. I graduated last year. I'm just passing through London to visit friends."

Miles swallowed hard. "I'm terribly sorry. Joy...of course. I mistook you for... Really this is most embarrassing."

"That is perfectly alright, it happens all the time." She gave a short bow. "Good bye Dr Mallalieu."

Miles stared after his former student with a deep sense of dismay. Two troubling encounters in one morning. The day could only improve. Yet Miles could not erase the image of Doug Allardyce from his mind. In a perverse kind of way, he decided that he rather envied the former academic's lot – the freedom from social norms, the licence to speak one's mind and above all, a release from the treadmill of publishing deadlines.

✦

En route home from the Department two evenings later, he was still pondering Doug Allardyce's fate as he waited on the corner of Great Titchfield Street before crossing the road. Miles checked his watch. It was almost six. He had time to kill if he was not to reach home until after Elspeth had left for her spiritualist meeting. He remembered guiltily that he had yet to make contact with Marian who had failed to return his phone calls. For all he knew, she may have been taken ill and might welcome a visit to cheer her up. He was also keen to discover what she might know about Tony Barstow's marital breakdown and his general state of mind. Decision made, Miles turned on his heels and headed south towards Marian's flat.

As he rounded the corner, Miles spotted him emerging from the entrance to Marian's block. The tall, angular frame and jut of the chin were all too familiar. Pausing at the base of the steps, the Director glanced up and down the street before scuttling away into the gathering dusk. Miles propped himself against the nearest wall and attempted to make sense of this sighting. Despite his badly-scuffed lenses, he felt sure that his eyes had not been playing tricks. As far as he was aware, Marian's relationship with her boss did not extend beyond office hours. Of course, Miles told himself, Tony may have been visiting someone else in the same block, or it would not even be too outlandish to imagine that he maintained a secret pied-à-terre if the rumours peddled by the gabbier members of the faculty were to be believed. Yet was it not also conceivable that, in his distressed state, Tony had called on his personal assistant to seek a sympathetic ear? Wherever the truth lay, Miles was sufficiently unnerved by the sighting to abort his plan to call on his friend. Instead, he headed for home.

✦

Miles heard the muffled voices as he was about to insert the key. Placing his ear to the front door, he could make out

Elspeth talking in an animated tone, followed by a peel of laughter shared with an unidentified female. He often suspected that his sister had a jovial side and here was proof. But who was she entertaining at a time when she was due to be elsewhere? It was as rare as hens' teeth for anyone to be invited to the flat. If there was a chance that the visitor was one of Elspeth's fellow dabblers into the spirit world, he would have to make his excuses and retreat to the pub.

In his attempt to unlock the door, Miles let slip the bunch of keys. They reverberated with a clatter as they bounced off the tiled corridor floor. The voices inside fell silent and footsteps could be heard. He glanced up. Framed in the open doorway stood Vera Petrovna.

"Good Heavens! What are you doing here?" asked Miles as he stooped to retrieve the keys. Aware that this response could be construed as frosty, he followed it with; "What a nice surprise! How on earth did you know where I lived?"

"Don't bombard your guest with questions, Miles," Elspeth interjected before Vera had had a chance to reply. "Vera's tired out."

"I thought you had your seance," replied Miles tersely.

"It won't do any harm to be late for once. You should introduce me to your friends more often." Elspeth smiled at Vera before turning to Miles. "Well, are you going to stand there all evening?"

"Your sister's been very kind, Miles. I am a stranger who arrived without invitation. I was telling Elzz..peth, is that how you pronounce it?" Elspeth nodded. "I was so worried about you in Chicago. I felt very bad for leaving you like that. How are you now?"

"I'm fine, thank you. It was kind of you but you needn't have worried," replied Miles, removing his coat. His excitement at seeing Vera again was tempered with nervousness. After all, he knew next to nothing about this woman.

"Well, I'll leave you two together," said Elspeth. "You've got a lot to catch up with. And by the way Miles, I've told Vera she can sleep in my room. I'll take the settee. I'm relying on you to give our guest some clean sheets. Poor thing's had a dreadful time. She'll explain. Make sure you don't tire her out. I'll be back about ten thirty." And with a broad smile directed at Vera, Elspeth headed out the door.

"Come and sit down Miles and I will explain everything," said Vera, patting the vacant space on the Chesterfield. "So much has happened since I left Chicago."

"Well before you tell me what brings you here, perhaps you could explain why you vanished from the conference."

Vera shifted awkwardly. "I had no choice. Can you imagine how I felt about it?"

"How did you find my address?"

"It wasn't so difficult. You're the only person in London I knew I could trust." Vera leapt up and started to pace the room as she talked.

"Trust with what?" asked Miles.

"It's my daughter, Claudia. You remember when we first met? I was having that argument with her on the phone. She was telling me she was dropping out of school. She's got in with a bad crowd, Miles. They do hard drugs, everything. Her father was supposed to be keeping watch on her while I was at the conference. He is worse than useless."

Miles was about to interject with a question about her current marital status but Vera was unstoppable. "Claudia has this friend from school, Irena. Her parents are both teachers. She made them very sad when she got a summer job in a hotel in Monte Carlo and refused to return home to continue her studies. She met some billionaire out there and now she's his mistress....Anyway, what was I saying?" asked Vera distractedly.

"You were talking about this friend of your daughter," said Miles, wondering what this girl had to do with Vera's appearance on his doorstep.

"Ah yes...anyway, that first night in Chicago, I got a call from the woman who keeps, how do you say?...an eye on my apartment. She told me Claudia had left a note to say she had gone to the South of France to be with Irena. She'd found my secret supply of dollars to pay for her flight. I have no address, nothing and she won't answer her phone. She's only seventeen for God's sake. I flew to France but I couldn't find her. Then somehow I managed to discover where this billionaire lived in Monte Carlo and the concierge was sorry for me after I was in tears. She told me that both girls had gone to London and may be staying at this man's apartment. You can see now Miles, why I had to come. The school will throw her out. She'll end up on the streets, or maybe even in prison." Vera slumped on to the settee again and began to sob.

"That's awful," said Miles, extracting his handkerchief. He was about to offer it to Vera when he noticed its less than pristine state and quickly stuffed it back in his pocket.

"Will you help me find her?" asked Vera.

"Me? I'm no detective..."

"I knew I could rely on you," said Vera, planting a kiss on his jowls.

✦

"It's wonderful to have you with me, Miles" said Vera, slipping her arm through his as they set out through the side streets of Mayfair. Somehow, there had been no alternative but to offer to help Vera find her missing daughter. Having finally opened a week-old email from his publisher, he had to admit though that the timing was far from perfect. It had contained an ultimatum: either produce the completed manuscript of his book in eight weeks time or...The threat was all too clear. Miles had promised himself there would be no distractions.

"It has just occurred to me that I have no idea who we're going to see," said Miles, trying to dismiss his uneasy thoughts.

"I was up early," replied Vera. "Elspeth helped me with the internet. We found this article from the newspaper about Bernie Prince and his wife. Their marriage is over. It's big news."

"Never heard of him I'm afraid, but then I'm no reader of the gossip pages," said Miles.

"Even in Russia we know about him. He's the British billionaire who is Claudia's friend Irena's sugar daddy. He's big pals with our beloved President. God knows what kind of business he does. Here, I'll show you where he lives." Vera extracted her phone and they paused while she located a photograph of a grand stuccoed London house illustrating the online article. "It says Eaton Square. Like the school maybe. Do you know it?"

"I'm afraid my knowledge of anything south of Marble Arch is rather sketchy."

"Maybe we should take a taxi?"

"We could always catch a bus," said Miles who regarded taxis as an extravagance.

✦

"Forgive me asking but what are you hoping to achieve by this visit?" asked Miles.

"Don't you see, Miles? This is the best chance we have of

finding Claudia. We will take her by surprise."

The prospect of stumbling across the errant daughter seemed far-fetched, but Miles said nothing. Besides, how would they identify the correct house? The notion of knocking on every door had little appeal. Meanwhile, the metered fare was escalating alarmingly. Miles checked his wallet to ascertain how much cash he was carrying. As he paid off the driver at the corner of Eaton Square, he found he had just enough left over for a meagre tip.

As the taxi drew away, they stood gazing at the gleaming terrace of Belgravia houses. Vera got out her phone and studied the newspaper article. "Look, his house has a bright red door and these stripy blinds on the windows should be easy to find."

Watched over by a security man guarding one of the neighbouring mansions, they finally pinpointed the most likely candidate and approached the front door.

"Who is it please?" asked a thickly-accented voice over the intercom. A CCTV camera mounted high in the portico swivelled downwards to investigate the new arrivals.

"You speak, Miles," whispered Vera.

"Better you. A woman and all that...less threatening."

Vera shrugged and leaned into the intercom. "My name is Vera Petrovna. I am looking for Mr or Mrs Prince. I hope I have the right house?"

"They're not here," the voice snapped. "If you are a journalist, please do not disturb us again or we will call the police." Vera and Miles exchanged glances. At least their sleuthing had proved accurate.

"No, no. I'm not a journalist. I am from Russia and I am looking for my daughter. I was hoping Mr Prince could help me," said Vera in an anxious tone.

The intercom fell silent and they were about to turn away when two blurred forms materialised beyond the opaque glass. As the door was opened tentatively, Vera and Miles found themselves under the scrutiny of a diminutive woman who Miles took to be the housekeeper. Hovering in the background was a lanky middle-aged female with an orangey tan and strawberry blonde hair.

"It's OK Caterina, I'll handle this," said the woman. Despite her air of caution, Miles noticed she had kindly eyes.

"Your daughter, you say? What's your name?"The woman moved towards the open door.

"Vera... Dr Vera Petrovna."

"And who's this?" asked Belinda Prince, staring curiously at Miles who found the directness of her gaze disquieting.

"This is my friend Dr Miles Mallalieu. He is helping me search for her."

"Are you quite sure you're not more scumbag journalists?"

"No,no...far from it." said Miles.

"I'm Belinda by the way. Bel for short." Her accent was tinged with a regional tone that Miles took to be Essex. "You'd better come in." She turned to address Vera. "I'm probably crazy to let strangers into my house but I have a hunch I know who you are. You and I might just have something in common."

They followed Belinda into an ornately furnished reception room hung with old tapestries of hunting scenes.

"Wanna drink?" asked Belinda. Miles glanced at the gilded clock on the marble mantelpiece. It was showing 11.45.

"Just water for me," said Vera.

"And for me," Miles interjected.

"Suit yourselves. I'm having a scotch. Are you two an item by any chance?" Belinda winked at Vera. "Two doctors, eh?"

"We're not medical doctors, if that's what you were implying," volunteered Miles.

"If you're not quacks, what's your game then?" asked Belinda.

"I'm an academic. I study Ancient History. That is also Miles' field," replied Vera.

"That figures. He's rather sweet. Mind you, he looks like he needs a bit of TLC," said Belinda. Miles coloured, unsure how to take this outspoken woman with her estuarine vowels.

"You'll have to excuse my sense of humour," said Belinda. "It comes from twenty years of living with Bernie. Sit down." Belinda indicated an elaborately carved settee before crossing to a sideboard, eventually returning with the drinks.

"I had a great auntie called Vera. Lovely old girl. So you're Irena's mum then?"

"Excuse me?" replied Vera.

Appearing not to have heard this remark, Belinda prattled on, in between sips of whisky and soda. "What she must see in him is anyone's guess. He may be loaded but, let's face it, he's no oil painting. What's she told you about him?"

"I'm sorry, Mrs Prince, but I think you've made a mistake," said Vera.

"You are Russian, aren't you, and you said you were looking for your daughter?"

"Yes, but my daughter is Claudia. She's a school friend of Irena's. She ran away from St Petersburg last week to stay with Irena in France. All I know is that they are together in London now and I was hoping so much to find her here."

Belinda appeared crestfallen at this revelation. She took a gulp before composing herself. "I see. You must be sick with worry, Vera. I know I would be. God knows what kind of things that bastard's got them into. Your Claudia. Is she a gold digger too?"

"Do you mean...is she a miner? asked Vera.

Belinda chortled. "Gold digger...miner. Got to hand it to you Russians. You like a laugh."

"Claudia's not yet eighteen. She still has time to make something of her life." Vera began to sniff and dab her eyes. Belinda crossed the room to sit beside her on the brocade settee. "I'm sorry to disappoint you but I haven't set eyes on your daughter, or Irena for that matter. Bernie's not going to show his face here, for obvious reasons."

"Please, I beg of you. If you have any information about where they might be, give it to me," said Vera.

"OK. I'll put you out of your misery," said Belinda, draining her glass. "When the bastard's in London, he keeps on the move to avoid the paparazzi. My spies tell me he's holed up in one of these service apartments in Brook Street. All very discreet. I've known about that little love nest of his for years. I've kept quiet about it until now." Belinda withdrew a small notepad from her handbag, scribbled down an address and passed it to Vera. "She'll be there, you can bet on it, and maybe your girl too. You'll probably catch them after they've got bored with burning a hole in Bernie's credit card."

Vera pored over the address. "Thank you so much. This means a lot to me. Come on Miles. We must go there at once." She approached Belinda. "If there's anything we can do for you, we will, won't we, Miles?"

"Well...just maybe there is," replied Belinda. "Maybe you could get your daughter to persuade her little friend to lay off my hubby. It's all been a nightmare, especially for the kids. If pigs could fly, eh? Mind you, I don't blame the girl. Knowing Bernie, he would have promised her the earth. She's only a two-bit waitress, after all."

"How can I say this?" replied Vera. "Irena is a strong personality. I doubt she will listen to my daughter, but you never know. First I have to find her."

"Do your best, eh Vera?" Belinda extracted a card from her clutch bag which she handed to Vera before turning to Miles. "Lovely to meet you. You hang on to him, Vera. You're on to a good thing there." She winked at Miles as she ushered them towards the door.

✦

"Couldn't we stop for a sandwich? I'm rather peckish," said Miles as they emerged on to the street.

"Peckish? What is peckish?" asked Vera.

"I'm rather hungry."

"There's no time for that now, Miles. Where is this Brook Street? We can't waste time getting lost." Vera extended her arm and a cruising black cab pulled into the curb. Miles was bundled in and they sped off before he had time to recover his balance.

"Don't you have a car?" Vera asked.

"It's gathering dust in a garage – needs a fortune spent on it. Morris Minor Traveller. A bit of a classic."

"A classic, you say? Just like you Miles," Vera smiled."You are not a modern man, this is part of your charm. I am so worried about Claudia," she added, her expression darkening. "What if we don't find her?"

"We will, I'm certain of it," Miles replied, summoning up a modicum of conviction that seemed to mollify Vera.

Number 50 Brook Street proved to be a residential building with an impressive portico. "May I help you? Which apartment are you visiting? " A well-groomed young concierge was stationed behind a large glass desk in the lobby. His accent placed his origins somewhere east of Ukraine. Vera and he launched into an animated exchange in Russian, a language of which Miles had no knowledge. Excluded from the conversation, he decided to maintain a benign smile. After all, this apparently helpful young man might hold the key to the whereabouts of the prodigal daughter. With luck, Vera might be reunited with Claudia by the end of the day, allowing him to attempt to resume work on the book. The barometer of guilt was rising with every hour he spent away from his desk.

Yet as they chatted on, Miles was struck by a troubling thought. Success in finding Claudia might also spell an end to any chance of deepening his acquaintance with Vera who would whisk her daughter back to St Petersburg. Although Miles had no inkling about Vera's intentions, he dared to believe that this fledgling relationship gave rise to a soupçon of hope.

"Miles, this is Dmitri and guess what? He's from St Petersburg too," said Vera, interrupting Miles' reflections. "He's being so helpful."

"How do you do, sir?" replied Dmitri, rising to shake Miles' hand before turning to Vera. "It will probably lose me my job to help you, but we Russians must look after each other, yes?" he said, grinning at Vera.

"Dmitri has confirmed it. Bernie Prince is staying here," said Vera, her eyes brightening. He says we should go a nightclub where they will be tonight for sure. You have to be a member but he can fix it. He is making us a reservation."

✦

"I'm not sure about that jacket," said Vera, as Miles paraded reluctantly before her.

"I'm rather fond of it. I've had it for donkey's years," he replied. Miles was not used to this level of scrutiny of his sartorial sense. The criticism of his green smoking jacket was particularly galling. It had become his perennial attire at formal do's since the 1980s.

"It looks a little ....tired. What do you think Elspeth?" said Vera.

"I agree," said Elspeth, flicking specks of dandruff from the jacket's velvet collar. "And that shirt cuff is frayed. Really Miles, is that the best you can do? If you're not careful, you'll be turned away at the door."

"I'm afraid it is," he muttered, sidling out of the firing line.

"Now what shoes are you going to wear?"

Elspeth had vanished into the kitchen but now reappeared with a tray bearing two cups. "I found some lemon, Vera. I know that's how you Russians like your tea."

It was evident that this operation to kit him out for their foray into London's high life had strengthened a bond between his sister and their guest. Miles found this both pleasing and perplexing in equal measures. Why is it, he mused, that women find it so much easier to develop an easy intimacy with their own sex than men do with their fellows? Perhaps Elspeth was eager for an injection of colour into her life and this vivacious Russian had provided the promise of just that? Pondering these questions, Miles retired to the bathroom for a rapid flannel wash.

✦

"Good evening Madam, Sir. Welcome to Annabel's." The uniformed flunkey held out a large umbrella to ward off the drizzle as they stepped out of the taxi in Berkeley Square. The spray from the rear wheels of the departing cab deposited a spattering of mud on Miles' shins. His attempts to brush it off left him with grubby hands which he was forced to wipe on his thighs. Miles had never entered a nightclub before, having studiously avoided such places. As Vera led him towards the entrance, he found himself grasping her arm nervously.

"How do I look?" she whispered. "Now it's your turn to be honest."

"You look splendid," he replied. He could not help but notice that the beaded cocktail dress borrowed from Elspeth complemented Vera's slender figure well.

"Do you have a reservation?" In the gloom, Miles found it hard to locate the owner of the silky voice, barely audible above the hubbub of background chatter.

"Yes we do. It's in the name of Petrovna. It was organised by Dmitri," replied Vera before Miles could assemble his response.

"Certainly. Here it is. Eight thirty for two."

Miles' pupils had adjusted sufficiently to make out the outline of the receptionist and beyond her, the gilded glamour of the nightclub itself, its cavernous interior illuminated only by pools of light from table lamps reflected in the polished brass pillars.

"Has Mr Prince arrived yet?" asked Vera tentatively.

"I don't believe we've had the pleasure of seeing you two here before?" Miles shook his head. "I'm afraid the house rules guarantee our members complete anonymity," the young woman continued, with a tight smile. "You might like to start with a drink at the bar. It's over there. You can't really miss it."

After pressing their way through the gilded crowd, Vera settled on an elevated stool at the end of the cocktail bar and began to scan the room for Claudia. Miles' attempts to clamber on to the neighbouring stool were soon abandoned and he was forced to lean awkwardly against the bar.

"Miles, keep looking," urged Vera. "Maybe they're here already."

Miles screwed up his eyes. It was impossible to pick out individual faces and having only been shown a distant snapshot of Claudia, he had no real idea of her appearance other than she had jet black hair. His eyes drifted to the small dance floor at the heart of the club. At this early hour, the floor was deserted except for two couples swaying lugubriously to the disco-type music. The males were elderly and of portly dimensions. Their svelte partners, on the other hand, appeared to be barely out of their teens. Miles watched with distaste as the diminutive men reached up to drape their arms around the lofty partners' necks, heads barely reaching chest height.

As if reading Miles' thoughts, Vera shook her head. "No, it's not her. My God, these people make me sick."

"Perhaps we should ask that girl on the desk to put a call out over the Tannoy?" Miles suggested, realising at once that this was a flawed idea, as Claudia might take flight.

"Tannoy? What is this," replied Vera. "Come with me. I have a plan." Before Miles could react, Vera had steered him towards the centre of the club. "Do what I say and try and look relaxed," she whispered in his ear as she manoeuvred him on to the dance floor.

"OK. Now put your arms around my neck, just like them." She indicated the two other males. "Not so much weight on my shoulders. You'll push me over."

"I must warn you," Miles muttered as he attempted to follow her instructions. "Anything involving co-ordinated movement is not my strong point."

"No one expects you to be Nureyev. Don't you see, this is the only way I can take a good look around the club without being suspicious? Keep turning me around. Slowly now. Slowly, I said."

In other circumstances, Miles might have found this clutch with Vera alluring, but the gravity of their mission dampened any hint of passion. He concentrated on revolving his partner in a clockwise direction at what he thought was a manageable pace.

"Not like a whirling dervish. You're going too fast," chided Vera as the tempo increased.

The electronic throb that passed for dance music had taken on a nightmare quality. Miles was beginning to feel nauseous. To his relief, there was a sudden break.

"Can we please sit?" he pleaded.

"Listen to me. I have a new plan. I'm going to the ladies' rest room. If Claudia's here, she'll check her make-up every half hour. It will be easier to talk there. Wait here, I won't be long," she added, vanishing into the throng.

Miles leant on the nearest pillar to steady himself. His head seemed disconnected from the rest of his body His ankles were threatening to give way and the opulent surroundings were beginning to fragment into a kaleidoscopic whirl.

"I loved the way you slid down that pillar. It was just like the cowboy movies."

Miles took in the piercing blue eyes set in a shaven bullet head looming over him. "A slight turn. I'll be fine" he replied.

"For a moment there I thought you were having a heart attack. If you don't mind me saying so, you look the type. You want to get up before the bouncers find you. They get very shirty about anyone who can't hold his booze," said his rescuer. A well-muscled arm was extended and Miles was restored to the vertical, his forehead still pounding. The man spoke with a soft Cockney accent. "Here on your own are you, looking for a bit of action?"

"My companion's just powdering her nose," replied Miles.

"Into the white stuff, is she?"

"I beg your pardon?" said Miles.

"I'm Bernie by the way."

"Miles...Miles Mallalieu."

"That's a fancy name. Pleased to meet you Mr Mallalieu. Here drink this." He leant over to a nearby table and passed Miles a glass. "It won't kill you. It's only water."

"Thank you," said Miles, gulping it down. "I'm not sure what came over me. It's Doctor Mallalieu actually."

"Here grab a pew, Doctor. My lot are in the little girls' room too. They'll be hours." Bernie made a great play of settling Miles in a chair at a nearby table.

Miles flopped down gratefully. "All this conspicuous consumption, it's rather too much to take."

Bernie waved his arms dismissively. "Crooks, wanker bankers, politicians, there's nothing to choose between them. You could put a bomb in here and the world would be a better place. You'd better tell me Miles what a decent sort like you is doing in this den of iniquity?"

"If you must know, this is not my usual milieu," said Miles.

"Milieu?" Bernie let the syllables roll off his tongue. "I like that word." Miles smiled at this seeming compliment before launching into a potted account of Claudia's disappearance from Russia.

"And what would this friend's name be?" asked Bernie.

"Irena, I think. She...the friend that is, has apparently latched on to a much older man... a multi-millionaire. Tax exile. You know the type. Very unsuitable by the sound of it. We had a tip-off that he's bringing both girls here tonight as his guests. That's the only reason we're here."

"This daughter of your friend, her name's not Claudia?" asked Bernie, leaning over to fix Miles with his steely gaze.

"Yes, that's it, Claudia. How on earth do you know? I've never met the girl. She sounds as if she's very headstrong."

"You can say that again. Moody sort of bitch."

There was a moment's pause then Miles began sliding down in his chair in an attempt to render himself invisible. "Your surname isn't Prince by any chance?" he stammered.

Bernie grinned. "In case you were wondering, I'm deeply unsuitable. If you don't believe me, ask my ex-wife."

Miles was about to blurt out that he had only that afternoon met the woman in question. He somehow checked himself and allowed Bernie to pour him a glass of champagne.

"Well, here's to a happy coincidence," said Bernie. No doubt at this very minute your lady and her Claudia will be having a tearful reunion in the khazi. To be honest, Miles, I'll be glad when she's off my hands. Both of them for that matter. Irena's gorgeous but she's too young for me. She's wearing me out something rotten." Miles cleared his throat nervously. "I know what you're thinking."

"What am I thinking?" replied Miles.

"I haven't touched Claudia. You have my word on that. Strange kid. She trails around after Irena like a bad smell."

Miles glanced anxiously in the direction of the ladies.

"Relax, Miles. They'll be back soon and it'll all be Happy Families again," said Bernie."Are you hitched? You don't look as though you are, lucky man."

Miles shook his head.

"I'm sure you've knocked around a bit. All those sexy nurses to pick from."

"I'm not that sort of doctor," replied Miles, weary at having to point this out.

"That's a relief. I hate them all. Bunch of charlatans. Tell me something Miles. I can see you're the brainy sort. Do you understand the workings of the female mind?"

Miles had never given this question much thought. "No, I can't say that I do," he replied instinctively.

"Well then, that makes two of us," said Bernie raising his glass. Miles reciprocated. There was something oddly endearing about this bull of a man. Miles was warming to his bluntness and lack of pretension.

Shrill voices drifted over from the far side of the club. Miles could just make out Vera and a young woman, whom Miles took to be none other than Claudia, locked in a shouting match. Vera was clutching at her daughter who was struggling to break free, while a second girl, whom he imagined to be Irena, looked on helplessly.

"Well, well,"said Bernie, with a broad smile. "It looks like mother and daughter have been reunited. Very touching. Leave this to me." He rose from his chair and strode across the club. Placing his not inconsiderable frame between the two warring parties, he virtually frog-marched them back to his table, Irena following sheepishly behind. "You two plonk your arses down here before you get us all thrown out." Bernie's menacing tone caused Vera and Claudia to quieten down and settle passively at the table.

Vera stared angrily at Miles and then at Bernie as if to say – who is this man who has interfered in this way? Miles observed that Vera's daughter was taller and broader in the face than her mother. After introductions had been made and Miles had explained Bernie's Good Samaritan role mother and daughter maintained a sullen silence. So this was the elusive Claudia. There was something about her challenging posture that made Miles thankful that he had not produced any offspring.

"While you two have been going hammer and tongs at each other, Miles and I've been doing a bit of male bonding, haven't we Miles?"

"Is everything alright here, Mr Prince?" They were interrupted by a stocky young man whom Miles took to be associated with security. Hovering by the table, he singled out Vera and Claudia for scrutiny.

Bernie's reaction was to extricate his wallet and slip him a bank note, patting the back of the man's hand as he did so. "Just a little local problem, Max. All over now. These good people are my guests. Rustle up some more Bollinger, there's a good bloke." Still eyeing up the two Russian women suspiciously, the employee pocketed the money without a word before withdrawing.

After only a brief lull, Claudia and Vera restarted their verbal skirmish, oblivious to the others at the table.

"Ladies please," said Bernie raising his hands to hush them. He turned to Irena. "You can remind your chums that I've just paid over the odds to stop them being thrown out. So do me a favour and get them to keep stumm, OK?"

Rolling her eyes, Irena leant over to whisper in Claudia's ear. Her reaction was to fold her arms defensively.

"Claudia wants to leave," explained Vera, grim-faced. "Of course she doesn't know where to go. She just wants to get away from me. You can imagine how that makes me feel."

"She's a big girl. She can look after herself," said Bernie.

"You don't understand, Mr Prince, I can't trust her," said Vera.

"It's Bernie, please. You can tell your daughter that if she upsets her gorgeous mother again, I'll personally put the dogs on her," he added. The force of his words rendered a translation unnecessary. Claudia shrugged and sank further into herself.

Bernie leant over to Miles and patted him on the shoulder before turning to Vera. "Do you know something? I like your boyfriend. He makes me smile. Do us a favour you ladies. Drink up and shut up!"

A young woman in a cocktail dress had approached the table. Without a word, she whipped out a smart phone and began photographing Bernie and his entourage. Out of nervousness, Miles found himself beaming obligingly into the lens. Bernie meanwhile leapt up and attempted to snatch the phone. Having failed to do so, he snapped his fingers. The club security man promptly appeared and whisked the woman away.

✦

The household was still asleep when Miles slipped out of the flat. It was well after one when they had returned from the club yet he had awoken early and felt surprisingly chipper. The latter part of their evening at Annabel's had passed without further incident. The supply of gourmet food and fine wines had been plentiful and Bernie Prince had insisted on settling the no-doubt extravagant bill.

Miles had left a scribbled note which he left by Elspeth's comatose form on the Chesterfield, alerting her to the fact that her own bed was occupied by both mother and daughter. He offered no explanation. He would leave that to Vera.

A drizzly wind propelled him towards Gower Street and he reached the Department ahead of schedule for his nine o'clock tutorial. Congratulating himself, Miles took a deep breath before ascending the stairs. The lack of motorised transport was slowly improving his physical stamina. He would use the available time to check whether Marian had returned to work. He had still not spoken to her directly since that sighting of Tony outside her flat. He had barely put his head round the door of her office when she popped out to accost him in the hallway. Miles was aware that she looked unusually strained.

"That was quite a night," she said, waving a copy of a tabloid newspaper under Miles' nose.

"How do you mean?" replied Miles. "Let me see that."

"That is you, isn't it? Unless you have a double." Marian pointed to a photograph on the society gossip page. Miles could just make out the scene in Annabel's with the group around Bernie's table prominently featured. Miles was alarmed to see that he appeared to be gurning into the camera.

"I...I can explain. I was only there to help out a friend. That photographer had no right....."

"I had no idea you frequented such places," said Marian with a strangely insouciant laugh. "I'm really quite impressed, and so, believe it or not, is Tony. He's keen to have a word."

"Tony's seen this?"

"Is that you, Miles? Do come in." Tony's voice was light and welcoming. The Director was stretched out on the burgundy leather sofa by the window. "Sling me that paper again, Marian," he yelled. Miles searched for signs of the previous despair he had witnessed but there was not a trace. Perhaps Tony's marriage had been saved, or had he moved in with Marian by way of consolation? The intricacies of other people's emotional lives were a constant puzzle.

Marian appeared from the outer office and deposited the Daily Mail in Tony's lap before returning to her lair without catching Miles' eye.

"It's not my usual haunt, if that's what you were wondering,"

Miles burbled as Tony studied the newspaper silently. He then wandered across to Miles who was hovering by the door.

"Well, well, Miles, you're a dark horse. Do sit down."

A smug grin spread over Tony's face as he launched into a spirited reading of the report: 'A night on the town for billionaire businessman Bernie Prince no doubt to take his mind off the acrimonious split from Belinda, his wife of 25 years which has caused the London divorce lawyers to start salivating.... Bernie holds court last night at this posh watering hole with a trio of female admirers. One of the two younger girls is rumoured to be Irena, his new Russian girlfriend who has been his constant companion since they met in Monaco. An unidentified male guest is also pictured getting into the spirit of the occasion..."' He offered the paper to Miles who let it slip to the floor.

"As it happens I was with a fellow academic... It's not what it seems."

"Be that as it may," replied Tony. "I'm not here to discuss what I always took to be your somewhat under-active private life. How well do you know this Bernie Prince?"

"Barely at all. I've only just met him. He rescued me after I'd had a turn in the club, if you must know. It was very stuffy in there."

"Will you be seeing him again?"

"It's possible, I suppose. As a matter of fact we got on rather well. He muttered something about inviting me on his yacht. I told him I was a useless sailor but he laughed it off."

"Excellent," said Tony, rising to cross to the window where he stood staring out at the square below. "As your ever-loyal confidante Marian has no doubt let slip, the Department's in deep shit, Miles. I need hardly tell you that Ancient History is regarded as a soft touch. Things are looking dire. Unless...."

Tony swivelled round to eyeball Miles. "Unless we can come up with a mug with millions to spare and who wants to gain some brownie points towards a knighthood. This Prince is the classic self-made man...he picked up some very suspect business associates on the way, but who hasn't these days?"

"What makes you think he's got any interest in what we do here?" asked Miles.

"The point is he left school at fourteen and apparently he's got a massive chip on his shoulder about his lack of qualifications. The university fundraisers have picked him out as someone who might fall for an honorary degree in exchange for a fat cheque to bail us out. Trouble is he won't answer their calls. Are you beginning to get the drift?" Tony returned from the window and crouched at Miles's feet. "We're relying on you Miles to get near him, to cultivate him...soften him up. In short, to squeeze large amounts of filthy lucre out of your new best pal."

Miles mopped his brow. "I hate begging. Even if I were to see this man again, I can scarcely ask him for a blank cheque."

"Eight million should get us over the worst of it. Fifteen would be a lot better. You can tell him that we'll splash his name everywhere. He can even have it printed on every sheet of bog roll for all I care."

"Fifteen million? You can't be serious?"

Tony returned to his desk and buried himself in his laptop. The meeting, it seemed, was at an end but then Tony spoke again, more quietly now, without glancing up.

"By the way, Miles, if you do get him to sign that cheque, I'm sure we can forget about those black marks over your teaching record. The slate will be wiped entirely clean. How does that sound? We're all depending on you. I know you won't let us down."

✦

"Ah Miles, can we have a wee word?" Gavin was in the habit of perching at the top of the stairs like a vulture waiting to feast on the entrails of gossip seeping from the Director's office. As ever, a copy of The Morning Star was tucked under his arm. He made a point of flaunting his allegiance to this last bastion of a Marxist perspective. At least he would not have seen the Mail, thought Miles with a modicum of relief.

"I hear your nine o'clock's been cancelled."

"How do you know?"

"I know everything." He tapped his nose with his index finger, a gesture that Miles found particularly irritating. Gavin took Miles' elbow. "You look as though you need a coffee. I'll treat you."

Miles had intended to make use of this sudden gap in his timetable to reflect on how he might respond to Tony's twisted demands. Yet he found himself following Gavin down the main stairs and out into the square. The early rain had cleared, leaving the pavements glistening in the watery sun. How was he going to withstand Gavin's grilling? When it came to sniffing out scandal, his colleague had an uncanny knack of extracting sensitive information to serve his nefarious purposes. They settled for Mario's round the corner.

"Fancy a pastry? That one's got your name on it," said Gavin, putting in their order at the counter. Having missed breakfast, Miles was unable to resist the sugar-coated Danish. Once settled at a corner table, Miles watched as Gavin spooned saccharin into his large cappuccino, taking care not to disturb the froth. He grinned at Miles. "So how are things between you and the Dear Leader? He seems to be summoning you a lot these days," he asked, affecting an uneasy nonchalance.

"Much the same really," replied Miles guardedly and took a bite. Gavin pressed on with the interrogation. "Do we take it that he's forgiven you for your transgressions...the business with that Chinese student?"

Miles made a grunting sound and scooped the residue of the icing off his Danish with his little finger. "You know Tony tried to have it off with her?" Gavin added.

"No I didn't know," said Miles.

"Apparently she's got quite a reputation for using her charms to up her marks, if you know what I mean." Wiping the froth from his lip, Gavin leaned towards Miles. "She didn't try it on with you, did she?"

"Look if you don't mind, Gavin, I can't be long. I've got a book to finish."

"Haven't we all?" Gavin paused. "Rumour hath it the said Tony's wife has finally got fed up with his philandering. Maybe he said something to you?"

"I fail to see what Tony's private life has to do with his running the Department," retorted Miles, already regretting his decision to lay himself open to Gavin's grilling.

"If his wife did kick him out, I imagine that Marian's been mopping up his tears. She's good with a mop is our Marian," said Gavin.

"Why don't you talk to her ? She's much closer to Tony than I am," Miles retorted, reining in his irritation.

"Marian's no fan of mine. She's got a thing about beards. But she does have a soft spot for you, Miles. Little dinners à deux, my spies tell me. Perfect for getting the lowdown on Tony."

"What Marian and I talk about is our business."

"Don't you see, Miles, we have to know everything about him. The little shit is dragging the Department down. It's time to topple him by whatever means it takes."

"I'm afraid I don't share your appetite for proletarian revolution."

"Screw the proletariat, Miles, it's about us, our future, our jobs."

"And who may I ask do you see as Tony's successor, or can one take an educated guess?"

Spooning the remaining froth from his cup, Gavin shuffled awkwardly in his chair.

"Thank you for the coffee, Gavin. I have to go."

Gavin placed his hand on Miles' wrist to restrain him. "I'll need a deputy of course. Help us and the post is yours."

Wriggling free of Gavin's grip, Miles drained his coffee and prepared to leave.

"Think about it Miles. Throw your lot in with the comrades and you won't regret it. We look after our fellow travellers. You'll see."

As he prepared to cut across the gardens opposite the Department, the square appeared deserted save for the resident army of scavenging pigeons. It was only after he had passed through the gate that Miles spotted a recumbent form on a bench. The blanket of newspaper and the trash-laden supermarket trolley bore the unmistakeable hallmarks of Doug Allardyce. Miles was about to change course when a bellowed greeting brought him to a halt.

"And a very good morning to you, Miles!" Doug had risen from the dead and was gesturing him to approach. "Come and chew the fat with your old friend."

CHAPTER THREE

Slings and arrows

Despite Miles' determination to avoid further awkward encounters that morning, there was something in Doug's tone that made his request hard to refuse.

"Great to see you again, Miles. Forgive the mess. I wasn't expecting visitors. Give me a moment, will you?" Removing the soiled newspaper and other debris, Doug made a play of creating a clear space on the bench for his guest. Beckoning to Miles to sit down beside him, he withdrew a packet of facial wipes from his coat pocket. "Want one? They're my little indulgence."

"It's kind of you, but no," said Miles with a weak smile.

"You don't mind if I do?" Without waiting for approval, Doug reached inside his tattered sweater to dab at his underarms. He completed his ablutions by dragging the used wipe over the small portion of his face that was not obscured by his matted beard. Miles edged away as far as was physically possible, which was not far enough to avoid the malodour.

"Now we can talk," said Doug. "How are things in the rat hole, Miles? Go on, tell your Uncle Doug all about it."

There remained an aura of wisdom about this shambles of a man who, before his spectacular fall from grace, had enjoyed an international reputation. Miles badly now needed advice on how to handle the Faustian pact that Tony had dangled before him that morning. In the past, it would have been Marian to whom he would have turned. She would have helped him place it all in a rational perspective. Yet, to his chagrin, he felt he could no longer count on her unswerving loyalty. There were too many unanswered questions about her relationship with Tony. Before any confessional could get underway, they were disturbed by a ringing tone emanating from Miles' briefcase.

"You'd better answer that. It might be the love of your life," said Doug.

"I quite forgotten I'd switched it on." Miles rummaged amongst the wodge of papers and fished out the elderly phone, once described by his nephew as a brick.

"Who is this?" Miles asked anxiously, holding the phone some inches from his ear.

"It won't bite you," said Doug, grinning.

Somehow, Miles had activated the loudspeaker key and Vera's voice rang out across the square.

"Miles, where are you?"

"Vera, is that you?" asked Miles, eventually locating the button to cancel the speaker function.

"Of course it's me. You must come back at once. It's Claudia. There's a big problem."

Miles placed his hand over the phone and turned to Doug. "Forgive me but I have to go." Rising from the bench, Miles began to back away. The residue of the night's rain had transferred to his trousers which now clung to his thighs.

"Whoever she is, it sounds like she's got you by the short

and curlies," Doug called out. "So long, Miles. Now you know where to find me, feel free to drop by any time." He gave a friendly wave which Miles felt obliged to return before hurrying off in the direction of his flat.

✦

As Miles reached his front door, Elspeth emerged, tweed-coated and unruffled. She brushed past him before he could question her.

"I've left them to it. I'm late for the chiropodist. There's some ham in the fridge that needs eating up," she called as she tripped lightly down the stone staircase. Miles braced himself before entering the flat. At first, he was unable to locate the Russians' precise location. Elspeth had been nagging him for weeks to replace the light bulb in the main corridor and little daylight penetrated its gloom. It was not until he groped his way down the corridor towards his study that he heard a low simpering from behind the bathroom door.

He almost lost his balance as he tripped over the pair of legs. Vera was squatting on the corridor floor, upper torso propped up against the wall, her hands pressed over her ears. As his foot came into contact with her shin, she let off a stream of Russian invective.

"Miles, are you blind?"

"I'm terribly sorry. Are you alright?"

"Help me up, will you?" He held out his arms to support Vera. "Claudia's refusing to go back to Russia. She has no money, nowhere to stay. She won't come out. We'll have to break down the door."

"That sounds a little extreme," said Miles, determining that Claudia must be coaxed out willingly to avoid unnecessary damage. He knocked gently but firmly at the door. "This is Miles here, Claudia. Can you hear me?" he asked, lowering the pitch of his voice to maximise the impact. The simpering ceased, to be replaced by a long silence. "Are you going to be much longer? I need to use the toilet," he added. As it happened, this was no subterfuge. There was only one lavatory and if this siege continued, he would have to resort to the facilities at the Maybury Arms, a good seven minutes away.

The door creaked open and Claudia emerged, with dark circles under her eyes, wrapped in a bath towel, and shuffled off meekly towards Elspeth's bedroom.

"Oh Miles, you're a genius!"Vera whispered as Claudia closed the bedroom door behind her. "She'll sleep now. I know her. She was awake all night. Why don't I make us some coffee and we can talk about all this?"

Having retreated to the sitting room, Vera had settled down next to Miles and was pouring their coffee. "That girl respects you. Her father could learn so much from you."

"Can't she go and live with him?" Miles asked.

"Are you crazy? Out of the question. He's refused to have her to stay for more than two nights. Anyway, he's an alcoholic and she hates his new girlfriend."

"In that case, I'm afraid I don't have any other bright ideas," Miles replied. The coffee was strong and his temples throbbed from the caffeine rush.

"Maybe, just maybe... it would be better for Claudia to stay here in London after all," said Vera, placing a hand lightly on Miles' knee. "She could learn English and get a part-time job."

Taking Vera's hand, Miles returned it pointedly to her own lap. "Is that a good idea?" he replied. "She may get into more trouble. And what about her education? Surely that's important to you?"

Vera bristled visibly. "Claudia's future means everything thing for me. Please don't doubt that."

"Well, perhaps Bernie can find her a job. Irena could put in a good word for her," replied Miles, having softened his stance.

"Irena won't talk to her. They've had a big fight. Apparently, she thought Claudia was, how do you say?...flirting with Bernie during our dinner."

"I didn't notice anything," said Miles.

"You wouldn't."

Before Miles could digest the implications of this rupture, Claudia emerged from Elspeth's room rubbing her eyes, dressed in an oversized black sweater and torn jeans. Miles was forced to shift sideways as Claudia virtually landed in his lap in her attempt to throw her arms around her mother. Extricating himself with some difficulty, Miles stood musing over this latest twist. Vera's affectionate response had elicited a broad smile from her daughter who eventually moved off to settle in the battered armchair, flicking idly through a copy of Elspeth's Psychic News.

"Claudia says she is sorry to have been so much trouble for you," announced Vera. "She says you are a nice man. She's changed her mind. She is ready to go home to Russia after all, but I have explained that we have another idea."

"Do we?" asked Miles.

"Actually you and I haven't had a chance to talk about this yet." She edged closer. "I've been thinking, Miles. If you can help me get a job at your Department then she and I can both live together in London. How would that be? Will you talk to your Director? Maybe he knows my work?"

Miles blinked repeatedly. The notion of tackling Tony at this time was out of the question. "I happen to know there are no vacancies," he replied. "In fact they are looking for excuses to get rid of people...that is not to say that the Department wouldn't be lucky to attract someone of your calibre," he added hastily.

"Don't you want me there?"

"No, no... I mean yes," Miles stammered, aware that the prospect of Vera remaining in London had more than a little appeal.

With a crestfallen look, Vera rose from the armchair and moved to the rain-smeared window. Her tone was colder now. "I'll be honest with you, Miles. My contract in St Petersburg may not be renewed next year. My future at the university is very uncertain. Anyway, I want a change and London is a wonderful city. If necessary, I will get a job doing anything, as a cleaner even. I'm not afraid of hard work."

"But where would you live?" asked Miles.

"Elspeth has had an idea about that."

"You've already talked this over with Elspeth? You and she seem to be getting on rather well."

"You're a lucky man to have such a sister, Miles. She's very kind. She's told me about the house."

"What house?"

"The one you own in the north of London... Brondersborry? She says that you've allowed an old friend to live there but he hasn't paid you any rent for more than two years. I am sure you have laws in this country about that. She says you could get him to leave, no problem, and then... maybe... Claudia and I could live there?"

Miles bit down hard on his lip. Elspeth's disclosure about the Brondesbury house was entirely out of order. After tasting blood, he resorted to drumming the nearest surface with his fingertips, a habit he had inherited from their mother when she was rattled. Elspeth had absolutely no right to discuss their private affairs with someone outside the family. He would speak to her severely when she returned from the chiropodist. Yet he could hardly deny that he and Elspeth each owned a share of the crumbling semi-detached house which had been left to them by an unmarried aunt whom they had barely known. It was also true to say that Elspeth had been nagging him for ages to reclaim the property.

Vera was fingering her hair nervously. "Perhaps you could too?"

"Could what?" stuttered Miles.

"Live there." Her eyes widened in anticipation of his response. "This flat is so small, Miles. You don't even have enough room for all your books." She pointed to the volumes piled in the corner awaiting a place on the over-stuffed shelves. Miles rose slowly from the settee and crossed to the window. "You must think about it. I won't rush you," she said quietly.

Miles was rendered speechless. Despite the spark of excitement Vera had undoubtedly kindled in him since they had first met in Chicago, he was not at all sure that he was ready for such a rapid escalation of their relationship, if that was what she was suggesting. Was his sister really encouraging him to set up home with this woman whom he had only known for a matter of weeks? If so, then Elspeth's motives were not hard to fathom. Miles could be reasonably sure that her own interests in such an outcome had not been overlooked. She would undoubtedly expect him to use the residue of his parental legacy to buy out her share of the house and she could then gain sole occupancy of the flat and enjoy greater financial security. It was not that Elspeth was especially devious, Miles reflected, but she was more worldly-wise than him. Their parents had considered their first-born to be the brighter, even though they had resisted sending her to university believing that a secretarial training would provide her with access to a suitable husband. Her subsequent impregnation by her first employer and her refusal to seek an abortion had led to a hasty marriage and an end to her chances of using her brain. Had Elspeth followed the academic route, who knows what might have happened? She could be running his department by now. The thought made Miles shiver.

Vera covered his silence by collecting up the coffee cups. As she retreated to the kitchen, Miles found himself blurting out; "It's a very small house. Only one decent-sized bedroom. Perhaps Elspeth didn't make that clear?" He paused but there was no reaction. Besides these practical issues, he reflected, there was the fate of his hapless old friend from university days Tristan, to consider. If Vera was to stay in London and succeeded in landing a job, she would be far better off, he decided, finding her own place with a room for Claudia. Vera and he could meet regularly but he would continue his independent existence as before. It was much too late, he concluded, to change his selfish ways. Much too late.

✦

"I could perfectly well have done this on my own," said Miles, addressing the road ahead. Despite the pressure from Elspeth and Vera, he had by no means resolved to issue Tristan with an ultimatum to quit. As far as he was concerned, this was merely to be an inspection visit.

"I don't trust you," replied Elspeth from the back seat of the minicab. "You're likely to fall for his hard luck stories. We're here to lend moral support." She turned to smile at Vera.

"It's that one, driver...half way up on the right by that lamp post," said Elspeth as they turned into a nondescript street of interwar semis, with once leafy front gardens now torn up for off-street parking. Overflowing wheelie bins cluttered the pavements. As the minicab drew up, Miles noticed that strands of loose paint were hanging off the battered window frames and the render on the facade was streaked with stains. It was over a year since he had last been to the house and he was dreading what he would find. Tristan had confessed to introducing several stray cats and on Miles' last visit an overpowering smell of cats' pee mingling with years of stale tobacco had permeated the interior. At the very least, it would require industrial-strength cleaning.

"That'll be twenty pounds," said the driver as they disembarked.

"Really?" said Miles "But we've barely come a couple of miles."

"That's what the office said to charge," said the driver.

"Just pay the man," muttered Elspeth.

Reluctantly, Miles let go the notes which fluttered onto the dashboard through the open window. Uttering an unidentifiable curse, the driver sped off, narrowly avoiding Miles' toes.

"Good riddance," he shouted after the cab, before leading the way up the narrow front path, ducking low under overgrown laurels. A scribbled sign informed callers that the bell was out of order. Miles knocked loudly on the cracked frosted glass panel but there was no response. Finally a blurred form could be made out approaching the door.

"Hang on, I'll just take it off the chain," said a disembodied male voice. A lengthy coughing fit delayed this operation. The door edged open and Tristan peered nervously out. Tall, thin, stooped, with bloodhound eyes and receding white hair, he was dressed in a murky maroon cardigan and olive green cords. A half-smoked cigarette with a drooping plume of ash was wedged between his fingers. As he raised the cigarette to his mouth, Miles noticed the onward march of liver spots on his wrist.

"Good Lord, it's you and...Elspeth too. What an unexpected pleasure! And who may I ask, is this?" Tristan's eyes lit up at the sight of Vera. Without waiting for an introduction, he took her hand and drew it to his lips. "Enchanté, mademoiselle." Miles had seen Tristan greet countless women in this way and it invariably made him squirm.

He studied his friend. Tristan had been regarded as something of an Adonis during their time at Oxford. Now a distinctly jaundiced patina had taken over his once finely chiselled features. His hands were shaking and Miles could smell the whisky breath. Years of alcohol abuse had blunted the wit that had once fuelled a popular column in The Spectator. That poorly-paid but prestigious sinecure had been lost some years before after a row with the editor who had threatened to kill him. There had been no apparent source of income after that. How he fed and watered himself remained a puzzle to Miles. After two childless marriages and countless casual girlfriends, there was no one left to keep watch on him.

"You'll have to forgive the mess. I'm afraid my cleaner has deserted me. Sorry about the pong. I've been having a bit of a fry up – burnt the bacon to a cinder. Even the cats rejected it." At least two of the creatures were encircling Tristan's legs as he spoke. He clapped his hands and shooed them way.

Unsure where to settle, Miles and the two women hovered in the hallway. Elspeth had taken the opportunity to look around disapprovingly at the overflowing cardboard boxes and piles of discarded newspapers.

"I've been meaning to unpack them for ages," said Tristan without conviction. "You wouldn't know how I could lay my hands on a nice Filipino couple who would take me on as a challenge, do you Elspeth?" The question having been ignored, he turned his attention to Miles, patting him heartily on the back. "It's good to see you, Miles. I was beginning to think you were avoiding me."

Any morsel of pity for Tristan's plight was soon dispelled by a brief glance at the state of the furniture they had inherited from their aunt. Ushering them into the front room, Tristan indicated some valuable, now battered, Regency-style dining chairs, one with a shattered arm.

"Do sit down. That sounds odd I suppose, considering it's your house," he said with a chuckle. Miles noticed Vera's eyes darting about the room, taking in the chaos. All three visitors remained standing as Tristan slumped into an armchair all but destroyed by cats' claws . "Suit yourselves," he said, as a hacking cough welled up from his chest.

Miles noticed that Tristan was eyeing the near-empty whisky bottle on the sideboard. There was little chance, Miles deduced, of them being offered a drink which was a relief. On the last occasion he had found something disgusting in his tumbler.

"As it happens, old pal, I've been meaning to get in touch with you. There's a nasty leak in the corner of the back bedroom. The damp's doing my books no good at all. There are some valuable first editions there, you know. I've put a bucket under it but perhaps you could send someone round?" There was an awkward silence before Tristan continued. "If it's money you're after, I'm afraid you're on a losing wicket." He turned out his trouser pockets and a few coppers clattered across the scratched parquet. Two bedraggled cats emerged from under the settee and shot across the room.

"Now look what's happened. We've upset Dido and Aeneas.

They're picking up the vibes."

"You're right," said Miles. "This is not a social visit. The fact is Tristan....the fact is..." He took a deep breath. "We need the house back. If you make it easy for us, we might be persuaded to forget about the debt," he added, surprising himself with his forthrightness.

"No problem," Tristan retorted brightly. "I can have the attic room. I wouldn't get in your way. Or here's an idea; we could do a swap. I could take over your room at the flat. Elspeth and I would rub along together well enough. Wouldn't we?" Elspeth glared at Tristan.

"I think not," she replied.

"Do you hear that Dido? They've come to give us our marching orders," said Tristan. The cat yowled and brushed suggestively against her master's shin. Tristan rose slowly and approached Elspeth, his arms outstretched. "Elspeth, Elspeth dear....Are you going to let this happen? Where's your legendary compassion?"

"Oh come on Tristan. You've been sponging for years," she replied, backing away.

Tristan flopped into his chair. The cats jumped up and perched on either arm, reminding Miles of Egyptian tomb guardians.

"If you don't mind, we'll take a look around," said Miles. Heading for the foot of the stairs, he beckoned to Vera and Elspeth to follow. His attention was caught by an exposed picture hook on the landing wall.

"Where is it?" Miles called out over the bannister rail.

"Where's what?" replied Tristan.

"You know perfectly well I'm talking about the Victorian watercolour of the Highlands." Miles was staring at the ghost of the frame's outline on the faded William Morris wallpaper.

"You've sold it, haven't you? Admit it."

"Whatever makes you think that?" replied Tristan who had wandered into view at the foot of the stairs. Miles cursed himself for having left this valuable item in place during Tristan's tenancy. A sense of having being badly let down now gave way to raw anger. Miles turned and hurried down the stairs, almost losing his footing.

"What else of ours have you sold?" he demanded, grabbing Tristan by the lapels.

"Leave go! You're hurting me."

"And don't insult me with more of your lies," said Miles.

"Alright...I flogged the picture a year or so ago. I was going to own up sooner or later."

"What else?"

"Just a couple of dreary etchings. You won't miss them."

Miles' right fist shot out and connected with the tip of Tristan's nose. A spurt of bright crimson spread over Miles' knuckles as Tristan slumped into the nearest chair staring disbelievingly at his unlikely assailant.

"Now look what you've done," he moaned. "Hurry, I'm losing pints of blood. Call an ambulance!" Tristan began to whimper.

Miles fished out his handkerchief and offered it to Tristan to staunch the flow. "He's right. He needs medical attention," Miles said anxiously, worried lest he had inflicted serious damage,

"Nonsense," said Elspeth, bending down to examine the victim. "It's only a nosebleed. Don't be such a wuss. Put your head back and it'll soon stop. We were quite prepared to make it easy for you Tristan, but your thieving spree put paid to that," she added, rising up to her full height. "We expect you and your menagerie gone within the month. Otherwise, it's the bailiffs." Elspeth looked to Miles for support. Still in shock at his uncharacteristic recourse to violence, he responded obliquely with a half nod. Vera meanwhile had been staring at Miles with an expression that appeared to waver between admiration and incredulity.

"I appeal to you... as an old friend," mumbled Tristan from behind the handkerchief. "How will you live with yourself if I bleed to death?"

"Well, Miles are you coming?" asked Elspeth, turning on her heels.

Casting a final uneasy glance at Tristan, Miles followed Elspeth and Vera to the front door.

Miles had neglected to note down the minicab firm's phone number and there was no alternative but to head for the nearest main road in the hope of picking up a black taxi. It was some time before Vera broke the uneasy silence.

"You're very quiet Miles. Do you feel bad...about what happened?"

"There's no need for him to, Vera. Tristan's been taking advantage of Miles for years. He had it coming to him," interjected Elspeth before Miles could summon his thoughts, yet alone reply.

Miles broke away from Vera and quickened his pace. Once level with Elspeth, he turned to block her path. "We're evicting him. Isn't that enough for you?" he snapped.

The drizzle had turned into a downpour and they were forced to take temporary shelter under a shop awning. Elspeth began to sniff as if attempting to stifle tears. "Miles, you can be so cruel."

Two passing youths sniggered on overhearing the row. The meaner-looking one spat out his gum which landed inches from Miles' shoes. He was about to reprimand the young offender when he thought better of the idea. There had been enough violence for one evening.

"I'm sure Miles didn't mean to upset you, Elspeth," said Vera.

"I don't know who you are any more," snivelled Elspeth. "Come on Vera. I want to go home. Find us a cab, Miles. That's the very least you can do."

Miles scanned the street before inserting his index and middle finger between his teeth. An apology for a whistle emerged which miraculously alerted a cruising black cab. Miles leant in to give the driver the address and then edged back under the awning.

"Aren't you coming?" asked Vera.

Miles shook his head. "I need some time to myself. I'll see you later."

"He's abandoning us, Vera. How's that for chivalry? " said Elspeth.

"You have me. I'll take you home. And you Miles, please take care of yourself," said Vera, kissing him lightly on the cheek before stepping into the cab.

✦

Miles was in no hurry to return to the flat. He needed time to reflect on the catalogue of dramas that had followed Vera's arrival, culminating in the aggression that had been uncorked in Brondesbury. In truth, he felt little remorse for striking out at Tristan. Although he would never admit it to Elspeth, at a visceral level the incident had felt oddly liberating. Had he been trying to prove something to her after her lecture on turning the other cheek in the face of his road rage incident? Miles had little time for indulgent introspection but maybe there was some truth in that.

As for the roots of all this, he reflected, a psychoanalyst would no doubt have a field day. Setting off in the rain down the deserted suburban high street, he was jolted back more than forty years to a night exercise on a windswept Dorset heath. Much to his chagrin, playing at soldiers was a key ingredient of the character-building school curriculum. A deeply miserable Miles is keeping guard on the platoon encampment amidst the dripping gorse. His sole companion on sentry duty is fifteen year-old Entwhistle, the ring leader of a relentless campaign to humiliate Miles on account of his less than sylph-like size. Entwhistle delighted in tormenting his victim while oozing oily charm when any member of the teaching staff came within view.

Without fear of being overheard on the gorse-strewn heath, Entwhistle's taunting reaches unendurable levels. Miles shoulders his rifle and points it at him.

'Go on Mallalieu, shoot. I dare you!" jeers his tormentor.

Miles removes the safety catch and takes aim. The bully spots a steeliness in Miles' eyes that causes him to turn and run. The blast force of the blank strikes Entwhistle in the lower back, knocking him to the ground. Standing triumphantly over his victim, Miles prods him in the ribs with the barrel. From this night on, the bully and his acolytes give Miles a wide berth. The incident is never reported. Miles had never mentioned it to Elspeth or anyone else since.

✦

Seated on the top deck of the near empty bus, Miles examined the knuckles of his right hand. The traces of his victim's blood had begun to congeal. He searched for his favourite spotted linen handkerchief to wipe away the residue but realised that he had handed it to Tristan. On impulse, he rang the bell and alighted at the next stop which happened to be near Warren Street. Setting off in the opposite direction to that of his flat, Miles' meanderings eventually took him in the direction of Marian's block of flats. He strode purposefully towards the main door. If she had been avoiding him, he needed to find out why. "It's me, Miles. I'm coming up," he announced, as if the notion of being refused entry was unthinkable.

Marian's voice crackled over the intercom. "It's rather late, isn't it? I warn you, I'm not looking my best." As he braced himself for the three-storey climb, Miles reflected that Marian would not have permitted this visit had she been entertaining her boss. Perhaps his suspicions on that front had been over-blown? Emerging breathlessly on to the landing outside her flat, Miles could see light spilling from the open doorway. There stood Marian, regally swaddled in a white fluffy dressing gown, hair piled high beneath a turbaned towel.

"So what brings you here at this wicked hour? Don't tell me you were just passing."

"Spur of the moment thing," replied Miles.

"You're kidding me Miles? Fisticuffs. Your life's become exciting at last," exclaimed Marian after Miles had relayed the details of the Tristan incident.

"He may press charges. I wouldn't put it past him."

"No way. He stole your property and he admitted it. Tell me honestly Miles, was it her idea...this eviction?"

"If you mean Elspeth...."

"I meant Ludmilla."

"I think it's Vera you're referring to," replied Miles stiffly. He was about to ask how she had found out about Vera but Marian interrupted.

"Such a quaint name. How did you two get involved? Go on, you can tell your old chum."

"We met in Chicago, if you must know. And we're not involved, as you put it."

"Be honest, Miles, you fancy her something rotten."

"That phrase is not to be found in my lexicon."

"Come off it. Even venerable scholars of ancient history look up from their books once in a while."

"Well you should know."

"What the hell are you talking about?" replied Marian.

"You and Herr Director. Are you...or aren't you?" demanded Miles, immediately regretting his question. Marian began scrutinising her nails. Miles took her silence as affirmative.

"I see," said Miles, biting down hard on his lip.

"What's it to you, Miles, what happens between Tony and me?"

"It's just that I don't like to think about that predatory creature taking advantage of you."

"We're quits there then...what with you and your Russian mystery woman." Marian tossed back her head, fighting off a suggestion of tears.

"Is that why you've been keeping away from me? I thought I was being paranoid," said Miles.

"It's not an easy thing to talk about, especially to a man." Marian appeared to sink into a sudden depression.

"What's not easy? You can tell me in absolute confidence."

"If you really want the gruesome details..." Marian sat down opposite Miles, pulling the hem of her dressing gown firmly down over her knees. "I agreed to have a meal with him after work at Mario's...that day you saw him go to pieces. He just wanted to talk and talk. All I did was nod in the right places. He walked me home. I found myself inviting him in for a coffee. Seemed the decent thing to do. He was going to have to book himself into a hotel and his phone battery was dead, or so he made out."

"Go on," said Miles.

Marian paused to expel a deep sigh. "Let's just say he wasn't gentle....far from it."

As Marian stifled her tears, Miles could sense the anger rising from his belly. "If I think you mean what I think you mean, you must report him, Marian. He should be made to face the consequences."

"Come on Miles, we both know I'd have a job being believed. He'd just say I consented. The worse thing about it is that I have to face the man every day. Now if you'll excuse me." Marian rose and headed for the bathroom. "I've said too much, You'd better go now. I need to dry my hair. You can see yourself out, can't you?"

His mobile rang as he left Marian's flat.

"Where are you Miles? It's almost two. Believe it or not, we were worried stiff about you. Vera made me ring every casualty department in London. Abandoning us like that in Shoot Up Hill of all places."

"As it happens I was just visiting a friend on my way home."

"Vera's convinced you've been with a prostitute."

"Nothing as colourful as that," replied Miles.

"I don't find that in the least amusing. And which friend would that be? I didn't know you had any."

"That dear sister, is none of your business. Now go to bed."

When he finally crept into the flat, he found that Elspeth had retired. Spotting a light on under the bedroom door, he slid past his sister's sleeping form on the Chesterfield and knocked gently. Vera was wide awake and brandishing a bottle of duty free vodka produced from her suitcase. Claudia, it transpired, would be out all night. They would not be disturbed. After much consumption of neat vodka came the welcome offer of a head massage. His lingering anger over the story that Marian had related began to wane as he succumbed to the soothing pressure of Vera's finger tips.

✦

After an awkward start, he later told himself he had acquitted himself tolerably well. Having undressed down to his string vest and boxers, he had climbed into bed to nervously await Vera's reappearance from the bathroom. He had debated stripping off completely but that would surely have been a step too far. As he lay there, Miles lamented the fact that his bed was unsuitable for dual occupancy. The pressure of his bodyweight had carved out a high-sided ravine at the centre of the elderly mattress, as if mirroring the process of glacial erosion.

Vera was taking her time and Miles had begun to wonder if she was having second thoughts. He distracted himself by experimenting with his pose. Would it be better to bury himself in his book or feign a light doze? Having plumped up the pillows, Miles settled for what he took to be a nonchalant position, propping himself up with fingers interlaced behind his neck. The lime green chenille bedspread had been hoicked up to chin-level so as to conceal what Elspeth uncharitably referred to as his 'man boobs.'

On catching sight of him, Vera burst into laughter. Before Miles could decipher this response, she nose-dived between the sheets and proceeded to curve her warm body around his middle section. Despite Dutch courage from the alcohol,

Miles was unable to overcome his coyness and insisted on extinguishing the reading light. In so doing, he accidentally tipped over a glass of water on the bedside table. Vera let out a shriek as a cold patch spread over the bottom sheet and made contact with their lower limbs. He held his hand over her mouth to stifle any further sounds. Vera bit down gently on his fingers and he uttered a feigned yelp of pain. Much to Miles' relief, this playful mood having been established, mirth became the oxygen of their pleasurable if short-lived entanglement.

"Bit rusty, I'm afraid," said Miles.

"Like metal, you mean?"

"I meant I'm out of practice," he replied sheepishly as they lay listening to the early morning sounds of the city.

"You were fine, Miles. More than fine," said Vera, stroking his stubble. "It's true what they say about Englishmen. They make love on their elbows. It's so considerate. Who taught you to do that? Your nanny maybe?"

He could have explained to her that, in his case her reference to British nannies had been somewhat wide of the mark. A succession of mousy German au-pairs had been taken into the Mallalieu household as live-in help during his formative years. To his continuing embarrassment, they had been preoccupied with ensuring the regularity of their charge's bowel movements, rather than any mission to enlighten him on the mysteries of sexual congress.

✦

It was after twelve noon when Miles and Vera ventured out of the flat. Vera had promised to spend time window shopping in Oxford Street with a now pacified Claudia who was either indifferent to, or appeared not to have noticed, her mother's new-found intimacy. Miles declined the offer to join them and out of habit, headed in the direction of the Department. He had no pressing reason to appear there that particular afternoon other than to check his pigeon hole. There was the book to finish of course, but perhaps not today. With the supremacy of electronic contact, he knew he would only find plaintiff notes from students whose emails he had failed to answer. But at least a hasty visit would enable him to check on Marian in the wake of her disturbing revelations.

A stiff breeze beat at Miles' cheeks as he stood waiting to cross the road at the junction of Great Titchfield and Mortimer Streets. He was startled by a tap on his shoulder. Swivelling around, he was confronted by a tall, spindly young man whose features seemed remarkably familiar.

"Uncle. This is a surprise!" It took Miles a moment or two to recall which of his two nephews had accosted him. He decided to take a chance. "Jeremy. You gave me a shock. I thought you might be a mugger."

His older nephew ushered Miles across the road, steering him adroitly out of the path of a speeding bicycle courier who had ignored the red light. They paused in a doorway away from the noise of traffic.

"What are you doing in London? I thought you were still at university," Miles ventured, conscious of his failure to demonstrate avuncular concern for either of Elspeth's charmless offspring.

"Graduated in the summer. Only a 2.2 I'm afraid."

"I see. Tempus fugit and all that," replied Miles who had no recollection of Elspeth having imparted this disappointing news.

"2.2 or no, got myself a proper job. Mother probably forgot

to tell you that too. I'm on my way to work now. I'm on the late shift."

"Shift? Do you work in a factory?" asked Miles, bracing himself for further disappointment.

"If that's your idea of a joke, Uncle...."

"Forgive me," said Miles recalling that as a child Jeremy had lacked any sense of humour.

"Do you have time for a coffee? It's on me," asked Miles, anxious to repair the damage.

"Here's your change, Uncle," said Jeremy appearing with the coffees. They had found a quiet table towards the back of Dino's.

"Please don't call me Uncle," said Miles, struggling to open the sachet of sugar.

"Why don't you let me?" said Jeremy, virtually snatching it from him. "How is Mother? I've been meaning to come round but what with the new job...."

"She's much the same," replied Miles, watching the sugar granules sink through the froth.

"What about academic life. Treating you well, is it? Can't be long now before we see that magnum opus of yours in the bookshops."

Miles grunted. "So what is it that you do exactly?" he asked, anxious to deflect further questions on the subject of his writing.

Jeremy glanced around the café before leaning in and whispering in Miles' ear. "Not really supposed to say but...security services. Fast track."

"Gracious. All that cloak and dagger stuff," replied Miles, unsure whether to be impressed or alarmed.

"I can tell you the selection process was no doddle. There

was a lot of competition. They said I had the right qualities." Miles detected a familiar note of smugness, implanted at the minor public school Jeremy had attended before scraping into a red brick university.

"Do they know your uncle was a paid up member of the Communist Party at Oxford?" Miles was unable to resist further teasing his po-faced nephew.

"As a close family member, I'm quite sure they looked into your past. They obviously don't see you as a threat," replied Jeremy.

"It's odd that your mother hasn't mentioned it....your job, I mean."

"She's not supposed to blab about it. Anyway, I'm still on probation."

"What does that entail?"

"It means that if I don't deliver on the current assignment, I may be working in a factory after all."

"And what assignment might that be?"

"You," replied Jeremy with a deadpan expression.

"I beg your pardon?"

"You are my assignment. Or to be more accurate, it's not you who my bosses are interested in but her."

"And who may I ask is her?"

"We refer to her as Heidi."

"I know no one of that name," said Miles.

A police siren obscured Jeremy's next response but Miles was left in no doubt about the identity of the alleged threat to national security. He clutched the edges of his chair to steady himself.

"You can tell your bosses they've been reading too many cheap spy novels," said Miles, regaining his equilibrium. "Are they seriously suggesting that Vera...Heidi or whatever you call her, has come to this country to subvert our precious democracy? Dr Petrovna's a respected academic. It's utterly ludicrous."

"I did ask if they could give the case to someone else," said Jeremy seemingly unmoved by his uncle's distress. "They just said you'd be more likely to cooperate if it was me. Flesh and blood and all that."

"I'm sorry Jeremy but you're just going to have to report that the subject was unconvinced by these absurd allegations. Now if you'll excuse me, I've got work to do on the book to which you referred," Miles added, as he prepared to disengage himself from this encounter.

Jeremy gripped his forearm tightly, effectively pinning him to his seat. "You don't understand Uncle...Miles...my career quite literally depends on you agreeing to play ball on this. The least you can do is to hear me out."

"Very well, if only to scotch this nonsense for once and for all," said Miles as Jeremy loosened his grip. A sudden thought sprung into Miles' head. "How much does your mother know about any of this?"

Jeremy nodded. "She had to be told. We need her cooperation. Her instructions were to make Heidi welcome. For all her weirdness, Mum has my best interests at heart. She wants me to succeed," he added, staring hard at Miles. There was a ping as a message came through on his nephew's phone which he examined. "There's someone I've arranged for you to meet. If I can't convince you then he will. He's not far away."

"And who might that be, M himself?" replied Miles, congratulating himself on recalling the acronym from the only Bond film he had seen. Jeremy's face hardened into a scowl.

As Miles allowed himself to be led him from the café, he still clung to the notion that this was some tasteless practical joke. Yet he had to admit that there was something about the set of Jeremy's jaw that seemed to belie that explanation.

"You might at least have the decency to tell me where you're taking me," said Miles, feeling more powerless by the minute.

"Let's just say you'll be meeting someone familiar to you," replied Jeremy, hailing a taxi which deposited them at the corner of the square housing the Department. As they alighted, Miles felt a sudden frisson of unease. Perhaps it was the Director himself whom they were going to meet? He would not put it past Tony Barstow to have cultivated a freelance attachment to MI5. A further paranoid thought occurred. Had the recent incident of his boss breaking down in tears merely been a charade to soften him up? Miles gave a shudder. Dissembling would come naturally to Tony, he decided, a talent that he himself lacked entirely. 'Where's your honesty got you?' being a favourite quip of Elspeth's to which he could never find a convincing reply.

Yet it was the public gardens facing the Department into which his nephew now steered Miles. At the entrance, Jeremy paused to make a phone call. Miles overheard "ETA two minutes," before Jeremy indicated that they should set off around the perimeter path. Miles looked around for a suitably sinister accomplice but the gardens appeared to be deserted.

"I think you two already know each other," said Jeremy, halting suddenly by a row of benches. As if on cue, a bedraggled figure rose Lazarus-like into view from a supine position. Doug gave Miles his usual friendly wave.

"Miles, great to see you again so soon. How's it hanging?" Doug reached out to grab his hand. Extracting it, Miles wiped his fingers surreptitiously on his trouser leg. Doug roared with laughter. "It's only make-up. I had a shower at the embassy before I came out."

"What on earth has brought you two together?" stuttered Miles.

"Let's just say that we're both on the side of the good guys. MI5, CIA, special relationship and all that," said Doug, breaking into a broad grin.

"You're working for the CIA?" gulped Miles. "An unusual career move for an ancient historian I would have thought. Are you telling me this...this get-up...all this is a sham?" It was certainly true that the odour of aftershave had replaced the blend of sweat and stale urine.

"Sit down Miles, there's a good guy," said Doug. "I'll fill you in. I guess I owe it to you."

Miles kept his arms tightly folded as if to protect himself from further unpalatable revelations. "After Princeton threw me out, no one would give me a job, not even as a janitor," explained Doug. "That was when Langley came calling. They wanted a piece of my brain and liked the fact they were doing me a favour. Gave them a convenient hold on me. That's the way they operate. Not so different from how the Russians do things, I'm told. Mind you, Langley gives me all the shitty jobs." He indicated the overflowing vagrant's trolley. "Convinced you though, huh?" Doug tugged at his ragged attire. "It's a great way to keep tabs on people. You can move round the city like you're invisible. Pity to have to junk it. I was beginning to believe my own performance." Doug held out a crumpled stick of chewing gum which Miles declined despite having a particularly nasty taste in his mouth. He felt a surge of fury at having been taken in by Doug's disguise.

"Okay, let's spool back," Doug continued. The pale sun had vanished below the roofline and Miles' extremities were beginning to feel the cool breeze. Doug glanced around as if to make sure no one had appeared to overhear them. "The Cold

War may be dead and buried but in case you hadn't noticed, the Big Chill is here and it ain't going away anytime soon. The old KGB mentality still hangs around the Lubyanka like the stench of dead rats under the floorboards. The point is Miles, they know the old ways still work. Remember all that sex scandal stuff in the 60s? Profumo, Ivanov ...using attractive women to inveigle their way into high places works every time. Never underestimate the power of pillow talk."

"You cannot be suggesting that the Russians would bother to send someone to spy on me?" snorted Miles.

"Don't take offence my friend, but the ex-KGB boys maintain a strange view of who's important to target in these damp and dreary isles," said Doug, patting Miles on the shoulder in a way he found profoundly patronising. "They've got this bee in their bonnet that British academics are respected and admired by your politicians who turn to them regularly for advice. That may be so in Russia, but in Blighty? Well... we both know differently." Doug smiled. "Don't get me wrong. It's not necessarily major secrets of state they're fishing for. They're perfectly happy with snippets of gossip. The point is they stitch it all together back in Moscow and hey presto, they get what they believe is a real insight into how your British political classes are operating, particularly when it comes to their attitude to Vladimir and his cronies."

"It's laughable. How could I possibly be of any use to them?"

"James Glendenning," piped up Jeremy, who was hovering nearby as if standing guard over the encounter.

"What about Glendenning?" asked Miles.

"You taught him as an undergraduate," replied Jeremy.

"As I recall, he showed remarkably little promise. What's he got to do with all this?"

"When did you last see him?" asked Doug.

"We've bumped into each other over the years at ghastly university fundraising do's. He always strikes me as dull as ditchwater. How he got to be Foreign Secretary is quite beyond me," said Miles.

"Be that as it may," said Doug. "That's precisely my point. As far as the Russians are concerned, it's entirely on the cards that you meet regularly and he may drop you juicy little nuggets of info on British foreign policy."

"And you're seriously suggesting they've sent Vera Petrovna over...to wheedle such things out of me?" asked Miles. "In case you were unaware, she's come to London in pursuit of her runaway teenage daughter. That rather undermines your theory, does it not?"

Doug and Jeremy exchanged looks. "You can call that a set-up or a convenient coincidence," said Doug. "Heidi would have been ordered to turn up on your doorstep on one excuse or another. Listen, Miles, we're both very sorry for you," he added. "I mean, being trapped by Moscow like this." Doug attempted to put his arm around Miles but was quickly rebuffed.

"It's a good yarn but it's pack of lies. Ergo I don't need your pity," replied Miles.

"We need your cooperation," said Doug, "...to beat the Russians at their own game. I can see that we're gonna have to prove all this to you. In the meantime, it goes without saying that you must not give her the slightest suspicion that we're on to her. Do I make myself clear?"

"You'll be expected to sign the Official Secrets Act," interjected Jeremy.

"I'm afraid, Jeremy, I don't subscribe to the concept of patriotic duty," said Miles, regaining the offensive.

"How can I put this? ....If you don't cooperate with us now, things could get very difficult and we may be powerless to help you," his nephew added. There was an icy chill in his voice which reminded Miles of Elspeth at her most threatening.

"How about it, eh? Your nephew working for the good guys. You should be proud of him," said Doug. Miles grimaced. The fact that Elspeth's eldest son was one of his tormentors added insult to injury.

"You take some time to think this through, Miles. We'll touch base later," added Doug.

"Just leave me alone now, will you!" snapped Miles. Doug shrugged and began gathering up the detritus which had spilled from his overflowing trolley. Their attention was diverted by an elderly park attendant wheeling a barrow in their direction. Whistling tunelessly he paused to glance at the strange cabal before giving Doug a cheery wave. Taking advantage of this distraction, Miles rose from the bench and edged away, clutching at the remnants of his dignity.

✦

As Doug and Jeremy made their separate ways out of the gardens, Miles stared at the pile of sodden leaves at his feet, as if attempting to read the dregs in a giant tea cup to determine his fate. He was still in a state of shock. However unlikely it may have seemed, he had allowed himself to believe that Vera found him appealing as a man. If the extraordinary tale spun in a London square proved to be true, he was left feeling beyond foolish. He had had his hopes raised and then cruelly dashed. He would have to face the fact that he had become, to use an expression gleaned from reading the odd American detective novel, a patsy.

The effort required to digest this unappetising prospect had brought on an attack of dizziness. In an attempt to regain focus, Miles fixed his attention on the façade of the Department. Its shabby familiarity may have been reassuring but the risk of bumping into tiresome colleagues such as Gavin or demanding students persuaded him against entering. He was about to turn away when his attention was caught by a Venetian blind blinking open on the third floor. He felt sure he could spot the backlit figure of Marian gazing out of Tony Barstow's office. After the disturbing revelations of that afternoon, he had never felt a greater need for a dispassionate confidante but the timing was far from right.

Dragging himself through Fitzrovia, Miles rehearsed what he might say to Vera. Would he defy Doug's edict and confront her outright with the allegations? Or would he stay silent, bide his time and maintain a lookout for anything remotely suspicious in her behaviour? By the time he arrived at the steps leading up to his block and took his customary deep breath before mounting the stairs, he had failed to reach any conclusion.

✦

"You were with Marian, weren't you?"

Miles had barely manoeuvred himself through the front door when his sister pounced.

"As a matter of fact we did have a drink together. Do give me a chance to get my coat off, Elspeth."

"I wouldn't have thought she was your type. A bit on the blousy side."

"Is Vera back yet?" he asked, with studied casualness.

Elspeth shook her head and busied herself in retrieving an overflowing pile of old issues of Psychic News which had slid off the overloaded coffee table. Miles meanwhile threw himself on the Chesterfield. Elspeth stood peering down at him with a stony expression. He needed no prompting to dutifully prise off his brogues. As Elspeth moved away, Miles found himself staring at her bony back. Had she been prepared to see him ensnared by a foreign power and helped set the trap? Could she really put her son's so-called career first at the expense of her brother's plight?

"Oh by the way, I forget to tell you I bumped into Jeremy on the way home." Miles said casually, curious to gauge her reaction.

"How is the boy?" replied Elspeth, shifting awkwardly as she turned to face him.

"Well enough, I suppose. But I think you know that. You neglected to tell me he was gainfully employed. Perhaps that's because he's got into something rather hush-hush, or at least that was the impression he gave."

"He doesn't like to talk about his work," replied Elspeth curtly and checked her watch. "Goodness, is that the time? I'm late for my colonic irrigation."

"Before you go, do you have any idea at all where Vera might be? She must have finished shopping by now surely," said Miles. "I've tried ringing her but there's no reply."

"You could always try that flat where the daughter hangs out with that other Russian floozy, the one who hooked the billionaire you're so chummy with. But before you go trotting round there, let me give you a piece of advice."

"And what would that be?" asked Miles, anticipating his irritation.

"If I were you, I'd take a shower first," said Elspeth, bustling out of the room.

✦

The tide of West End shoppers was at its high point as Miles battled his way across Oxford Street heading towards Bernie Prince's Mayfair flat. Above the wail of an approaching siren he became vaguely aware that his mobile was ringing and scrambled to withdraw it from the recesses of his pocket. His spectacles being badly in need of a clean, he was unable to decipher the caller's details.

"Miles here. Who is this?"

"It's Jeremy."

"What is it now?"

"In a few minutes time you'll be crossing Grosvenor Square. I just wanted to alert you to the fact that you'll see something relevant to our earlier conversation. You'll find Heidi on a seat at the south east corner of the square. The south east, OK? I should warn you... she's not alone."

"Haven't I made myself clear, Jeremy? I want no further part of this. It's time you got yourself a proper job."

"And Uncle...for Christ's sake, don't let her spot you spying on her, if you get my meaning," Jeremy continued unfazed, "I'll have a transcript of their conversation for you by this evening. I'm pretty sure it'll give you the proof you asked for. Cheers for now. Talk later."

Miles stood staring at his phone. No doubt he was naive when it came to modern snooping methods but how on earth did the security services know where to pinpoint both him and Vera, yet alone record her discussions in a public place? Miles' more politically-aware colleagues were always bleating on about the dangers of the 'surveillance society' and here seemed to be proof. His initial instinct was to take a diversionary route but he succumbed to the compulsion to discover whether Vera was indeed involved in an assignation of some kind.

A sense of direction had never been a Mallalieu attribute and it took several moments to establish where the south east of Grosvenor Square lay. Miles berated himself for conniving with Jeremy and Doug Allardyce's absurd hypothesis. Yet curiosity dictated that he would at least make a visual sweep of the elegant square. By squinting he was able to make out a female figure in the distance seated next to a man on the only bench occupied in that particular corner. There was something about the tautness of the woman's pose that immediately brought Vera to mind and he thought he recognized her blue overcoat. In defiance of Jeremy's edict, Miles was about to move closer when some inner trip wire stopped him dead. It would be more sensible, he decided, to keep watch from the middle distance.

A line of mature plane trees bordered the perimeter path and Miles concluded they would offer him convenient cover. After moving stealthily from trunk to trunk, attempting to keep out of the couple's line of sight, he paused at the halfway point and peered out from behind the broad-girthed trunk. Vera, for it was she, sat a foot or so away from her unidentified companion who was probably in his early thirties. His inaudible entreaties were accompanied by exaggerated gestures of the hands, suggesting to Miles that his origins were other than Anglo-Saxon.

Raw jealousy welled up from the pit of Miles' stomach, a sensation he had not experienced for decades. Who was this man and what was he to Vera? She was, after all, the woman with whom he had made love the previous night and who had given physical expression to the warmest of feelings for him. Yet some minutes into his clandestine vigil, rational thinking returned. This, Miles concluded, was most unlikely to be a tryst. The young man was dragging furiously at his cigarette while continuing to talk in a hard-nosed fashion at Vera who nodded morosely. His head was close-shaven and his features appeared Slav-like. A heavy brown leather jacket added to the stereotypical portrait of an espionage agent, an image dragged from Miles' store of cinematic clichés.

If they were not quarrelling lovers, could the alternative really be as unpalatable as it seemed? Miles struggled to shake off the germ of paranoia that Jeremy and Doug had implanted. If these were Russian spies, it was highly unlikely they would meet in the shadow of the American Embassy in this brazen way. Perhaps the young man was a friend or colleague of Vera's from St Petersburg? Miles shuffled over to a closer tree, sliding behind the trunk which barely matched his own girth. He glanced down and saw that he had forgotten to fasten his flies before leaving the flat. He made a hasty adjustment, only to find that the zip had become stuck at half mast. He tugged at it without success. The Slav meanwhile was preoccupied in handing Vera a small package, before rising abruptly and striding away. Vera remained quite still, staring vacantly ahead.

"Excuse me sir, can you tell me what you're doing behind that tree?" The police officer had appeared without warning and caused Miles to jump.

"Nothing, officer, nothing at all. What on earth do you mean?"

"There's been a complaint." The officer nodded in the direction of a young mother with a large buggy who scowled at Miles as she caught his eye.

"According to the young lady, you've been seen acting suspiciously. We could be looking at a breach of the peace or something altogether more serious, if you get my meaning." He indicated a small group of toddlers playing noisily on a patch of grass nearby. A gaggle of mothers were gathered close to their offspring and the complainant had returned to join the circle. Miles felt their joint stares bore through him.

"I was taking a stroll. Is that a crime these days?" he replied, somehow maintaining his surface composure, aware that his zipping action had been misconstrued. The officer gave no reply and maintained a deadpan expression. "Look.... I can explain, officer. The fact of the matter is I've come here to meet someone but she's late. I was simply killing time. There she is now. Over there!" he blurted out, pointing to Vera without a thought for the implications of his invented alibi.

"In that case, you won't object if we check your story with your friend? If she vouches for you then all's well and good."

"If it's all the same to you officer, I'd rather you didn't. It's rather delicate," replied Miles. "Perhaps we could continue this conversation elsewhere?" he added, turning his back on Vera while attempting to draw the policeman away from her line of vision.

"You're beginning to waste my time sir. If you don't cooperate, I'll have to ask you to come with me to the station for further questioning."

"You're making a huge mistake, officer," exclaimed Miles loudly. In an attempt to control his rage at this suggestion, he sucked in the air between his teeth which produced a whistling sound, shrill enough to alert Vera to his presence. Startled, she jumped up and scurried away without looking back at him. She was halted by the police officer calling out after her. With obvious reluctance, Vera waited for him to draw level. Miles strained to catch their brief exchange but traffic noise reduced it to an inaudible murmur. He could not be entirely certain but he thought he detected a shake of her head.

◆

Miles woke with a start. He had no idea how long he had been dozing but he berated himself for this lapse in watchfulness. He knew he had to maintain his concentration at all times if he was to have any chance of extricating himself from this debacle. After Vera had made her hasty exit, Miles had continued to argue his innocence in vain. He had endured the humiliation of being cautioned, handcuffed and led to a waiting police van in full public view. As the rear door was about to close on him, he noticed a satisfied smirk on the face of the young woman who had reported his so-called suspicious behaviour. The police van had delivered him to West End Central police station at high speed with siren blaring. During the short journey he had been wedged between two burly policemen who had amused themselves with comments such as: 'Looks like a stuck pig, doesn't he?' 'More like an over-inflated balloon to me.' 'You need to lay off those sponge puddings, sunshine...' Miles winced as their barbs echoed in his head.

On arrival, he had been searched, his possessions removed and for what seemed like hours, he had been left alone to ruminate in a windowless interrogation room. His demands that a lawyer be summoned had so far produced no result. He had had ample time to pour over Vera's refusal to vouch for his identity. It was both puzzling and deeply dispiriting. Was this a de facto confirmation of her involvement with the KGB or whatever it was called these days, or had she merely taken fright and been reluctant to involve herself with the forces of the law?

He was jolted out of his deliberations by the sound of footsteps and voices in the corridor. The door of the interrogation room swung open and a barely recognisable Doug Allardyce appeared, now fully scrubbed up and grey-suited. He was flanked by nephew Jeremy, his bland features betraying no emotion at the sight of his uncle in distress.

"Don't get up," said Doug. Miles had no intention of doing so. His braces, along with his sock suspenders, had been confiscated on arrival at the police station and his unsupported corduroys were in danger of joining his socks which were hanging limply around his ankles.

"What are you two doing here? Have you come to gloat? I thought you might be lawyers."

"Well, well, you do seem to have got yourself in a real spot of bother this time," said Doug. He turned to Jeremy. "Your uncle has no one else to blame but himself, has he?" Jeremy nodded in confirmation. His expression had remained utterly impassive and Miles began to wonder if his nephew's induction into MI5 had involved a lobotomy. "You gotta admit it was very careless of you to attract suspicion like that," added Doug. "But have no fear, we're here to help limit the damage."

"There's no point asking how you knew about this," replied Miles. "I'm beginning to understand how you people operate."

"We all need friends when we're in trouble," interjected Jeremy.

"I choose my friends rather carefully but family, one is stuck with," replied Miles glowering at his nephew.

"Let's not kid ourselves," said Doug. "A court appearance on a juicy charge of indecency is unlikely to impress your paymasters at the university. The tabloids will have a ball. It'll spell the end of an illustrious, or should I say already tarnished, career? Those student complaints that keep piling up must keep you awake at night." Doug leant in towards Miles and spoke in a semi-whisper: "We can pull the right strings to get you out of here without a blemish on your character. As a bonus, we could even arrange for your nemesis, Tony Barstow, to be eased out of the picture. How does that sound?"

Miles snorted and folded his arms tightly. The prospect of being indebted to them in this way made him squirm. "You're assuming that the so-called evidence of my nefarious activities would stand up in a court of law. Supposing I was to decline your offer and take my chances?" he added, suddenly discovering new reserves of resistance.

"That would imply that you have an exaggerated faith in British justice," replied Doug firmly. "As it happens, the mother who reported you turns out to be the daughter of a prominent German industrialist whose company invests heavily in the UK. Believe me, her word will carry a lot of clout."

"Are you seriously implying that courts would be swayed by such things?"asked Miles.

"I'd be happy to give you a character reference myself, but these days you'll appreciate I have to keep a low profile," said Doug with a wry smile.

Jeremy now approached Miles, brandishing a large brown envelope. "Hot from the press. We promised you the transcript of what Heidi and her minder were discussing. I think you'll agree it makes interesting reading. As you see, it's long and rambling. The translator did the best she could. I've highlighted the most striking bits. "Jeremy proffered the envelope to Miles whose hands remained firmly planted on his knees.

"Go on, Miles. Take a look, you owe it to yourself," said Doug.

With a deep sigh Miles withdrew the stapled document and studied the first page superficially. It was laid out in a format that reminded him of a play script with dialogue labelled H, presumably a reference to the codename Heidi, and X for her apparent Russian contact.

"Read it now. We can't leave it with you," said Jeremy, adding: "We're pretty confident you'll want to come on board after you've got the gist."

Miles could not bring himself to read the transcript in any detail. Instead he skimmed the highlighted sentences. 'You must work harder to gain his trust...' said X. H replied: 'You don't understand. He's not an easy man to get close to. He is emotionally very well defended.'

X 'Have you slept together yet?'

There was no recorded response from H then another question. 'Has he asked you to live with him? We agreed that must be your goal.'

H 'I'm working on it, for God's sake.'

Miles thrust the document away. "How do I know it hasn't been doctored to suit your cosy little thesis?"

"It hasn't. You have to believe me," replied Doug gravely, as Jeremy stooped down to retrieve the document from the interrogation room floor.

✦

However much Miles despised the nature of the bind in which Doug and Jeremy had placed him, he knew then that he was not prepared to see the last vestiges of his academic career snatched away. He knew also that this reassurance would come at a high price.

"Very well," he said, taking a deep breath. "What is it exactly you expect me to do?" Fuelled by his fury with Vera, the words had slipped out. The prospect of the murky arrangement into which he was about to enter caused the bile to rise. He swallowed hard to hold it down.

Doug exchanged a look of relief with Jeremy. "We need you to be on standby to follow our instructions and I'm talking 24/7," replied Doug.

"Your job will be to help us feed the Russians with what we call disinformation," added Jeremy in his irritatingly clinical tone. "You'll be playing a really important part. You should feel good about it."

"I hope you realise what you've got yourself into, Jeremy?" said Miles, fixing his nephew with an icy stare. "Entrapping family members into the espionage game is not everyone's idea of job satisfaction."

"Don't be too hard on the boy," interjected Doug. "I don't need to tell you that these days, Moscow is keen to wrong foot us at every turn. We need to strike back in any way we can. You may not be a political animal Miles, but you can surely appreciate that."

"Just before we go any deeper into this quagmire," said Miles, turning to Doug. "If you're so sure Vera is what you say she is, why don't you simply arrest her?"

Doug smiled. "That's a no brainer, Miles. Apart from the juicy bits of disinformation you're going to help us feed her, she's far more useful left in place here. With luck she'll lead us to others operating undercover in London."

"If we nab her, she'd be deported and on the next plane back to Moscow to be treated as surplus to requirements,'" interrupted Jeremy. "We learnt about the way they work on our induction course."

"What Jeremy is trying to say is that they don't tend to reward failure. She'd probably be disappeared, if you catch my meaning," said Doug. "The upshot is that you'd be extremely unlikely to ever see her again. I wonder how you'd feel about that. You two have been getting on so famously."

"I need a glass of water," said Miles, his mouth dry as a wadi. He was on his feet, clutching the waistband of his unsupported trousers. "Before we part, I don't want you to imagine that I am helping you out of some distorted sense of patriotism."

"You've made the right choice, that's all that matters," said Jeremy, breaking into a smile that Miles found repugnant.

"OK. Session over," said Doug crisply. "You're free to go. How does that sound?" He headed for the door to the interrogation room which he held open.

"After you, sir," said Doug, allowing Miles to pass through into the corridor before following him and closing the heavy steel door behind him. "Do you still want that water or maybe something stiffer would be more appealing?"

"There's a decent little watering hole round the corner. Are you sure we can't tempt you?" asked Jeremy as they emerged from the police station on to Saville Row. Miles shook his head. Taking a welcome gulp of what passed for fresh air, and without any form of farewell, he strode away with as much speed as he could muster.

✦

The pungent smell of frying onions had greeted Miles as he climbed the stairs.

"How do you like the goulash? It's the recipe my grandmother used. You said it was one of your favourites. I don't cook it for everyone." Vera paused, waiting for his reaction as they faced each other over the kitchen table. Elspeth, he discovered, was at a whist drive and Claudia was out with Irena.

Miles grunted non committedly and wiped his mouth with a sheet of kitchen roll. He had managed to maintain his silence while eating, aided by Vera's unstoppable diatribe about the shame that the wealthy oligarchs brought on their less affluent but largely law-abiding fellow countrymen.

"Thank you. Now if you'll excuse me, I have some work to do." He rose from the table and headed for his study. Closing the door firmly behind him, Miles stood motionless, feeling his heart hammering with the tension of maintaining this charade. The first contact with Vera after the day's revelations was never going to be easy. He longed to extract the replica statuette of Astarte from his cupboard and seek the goddess's wisdom and solace in this time of crisis. He had not done so since that morning of the scooter accident. It occurred to him that Astarte may be feeling neglected or even jealous of his new female interest. He decided though to bide his time. There was the risk of being disturbed and he had no wish to have to explain such eccentric behaviour even to a fellow ancient historian. Was she even a bona fide academic? Miles had begun to doubt everything Vera had told him about herself.

Miles switched on the computer and sat idly waiting for the screen to settle down. He was disturbed from his reverie by his phone ringing deep in his trouser pocket. He had quite forgotten carrying it, yet alone leaving it switched it on.

"Can you talk?" It was Jeremy's flat tones.

"What kind of question is that?" snapped Miles.

"Please don't make life difficult for me. You do want me to succeed, don't you?"

"I'd be a great deal happier, Jeremy, if you were stacking shelves at Tesco, though I doubt that your mother would approve. What is it you want now?"

"You're going to a party tomorrow tonight and you're taking Heidi...Vera... as your plus one."

"A party? I'm hardly in the mood. Where?"

"The FCO, Whitehall. It's a formal thing so I suggest you smarten yourself up. We'll send a car for you both at six. The

Foreign Sec's been briefed. He'll make a point of seeking you both out. He'll be acting as if he's pleased to see you. That's all Doug said you need to know for now. Will fill you in later. Gotta go. Ciao."

✦

Vera had greeted the news of this grand invitation with what seemed to Miles like a suspicious degree of enthusiasm. He assumed she would be in contact with her chain-smoking controller to pass on the news. Her choices being somewhat limited, she had elected to wear the same dress borrowed from Elspeth which she had worn to Annabel's. Miles had dusted off the grey double-breasted suit he kept for funerals.

As they inched into the crush filling the Foreign Office's vast Durbar Court, Miles was alert to every nuance of Vera's behaviour amongst the Great and Good. Gulping down a fortifying glass of champagne and a meagre canapé proffered by flunkeys, they stood on the periphery eyeing up the intimidating groups of clearly well-acquainted fellow guests. A mingling of expensive fragrances clouded the air and shards of light from the great glass roof splattered the coiffed hairdos and gleaming bald pates. African and Asian traditional attire sung out amongst the blur of dark business suits and restrained cocktail dresses. Miles' eardrums throbbed from exposure to the conversational roar.

They had not been there more than a few minutes when their host pounced. "Miles, it's good to see you. And in such delightful company!"

"This is Dr Petrovna, Dr Vera Petrovna," stammered Miles for whom introductions were never straightforward. "This is.... James...Glendenning...our Foreign...err..." In truth, he scarcely recognised his former pupil. He appeared to have both shrunk in stature and filled out in girth since their last meeting some years previously at a university event. The piggy eyes, however, remained a distinguishing feature which newspaper photos failed to capture.

"It's a pleasure to meet you, Dr Petrovna." The Foreign Secretary turned to Miles with a well-oiled smile. "I'm so pleased you could both make it to this little celebration." He stretched out his palms as if to encompass the glittering assembly in what Miles felt was a misplaced emulation of a papal gesture. "I'm sure that Miles has told you, Dr Petrovna, that I was fortunate enough to have him as my academic supervisor. What a mind. Such a remarkable grasp of realpolitik."

"We ancient historians are not as out of touch as some people might think," replied Vera with a winsome smile.

"So you're of the faith too?" exclaimed Glendenning. "Well said. Indeed not. That's where the long view of history really comes into its own, helping to put the modern world into perspective," the Foreign Secretary added, his eyes wandering up and down Vera's frontage. Having clasped her hand, he had continued to cradle it in a way Miles felt to be bordering on the inappropriate. "And what, if I may ask, brings you to London?"

"I'm here to visit my good friend here." She smiled at Miles. "We have much in common." Finally freeing herself from Glendenning's grip, Vera squeezed Miles' arm affectionately. Miles tried not to tense up. She was putting on a good performance, as indeed was Glendenning whom Miles recalled had spent far too much time away from his studies with the university drama society.

"I trust your visit isn't entirely work-related," the Foreign Secretary continued. "You're a lucky man," he added, beaming at Miles before returning his gaze to Vera. "You do know that I rely on Miles' judgement. Have done for years. He's indispensable to me. Perhaps he hasn't told you? Not only is he brilliant but he's also very modest which is why we consider him to be something of a national treasure."

This is going too far, thought Miles. Vera was attempting to gain his attention by tapping her upper lip in a curiously insistent way. On a reflex, Miles rolled his tongue over the corresponding area and tasted the saltiness of salmon, a residue no doubt of a hastily grabbed canapé. He used the back of his hand to wipe it away.

"Will you forgive us for a moment for talking shop, Dr Petrovna, but I've been meaning to consult your Miles about something rather pressing. I want to seize the moment, as they say."

"Would you like me to shut my ears?" suggested Vera, playfully raising her hands as if to block them.

"I'm quite sure we're among friends," replied the Foreign Secretary with a smile. He had moved closer to Miles but remained well within earshot of Vera. "It's just that we're thinking of increasing our support to the Yemenis. Nothing too drastic. A few more military advisers. Boost the training programme to keep their army on their toes. That sort of thing. Do you think that will send the right signals?"

Miles blinked. He was struggling to recall exactly where Yemen was on the map or anything about the current situation it faced. He'd scarcely glanced at a newspaper for weeks and had been meaning to buy a new battery for his ancient Roberts radio. Whilst struggling to come up with a credible response, he was distracted by the sight of Doug Allardyce in a grey suit, propping up a nearby pillar, no doubt keeping a close watch on the encounter. He gave Miles a cheery wave which was not returned.

"So what do you think, Miles? I am all ears," prompted the Foreign Secretary.

"Ah Yemen," replied Miles, in a tone that suggested it was uppermost in his thoughts. "I'll have to think about that one," he spluttered. "Probably worth a try though."

"My sentiments exactly. I knew I could rely on your judgement. You've just got a nous for these things," exclaimed the Foreign Secretary batting Miles playfully on the shoulder. At that moment a short woman in a low cut vermilion dress popped up and stood clutching Glendenning's arm, waiting to be introduced.

"Ah, there you are, dear," exclaimed the Foreign Secretary with an obvious lack of enthusiasm. "May I introduce Dr Vera Petrovna. This is my wife, Patricia. Miles Mallalieu, you know of course."

"Do I?" replied his wife. Glendenning smiled awkwardly. "You'll have to forgive me. As James will tell you, remembering people isn't my strength," his wife added.

"I taught your husband at university."

"You have my commiserations," replied Mrs Glendenning.

"I'm sure Dr Petrovna would appreciate your ideas on what to do in London at this time of year, dear," said the Foreign Secretary, barely disguising his irritation. "Why don't you give her a briefing?"

"How am I doing?" Glendenning asked, drawing Miles aside as the two women began to converse separately.

"Doing?" asked Miles.

"We both know what we're talking about, Dr Mallalieu."

"I'm sure she's impressed with our little charade, if that's what you mean," replied Miles.

Glendenning smiled and stood back, examining Miles

carefully. "It's good to see you again. I can't perjure myself and say you don't look a day older, but then no doubt you'd say the same of me. I really want you to know that we appreciate the help you're giving our friends in the Firm. Keep it up and we'll see about a gong for you. Now we must rejoin the ladies."

Miles had noticed a square-jawed man with piercing blue eyes who had been hovering some feet away. He now seized his moment to home in on the Foreign Secretary. "Ah, Sergei," said Glendenning. "There you are. Come and meet a fellow countryman, or should I say countrywoman? May I introduce Dr Vera Petrovna and this is her friend and colleague, Dr Mallalieu. They're both ancient historians. And my wife Patricia you know of course." He turned to Miles and Vera. "Mr Kutuzov is the ambassador for the Russian Federation and a great chess enthusiast. An interest we share, don't we Sergei? Perhaps one day I'll beat you."

The Russian ambassador grinned. "I don't believe we've met," he said, shaking Vera's hand formally. "Which is your university?" he asked in heavily accented English.

"St Petersburg."

"My old alma mater. How are things there?"

"We can't complain," said Vera with a tight smile.

"What brings you to this great country?"

"I was asking Dr Petrovna precisely the same question," interjected the Foreign Secretary, indicating Miles. "I think we have the answer." Miles felt his face flush.

"Excellent. A living example of Anglo-Russian solidarity," declared the Russian ambassador. "That is very touching." He raised his glass as if to salute the relationship. "Nah zda-rovh-yeh! Cheers."

"I was just telling Dr Petrovna that Dr Mallalieu and I go

back a long way, "said the Foreign Secretary. "Now he's one of my most valued advisors."

"Perhaps we should make him a counter offer he can't refuse?" said the ambassador with a grin.

"I doubt whether you could afford me," replied Miles, surprised by his own repartee. The ambassador chuckled at this response and the others broke into dutiful laughter. Miles, who had been studying Vera, noticed a flicker of nervousness cross her eyes.

As the mirth subsided, Miles felt a heavy hand on his shoulder and a familiar estuarine voice rang out. "Well if it isn't my favourite nutty professor? How are you doing Miles, old son? Haven't seen you in Annabel's lately."

Resplendent in a shiny charcoal suit, Bernie Prince had burrowed his way into the centre of the group and proceeded to slap first the Foreign Secretary and then the Russian ambassador on their backs. "James, Sergei... Nice to see we're all pals. All's fair in love and business, eh?"

Both men appeared to Miles to show distinct signs of unease at this intrusion but made a point of shaking Bernie's hand warmly.

"It appears to be a very small world," said the Foreign Secretary, gazing round at Miles, Bernie and the ambassador.

"And if it isn't the lovely Vera!" He moved over to kiss her on both cheeks. "Must fly. Great do, James. Got the chopper waiting at the heliport." As he turned to go, Bernie called out to Miles: "Have to get you and your lady on the yacht before the weather turns. I could do with a bit of intellectual stimulation. Come to think of it, make it next weekend. Call my PA and she'll fix the flights. That's settled then." Extracting a business card from his wallet, Bernie strode over to slide it into Miles' breast pocket.

"Adios one and all," he added, giving a mock salute before vanishing into the throng.

✦

"That was amazing. Your Foreign Minister treats you like a guru," said Vera, attempting to gain Miles's attention after a lengthy silence. He was gazing out at the blur of West End crowds through the darkened windows of the official car returning them to his flat.

"I wouldn't put it quite as strongly as that," replied Miles tersely.

"And now we have an invitation to spend the weekend on a billionaire's super yacht. Since we found Claudia, everything is becoming like a dream."

Miles was tempted to comment that it seemed more like a nightmare. Having consumed large quantities of Foreign Office champagne, Vera had maintained a garrulous stream of consciousness which Miles managed to ignore. He was distracted by distress signals from his stomach. The meagre quantity of canapés at the reception had done little to assuage his hunger. Yet the notion of engaging in small talk with Vera over another intimate meal was unthinkable now.

On their return to the flat, Vera professed not to be hungry and busied herself with checking her phone. Elspeth had retired early, leaving a 'Shocking migraine, do not disturb' note on the kitchen table. In Miles' experience, his sister's headaches were little more than excuses to avoid him. On this particular occasion, he was grateful for her absence as it delayed the need to consider the thorny question of her complicity in 'Operation Heidi'.

Having made do with a lump of out-dated Cheddar accompanied by two limp sticks of celery, Miles announced that he was tired and would be turning in for the night. Vera's attention was still fixed on her phone. Was she, he wondered, sending a coded message to her Russian controller?

"That's fine. You go ahead," she said. "I won't be long I promise, but I need to make arrangements for tomorrow with Claudia. Irena is driving us to the airport."

"Where are you going?" asked Miles, thrown off balance.

"Not me, her. I'm staying with you. You know that, Miles," She smiled winsomely. "I will just see her off and come straight back."

"This is all rather unexpected, isn't it?" said Miles.

"I can't believe I forgot to tell you," replied Vera. "It wasn't confirmed until this morning and there's been so much happening. Forgive me but you should be pleased for her, Miles. She's been offered a chance to study website design at the Technical College in St Petersburg. It's not exactly ancient history but it's something at least. She must start immediately. Oh Miles, you can imagine it's such a relief for me. You know I worry so much about that girl."

"I thought you told me that she had no chance of getting a place anywhere, except behind bars."

"Miles, please don't joke about such things. I spoke to a family friend who has influence and well...it's like a miracle. They will take her even without an interview. In my country like in yours, it's important to know people in, how do you say? ...high places."

"A family friend, you say?"

"Yes, a family friend." Vera shifted awkwardly. "What do you mean exactly?"

"Nothing," Miles replied.

With her angry eyes and nostril piercings, Miles had found

it hard to warm to Claudia. Vera had made it clear that her daughter was one step away from being incarcerated for drugs offences. Yet, despite this, he had deduced that Vera was exceptionally close to her only child. It was almost as if they were sisters. There was perhaps an unhealthy aspect to their relationship but as Miles reminded himself, who was he to judge? He was a childless single man after all. Vera would undoubtedly want the best for her offspring, especially if her accounts of the useless absent father were to be believed.

Miles was still grappling with these thoughts as he brushed his teeth in a desultory way. His deep sense of hurt was impossible to throw off, but could it be that he had misjudged Vera? Perhaps the story he had been spun was not as black and white as it might appear? Neither Doug nor Jeremy had given any clue as to her motivation. Yet if he were to confront her directly on the subject, she would undoubtedly deny any involvement and, with her cover blown, would be forced to return to Russia to meet an uncertain fate. As he stared vacantly into the toothpaste-spattered mirror, Miles was struck by an unshakeable thought: even if Vera was a cold calculating servant of the Russian State, he had no real inclination to wriggle free from the emotional lasso she had thrown over him.

"Are you ready to turn off the light?" asked Vera, slipping into bed beside him and snuggling closer.

"Yes. Good night," replied Miles, without turning to face her. Donning his face mask, he drew himself up into his customary foetal position to await the release of sleep.

As he drifted towards unconsciousness, the image of a gleaming private yacht came into his mind. Perhaps a luxurious weekend afloat would act as a diversion from the tangle of intrigue in which he now found himself? It would also give him a chance to test Vera further. Besides, although he was no sailor, Miles had always had a thing about boats. A rare bright memory from childhood was that of summer holiday excursions in his Uncle Nigel's speedboat racing back and forth across Poole Harbour. He had revelled in the sensation of speed as he was towed behind it on homemade wooden skis, somehow managing to keep upright, the salty spray stinging his cheeks amid shouts of approval.

✦

Miles had barely finished breakfast when his enthusiasm for the forthcoming weekend was dampened by a phone call from Tony Barstow demanding a progress report on what he described as the 'schmoozing' of Bernie Prince. Tony had become euphoric at the news of the last-minute invitation on board the yacht, reminding Miles that time spent with Bernie at such close quarters would be the ideal opportunity to pin him down to write that cheque. Miles' attempts to persuade Tony to lower his expectations to zero were to no avail. As it was, he could hardly bring himself to speak to Barstow after Marian's revelations. After he had hung up, Miles reflected that it was all very well entering into dubious deals with Doug Allardyce and Jeremy to remove the threats to his career if the Department was to be shut down for the lack of a financial saviour. He would just have to fight off his revulsion at producing the begging bowl.

The flat was mercifully quiet. Vera had left early for the airport to see off Claudia and Elspeth appeared to still be asleep, confirmed by the odd snore emanating from her bedroom which she had re-colonised, having accepted that Vera would be sharing Miles' room. While he was in the midst of dressing, the phone rang once more.

"It's Doug. Are you alone?"

"As it happens I am. What is it?"

"We thought you'd like to know that we've just intercepted a message from their embassy back to Moscow. They fell for it, your little scripted melodrama with Glendenning. Operation Heidi's off to a good start, Miles. It's all going very nicely, very nicely indeed."

"I'm pleased for you," replied Miles.

"Oh and we've just heard about your weekend jaunt on the Prince yacht. Heidi must think she's on to a good thing. Don't forget to send us your updates. You're certainly living the high life these days, Miles. Not bad for a crusty academic, huh?"

CHAPTER FOUR

Mediterranean madness

Word had reached Miles via a telephone call from Bernie's PA that they should be ready to be collected by car from the flat at eleven the next morning promptly. All they would need to bring were some lightweight casual clothes, not forgetting swimming attire. The PA assured them that the Riviera was enjoying an Indian summer. This presented Miles with a slight problem. Rooting though the chaos of his drawers, he had discovered nothing more suitable than two elderly short-sleeved Aertex shirts with several buttons missing, a battered Panama and a linen suit that he had acquired during a sabbatical in Cape Town some twenty years before. There were no shorts of any description to be found.

"What's the point of exposing yourself anyway? You go red as a lobster after five minutes in the sun," had been Elspeth's response when Miles enquired if she had happened to notice any swimming trunks tucked away in some forgotten corner. He had managed to avoid communicating with her until this sartorial crisis weakened his resolve. The graver issue of her supporting role in his entrapment would have to remain un-explored, at least for the time being.

❖

The waiting limousine appeared to stretch halfway down the street. Despite being double-parked, an obliging traffic warden was waving traffic on past it. The uniformed chauffeur pressed something into the warden's hand before taking hold of Miles' shabby case and Vera's red plastic hold-all. Having been ushered into the cavernous interior, they settled back as the limousine purred towards the suburbs.

"You know, Miles, I could get used to this," said Vera, kicking off her shoes and stroking the suede upholstery.

"It's not going to be all fun and games," Miles replied. It's what we call a busman's holiday."

"I don't understand...why busman?"

"Please don't ask me to explain," said Miles wearily. The pressure to act as if his attitude to the relationship was unchanged had begun to manifest itself physically. The muscles in the back of his neck felt as if they were being squeezed in a vice.

✦

The Gulfstream private jet climbed sharply through the blanket of heavy cloud above Luton airport where they had boarded through the gate reserved for VIPs. Miles allowed his body to sink into the generously proportioned soft leather seat. After enduring decades of flying 'cattle class' to conferences on many continents, it was hard to take in the fact that Vera and he were the sole passengers on this flight with two air hostesses dancing attendance.

A burst of sunlight filled the cabin as the aircraft broke through the clouds, infecting Miles with a momentary sense of optimism. He gazed at Vera who had dozed off beside him. Despite all he had heard, he could not help but still feel something akin to affection for this vivacious woman who had parachuted into his lacklustre life. As the plane levelled off at its cruising height, champagne cocktails appeared. After two of these concoctions, Miles concluded that there was much to be said for the trappings of the material world.

The flight was over all too soon. As it began its approach into Nice, the Gulfstream appeared to skim over the surface of the postcard blue sea dotted with pleasure craft idly carving their courses along the Cote d'Azur, as if defying the close of summer. After the smoothest of landings, the jet taxied into a corner of the airfield reserved for private aviation. As the cabin door was opened, Miles paused at the top of the aircraft steps and raised his chin to the sky, soaking in the still warm autumn sun.

His ears were assailed with a deafening clatter as Vera and he were guided across the tarmac towards a waiting helicopter with rotor blades spinning. Moments after they had been bundled aboard, the machine leapt from the ground, the rapidity of its elevation taking Miles by surprise. He had never before flown in a helicopter and the prospect of entrusting one's life to a single set of revolving blades seemed alarming. Vera also seemed perturbed and grasped Miles' hand for reassurance. The pilot was squawking into the intercom but Miles was unable to catch a word of what he was saying. He thought it prudent nonetheless to give the man a thumbs-up. It was always sensible, he believed, to be on good terms with those entrusted with one's life.

The helicopter appeared to be heading directly out to sea. Unnervingly, Miles was unable to recall whether it had been fitted with floats for a liquid landing. He was still grappling with this when, after a few minutes, the machine began to drop from the sky apparently heading directly for the waves.

Vera's nails dug deep into the flesh of Miles' arm. With eyes tight shut, Miles struggled to recall the words of the Lord's Prayer. He had not recited it since schooldays and then only under duress. Stumbling after 'And forgive us our trespasses...' gingerly he opened one eye. To his astonishment, instead of the azure Mediterranean waters rising to meet them, a vast pleasure yacht, seemingly the size of a cross-Channel ferry, had loomed into view directly below.

Mimicking a giant insect settling on its prey, the helicopter now lowered itself onto a giant letter H painted on the yacht's upper deck. Once the rotor blades had finally come to rest, Miles and Vera were helped from the aircraft by a uniformed crew member dressed in a dazzling white high-collared jacket with gold epaulettes.

"Welcome aboard La Celestia! I'm Andrew, your steward but you can call me Andy. I'm here to make your stay on board as comfortable as possible," he shouted above the noise of the dying motor. "First off, I'll have to ask you to remove your shoes. House rules to protect the decks. He handed them each a pair of espadrilles embossed with the ship's name and indicated a nearby bench for them to sit on. "We had to guess your sizes," he added, glancing at Miles' boat-like feet.

Vera appeared equally dazed after their dramatic descent. Miles was perturbed to see that his big toe was poking through a hole in his left sock like a bulb in early spring. No doubt registering Miles' embarrassment, Vera smiled reassuringly as he attempted to squeeze into the espadrilles.

"Now if you'll both be so kind as to follow me to your quarters," said Andy whose boyish face Miles found strangely irritating. "It's your first time on board I believe. Bit of a rabbit warren. Takes some getting used to. We'll give you a map of the ship's layout or there's an app, if you have a compatible smart phone, that is." This remark was addressed to Miles who was not about to confess that he had yet to fully master the rudimentary functions of his decidedly low-tech mobile.

As they followed the steward through lavish lounge area after lounge area, the sheer opulence of the yacht's interiors became apparent. Miles had neglected to pack sunglasses and the expanse of white leather seating, chrome fittings and highly polished flooring caused him to squint.

"You're both professors I understand? Makes a change. We usually get politicians and business types on board. You'll definitely raise the tone. Don't tell Mr Prince I said so though," said Andy nervously as they descended to a lower deck.

"Where is our host?" asked Vera, clearly as awestruck as Miles by the extravagance of their surroundings.

"The Prince, as we call him, madam, is on a business trip. Beirut, I believe. He'll be flying back in time for dinner. He asked me to apologise. He would have liked to be here to greet you in person."

"What kind of business is Mr Prince involved in?" asked Vera.

"I am not party to that kind of information. This is your stateroom. Mr Prince wanted you to have the best one on the ship," said Andy, opening double doors to expose a palatial cabin furnished in a sleek, ultra-modern style and dominated by a vast bed. The entire wall opposite was taken up with a flat-screen television.

"Can I bring you some champagne?"asked Andy.

A cup of tea would be nice," was all Miles could think to reply.

"And for madam?"

"Yes tea will be fine thank you," replied Vera.

"Very well. Tea it is," said Andy, clearly disappointed by their choice. "I'll be right back. Please feel free to watch TV. There over five hundred channels. All tastes catered for," he added, with an unreadable smile.

✦

"You're not going to leave that? Remember all those starving children in Africa, as my old Nan used to say," exclaimed Bernie.

A virtually untouched lobster in its rosy-hued shell stared up at Miles from his plate. Despite a predilection for crustaceans, dissecting them daintily had never been Miles' forte. Vera and he were seated at lunch the next day with their newly-arrived host and his young Russian girlfriend, Irena, on the upper deck of the floating colossus.

"Bernie, it's so beautiful...your yacht...everything and you are the perfect host. You do know that we are really honoured to be your guests?" Vera raised her glass. "Cheers!"

"So you should be my girl, so you should be," replied Bernie, fixing her with his ice blue eyes. That's it, Miles, my man. Get stuck in!" he exclaimed, as Miles finally succeeded in gouging out a thin strip of lobster flesh and popping it in his mouth. There was an audible crunch as he bit down on a fragment of shell he had failed to detach. Expelling a cry of surprise, he nursed his jaw.

Despite his hunger, Miles would have given anything to be able to crawl back to his cabin. He had a headache and his espadrilles were rubbing on his swollen feet. Yet there was the pressing matter of his mission to hook the Prince millions to save the Department. He decided he had better begin making an effort to engage their host in convivial conversation. He had read somewhere that there was nothing that the rich liked better than a chance to boast about their material possessions. Miles decided to put this theory to the test.

"Am I right in thinking that that is the real thing?" he enquired innocently, pointing in Bernie's direction.

This?" his host asked. "What do you take me for Miles – a cheapskate?" Bernie roared with laughter and fingered the chunky gold chain around his neck.

"No, no," Miles stammered. "The picture... behind you." Miles's knowledge of art was patchy at best. Yet he felt sure he could detect a strong influence of Renoir in the sugary but charming portrait of a young girl in peasant dress hanging directly behind Bernie's left shoulder.

"Gotcha," Bernie roared with laughter. "So you like my 'Renwower'? It was my ex's favourite. I almost flogged it off. Came with the ship. Bought the job lot off one of your fellow countrymen Vera. Let's just say he ran into a little problem with the Kremlin and had to divest himself of his assets in a hurry. Mr Prozikov's loss is our gain, eh?"

Vera smiled and again raised her glass to Bernie. Miles had to admit that Vera was looking particularly fetching in a closely-fitted summer dress she had acquired in a sale for twenty five pounds. It was all too obvious that this had not been lost on Bernie. Irena was silent and sulky. She had clearly noticed his interest too.

"Remind me, Bernie, what happened to Prozikov?' asked Vera, idly trailing her fingertips in a silver finger bowl strewn with rose petals.

"Not a pretty business,"replied Bernie, leaning in towards her. "He is, as our Italian friends put it, 'swimming with the fishes.'"

After this conversation stopper, it was time for more overt

flattery. Miles cleared his throat.

"You seemed to have done alright for yourself Bernie, if I may so," he declared, inwardly cringing as he indicated the yacht's towering superstructure.

"Any idiot can make money," replied Bernie.

"There's no money in ancient history, believe me," said Miles.

"I can confirm that," interjected Vera, seemingly renewing her attempt to gain Bernie's attention.

"Education is a beautiful thing. The world needs people like you, Miles."

"That's very gratifying to hear," Miles replied.

"OK, let's cut the crap. We need to talk, right? Come." Miles drew his chair closer to Bernie.

"How much do they need?"

"How much do who need?" Miles replied.

"Your people. Come on Miles, don't be shy. I know why you're here. I have my spies. I've done my due diligence."

Miles hesitated. It was hard to believe that the need for further soft soaping of Bernie's ego had been circumvented. "Very well. Since you ask, I'm told that eight million should see us out of the woods." Then he recalled Tony's instructions. "Well actually...fifteen would be ideal."

Miles waited for the inevitable rejection. Instead, Bernie leapt up and seized his hand in a vice-like grip.

"Miles, my old son, we'll make it happen. Comprende?"

` "Splendid," replied Miles, utterly dumbfounded. Had it really been this easy?

Bernie began pacing the deck. "Just one thing though. I'll get my name plastered all over the building, won't I? Nothing too naff, mind. I'm not talking neon here."

"Well... I'd have to...." Miles muttered, before recalling that

Tony had joked about even permitting toilet paper bearing the Prince logo.

'The Bernard Prince Department of Ancient History. You've got to admit it's got a neat ring to it. I fancy one of those honorary degrees. You can you fix it for me, Miles. That's settled. No time to waste then," Bernie continued. "I'll need to get it all done and dusted before the end of the month," he continued, lowering his voice. "My ex is trying to take me to the cleaners. The faster I can divest myself of some serious assets the better, which happens to be your good fortune. Besides, I want to do my bit for British education, don't I?"

"I think it's wonderful news, isn't Miles? You're so generous Bernie," said Vera.

"I know," he replied with a smirk "I like to make people happy." He clapped his hands. "Now we've got the business out of the way, time for a tour of the tub, eh?

"If you'll forgive me, I think I need to lie down," replied Miles who was still in shock.

"You can take me, Bernie" said Vera. "I'm sure Miles will be happy with that, won't you? I'll join you later."

"Why not?" replied Miles.

"That's settled then," said Bernie, placing his other arm over Vera's hand and preparing to lead her away. "Where shall we start?"

"At the beginning," replied Vera with a broad grin.

"OK. Bow to stern it is," announced Bernie before turning to Miles. "Off you go and get your shuteye. I'll look after her, don't you worry."

Miles turned away without acknowledging Vera's farewell wave as she disappeared down the deck arm-in-arm with Bernie.

✦

Miles awoke in a sweat from a chaotic dream. He checked the bedside clock. 16.45. He had been in a deep sleep for more than two hours and Vera had not yet returned. Was there a possibility this could this be an attempt to make him jealous? Her behaviour with Prince had bordered on the flirtatious after all.

"Oh Miles, this yacht has two pools and a big movie theatre! It's incredible to believe it all belongs to one man." Vera had reappeared as he was reviving himself by splashing water on his face from the gold-plated tap.

"Yes and that man seems to be very taken with you," replied Miles, calling from the marble-lined bathroom.

Vera shrugged. "Listen, I've met guys like him before. He thinks he can buy anyone."

"Well, that's the point, isn't it? He can buy anyone," replied Miles. "He's as good as bought the Department."

Vera placed her hand on his shoulder. "Listen to me, Miles. You think you've got what you need from Bernie. But he could change his mind at any time. I'm only helping to make sure he keeps his promise to you. We have to keep him happy."

"How do you think it makes me feel, kowtowing to a crook?" replied Miles.

"What is 'kowtowing'? ..never mind, think of all your colleagues who would also lose their jobs too. And one day maybe I would work there too just like we talked about."

"Did we?"asked Miles, aware of his disingenuous tone.

"Relax Miles, and please try and enjoy our little adventure." Vera moved forward to plant a kiss on his lips. Miles turned away. Vera moved off with a shrug.

"For God's sake Miles, you're behaving like a jealous teenager. You've been strange for the last few days. Now don't forget we have water skiing at five. I can't wait."

"I'm not going and that's that," said Miles. "Besides, I haven't got any swimming trunks."

"These will have to do," replied Vera producing a voluminous pair of paisley boxer shorts from a drawer. "No one will know the difference. Put them on quickly or we'll be late."

Two crew members clad in pressed white shirts and shorts were stationed on the lower deck ready to decant Bernie and his guests into a sleek mahogany Riva speedboat moored by the ship's stern. Bernie greeted Miles with a bear hug and Vera with a fulsome kiss. There was no sign of the sullen girlfriend and Miles found himself enquiring after her. "Irena?" replied Bernie. "She's no water babe. Gone ashore to empty a few jewellery shops, just the three of us then. Nice and cosy, eh?"

The roar of the engine rose in pitch as they skimmed across the bay of Villefranche with Bernie at the wheel, until the mother ship had become a speck in the pale blue distance. Miles clutched the chrome rail as the boat wove an intricate path between yachts at anchor. Miles cranked his neck round to check on Vera. He had to admit that she cut a splendid figure as she zigzagged artfully back and forth at the end of the tow rope on her single ski.

"Are you thinking what I'm thinking? That girl's a natural," yelled Bernie, competing with the throb of the motor. "She's been lying to us. Can't believe she hasn't done it since she was a kid." As if acknowledging the compliment, Vera nonchalantly raised one hand from the bar attached to the rope and waved. Wiping the salt spray from his lenses with his handkerchief, Miles settled back, yielding himself up to the warm breeze.

After signalling to Bernie to cut the engine, Vera relinquished the tow rope and with a final flourish, sank into the waves as gracefully as a Nereid. Bernie manoeuvred the boat alongside her bobbing head, and with a "Well done that girl," kissed her on the lips as she climbed back on board, "How was it for you?"asked Bernie with a grin.

"Fantastic," replied Vera, shivering as Bernie made much ado of wrapping her in a large beach towel. Vera smiled at Miles as if to say 'How about that?' before stretching out full length to dry off in the sun, beaming with contentment. Miles attempted in vain to interject his own plaudits but Bernie continued to hog Vera's attention.

"It's my turn now," blurted out Miles. There was a lengthy pause. Bernie and Vera exchanged bemused glances.

"Ever done it before?" Bernie asked warily. Miles shrugged. "I like a man who goes outside his comfort zone. Good on you," Bernie added.

"Are you sure you want to do this Miles?" Vera asked nervously.

"Of course I'm sure. Now pass me that life jacket, will you?"

Although the speedboat was becalmed, the process of extending and buckling the straps around Miles' middle took several minutes to complete. Once he was fully encased in the bulbous orange jacket, Bernie and Vera stood back to inspect him.

"There you go. How's that feel?" asked Bernie, barely suppressing his amusement. "And no remarks about the Michelin man, I promise....there goes that tongue of mine again."

The jibe went unanswered as Miles was buffeted by a strong gust of wind and all his efforts were required to maintain his balance. He took in a deep gulp of air to induce a semblance of calm before forcing himself to move to the rear of the speedboat. Without waiting for instructions, he now prepared to enter the sea via the short ladder hooked over the stern.

"The man's unstoppable," said Bernie, peering over the side as Miles lowered himself backwards into the brine, emulating Vera's earlier actions. To his surprise, the water temperature was tolerable and the sensation of bobbing around in the gentle swell supported by his lifejacket was not unpleasant. "Just stay where you are and I'll pass you down the skis," shouted Bernie. "Keep your knees up to your chin while you get them on. Don't you worry old son, we'll have you up on your feet in no time."

The operation was hampered by the fact that Miles' arms were unusually short, so he had been told by his doctor father who regarded his child as a medical curiosity. Shoehorning his toes into the rubber ski bindings whilst bobbing around in the swell proved a lengthy and exhausting process. Spray was whipping in Miles' face and obscuring his vision. With hammering heart, he persevered and after several false starts, his feet were finally attached to the skis as he bobbed about buoy-like in the water.

"Keep those skis up at ninety degrees and face me!" yelled Bernie. "Here, catch, and whatever you do, don't bend your arms and don't let go."

The current was now threatening to pull him away from the boat. As Miles struggled to grasp the handle of the tow rope which was by now floating three or more feet away, his teeth and jaws began chattering uncontrollably and for the first time in his adult life, he found himself calling out for his mother. A voice in his head exhorted him to remain calm. He was after all wearing a life jacket. He would show the Bernie Princes of this world the true mettle of the Mallalieu line.

"Miles, you don't have to do this, you know," Vera yelled above the engine which was burbling lustily as it strained for the off. A sudden eddy sent the tow rope conveniently floating towards him and Miles succeeded in gripping the bar attached to it with both hands.

"Here. You'd better take these," he called out through knocking teeth. By assuming a vigorous paddling motion with his spare arm, he had managed to manoeuvre himself within range of Vera who leant over to scoop up his spectacles.

"How will you see?" she asked, peering down at him with a look of increasing concern.

"Better I don't," replied Miles, coughing violently, having swallowed a mouthful of sea water. "Now just tell me what to do next."

"If you're sure?" shouted Vera.

"Yes, I'm quite sure."

"Ok, this is what you do..."

Before Miles could think of confirming receipt of the ensuing instructions, Bernie began revving the powerful engine. As the boat gathered speed Miles curled his knees up into his chest in a womb-like position. The resulting pressure on forgotten muscles caused a sharp stab of pain to shoot through his thighs. To increase his discomfort, sheets of spray were blurring his depleted vision.

"You're letting your skis drift! Keeps them pointing upwards, parallel to each another," yelled Bernie.

By twisting his calves clockwise, Miles found he could separate the unwieldy planks of plastic that had become entangled. His skis were now pointing skywards at exactly ninety degrees.

"Good on you, Miles!" shouted Bernie. "Hold that position. Thumbs up means you want me to go faster. Down means slower. Got that? Remember to keep those arms stiff as a tom cat on heat and just hang on. Here we go."

Miles felt the tow rope tense as his fingers tightened around the bar. Arms taut, eyes screwed up against the spray, he was propelled forward with a sudden lurch, ploughing through the froth of the boat's wake. The wind was shrieking in his ears as he gingerly raised himself into a semi-squatting position. He was now skittering across the surface and Miles could hear the whoops of encouragement. Yet sustaining the momentum of this near-flawless take-off seemed unlikely and Miles braced himself for the inevitable capsize. Miraculously, his semi-upright stance was maintained and his skis continued to clatter cheerfully over the swell.

Feeling emboldened as the speed boat swooped around the bay, Miles slowly elevated himself to a vertical position without mishap. He was experiencing a sensation of near weightlessness. It was as if his corporeal being had been dissolved. Through the spray, he could make out Vera applauding him from the stern of the boat.

Although elated by his unexpected prowess, Miles decided that fate had been tempted far enough. Releasing one hand from the bar, he gave the agreed thumbs down signal for the boat to slow. Yet far from slowing down, the boat now appeared to be gathering speed at an alarming rate. Again, he gave the thumbs down signal but to no effect. Every fibre of his strength would be required if he was to retain a grip on the rope. His ankles, weak at the best of times, had become involuntary shock absorbers and the pressure on them was becoming intolerable as he bounced over the waves. To ease the pain, Miles sank to a near squatting position on his skis and buried his face in his arms to avoid the worst of the buffeting. His jaws were chattering to such an extent that his teeth could be heard clashing together.

Surely Bernie and Vera had seen his signal? They were entering a stretch of choppier water and the seascape was turning a monochrome grey. Miles clung on to the bar. He knew that he was losing the last semblance of control when the tips of his skis began to veer alarmingly to left and right, slapping up and down against the swell, sending shock waves through his body.

It was all over in a fraction of a second. As the skis rose from the horizontal to meet him, one ski struck his cheekbone a glancing blow before it prised itself free from the ankle bindings to be lost in the waves. The remaining ski also went its separate way. Sea became sky and sky became sea. Twisting and turning on the end of the line, he was dragged along like flotsam caught in a trawler's net. One moment he was underwater, the next, inches clear, retching and gasping for air. Still Miles hung on to the rope until the last sinew of will snapped. As he felt the bar slide through his fingers, a wall of water rose up to meet him and he was lost in a cloud of bubbling liquid.

He found himself floating face down. Despite rising panic, Miles somehow succeeded in raising his nostrils above the surface, taking deep gulps of air while expelling mouthfuls of water. He was bruised, cold and in shock but apparently still alive. All he had to do was to remain calm and wait to be rescued. Executing his version of doggy paddle, Miles searched for a blur that would indicate the reassuring proximity of the speedboat.

It was the throbbing of the engine that finally gave away its position, some distance to his right but close enough to hear voices. He shouted and waved frantically to attract Bernie and Vera's attention. It would surely only be a matter of minutes before he would be hauled aboard.

To his astonishment, far from moving in for the rescue, Bernie was now steering the speedboat away from him at full pelt. "What are you doing? Come back!" Miles cried out feebly, any remaining shreds of strength fast ebbing away. A glance at his thighs beneath the surface, revealed a mass of blue-tinged flesh. He could not survive much longer in the open sea without hypothermia setting in. A sense of paranoia began to take hold. Was Bernie leaving him to die of exposure? Why else would he be deliberately heading away? Miles felt his body go limp and his mind blank. He closed his eyes.

The mahogany hull finally hoved into Miles' vision. As the boat drew alongside, Miles found himself gazing up into Bernie's bullet-like features. Miles could see that his host was wearing a broad grin as he reached over the side to extend a rescuing arm. It took several failed attempts to haul Miles out of the water. He yelped with pain as his ribs knocked against the side. Finally, he lay on his back in the well of the boat shivering and spluttering like a beached amphibian..

"You should've seen yourself. You should've seen yourself!" exclaimed Bernie." "Don't worry, old son, I'm not going to throw you back. Here, wrap up. Don't want you dying on us," he chuckled, throwing Miles a beach towel.

As the speed boat headed at full throttle towards the mother ship Vera crouched down and leant over Miles, "You did so well. I'm proud of you for trying," she said, tucking a second towel around his shoulders.

"The man's a sadist. Why didn't you stop him?" Miles snapped."

"I tried to, Miles, believe me," replied Vera. "He wouldn't listen."

"Well you didn't try hard enough."

"This'll help," said Bernie, turning to toss over a small silver hip flask. Miles made no attempt to catch it.

"Suit yourself. Just a bit of harmless fun. If we're going to do business together Miles, you're going to have to get used to my warped sense of humour. Looks like our boyfriend's getting uppity," he added, turning to Vera. "Seems he can't take a joke. Don't sulk, Miles. It doesn't suit you."

Miles turned away and fixed his gaze on the disappearing wake. Had Bernie's plan all along been to humiliate him in front of Vera? As Miles stared at the thick set of his host's bulldog neck, his stomach began to churn with fury.

✦

His anger still simmering, Miles had slunk off to the cabin to be alone as soon as they had re-boarded La Celestia. Every cell of his body was aching from his aquatic ordeal and strands of seaweed were still embedded in his chest hair. Having prised himself out of salt-stiff boxers, Miles had wrapped himself in a towelling dressing gown and rolled on to the bed with no intention of stirring.

As he lay with his eyes closed, Bernie's sabotaging of the brief, unexpected moment of triumph on water skis propelled him back into a dank corner of his childhood. Miles' parents had made it clear that when it came to physical prowess, their second born was a disappointment. One incident, seared into Miles' memory, now resurfaced. Mallalieu senior had considered mastering the art of riding a bicycle to be an essential milestone on the path to manhood. Miles had not the slightest interest in abandoning his tricycle which, by the age of five, he had long outgrown. His father decided therefore that it was time to force the issue. During a summer holiday on the Isle of Wight, he announced that young Miles would be pleased to demonstrate his cycling skills, a two-wheeled machine having been commandeered from a neighbour. Miles begged to be spared this ordeal but his father would brook no refusal. Having gathered the family ceremonially at the summit of the gravelled drive leading from their holiday cottage, Mallalieu senior launched his son forth with a sharp shove to the back of the saddle. As Miles sailed downwards, for a few seconds he remained miraculously vertical. Yet as the iron gates leading to the public road grew closer, the bicycle gathered speed. Applying the brakes, the machine slid from underneath him. He rolled off the driveway through a bed of nettles before finally coming to rest in a weed-clogged garden pond. Miles hauled himself from the stagnant water to a chorus of familial laughter, his skin on fire with nettle burn, hot tears carving channels in his cheeks. "Well, aren't you at least going to pick up the bike, boy?" his father called out with barely disguised disdain.

✦

He was startled from his reverie by his mobile phone.

"How's the schmoozing going?" Tony Barstow's supercilious tone was as grating as ever. "Well, have you hooked the fish?"

"I presume, Tony, that you're referring to my efforts to extract large amounts from someone you would normally dismiss as a jumped-up spiv?"

"This is no time for niceties, Miles. Has he or hasn't he? I've just come from a meeting with the Vice-Chancellor. He's given us three months to come up with a major donor to fill the funding hole. If no go, he made it quite clear that they'll close us down at the end of the academic year. We're relying on you Miles. So what have you got to tell me?"

"All I can say is that he's making the right noises."Miles was taking delight in keeping his boss dangling. The good news could wait until he returned.

"Keep up the pressure," said Tony. "Get your new lady friend involved. She knows how to roll out the charm."

"I wasn't aware that you and Dr Petrovna had met," said Miles, unable to conceal his surprise.

"She dropped in to see me last week. Didn't she tell you? Oh and by the way, just so you know, my wife and I have decided to give it another go."

✦

"Ah, there you are, my learned friend," said Bernie, rising to greet Miles from the dinner table. "No need to be shy. We'd given up on you. No hard feelings ?" he said, grinning at Vera. "Go on, Miles. Tuck in. We've had our fill. I know you're a man with a healthy appetite." Bernie winked at Vera. "Am I right?"

Much to Miles' dismay, Vera responded with an enigmatic smile. Miles had noticed the table was only set for three. "Aren't we missing somebody?" he asked.

Bernie shrugged. "You mean Irena. You must've heard the chopper leave? The little minx demanded to be flown back to London. Some big party she was desperate not to miss. Suppose I can't blame her. She's been getting cabin-fever. Good riddance, I say."

Miles glanced over at Vera before replying to Bernie. "No doubt a man in your position has no shortage of new offers."

Bernie pinched Miles' jowls between his thumb and forefinger, forcing Miles to delay the delivery of the next mouthful of giant prawn. "Do you know something, Professor? I like you," he roared. "Have done since I scraped you off the floor at Annabel's. You're a one off. Quite a change from the sleazy bastards I spend my life dealing with. Hope my generous offer's gone down well with your bosses in the ivory tower," he added. "Expected a bunch of flowers at the very least, to keep me sweet."

Miles gave no reply. Bernie refilled their glasses and took a large swig himself. "Just before we get stuck in though, a word of warning in your shell-like ear. There's one thing we need to get straight," he said, placing his arm round Miles' shoulders.

"And what would that be?" asked Miles, bridling at this gesture. He was fully expecting to hear Bernie was having second thoughts.

"They're not going to go all ethical and get their knickers in a twist about my business interests, are they?" asked Bernie. "Not if they want my money, that is." He tapped the side of his nose. "No point looking for trouble, eh?"

"I see," replied Miles, uncertain how to react.

"As you might have sussed at that fancy do, the British government love me, or put it this way, they tolerate me because they need my services when certain factions they support in the Middle East say, need that little bit of extra muscle," Bernie added. "Mind you, it's not only the Brits. Mr P never fails to send round a bottle of Bolly to my suite when I check into the Kempinski."

"Are you talking about our President?" demanded Vera, wide-eyed.

"He's Vladimir to me," said Bernie. "All things to all people, that's Bernie Prince. Enough said. If your boffins want my filthy lucre, they'll have to take that on board. Comprende?" He grinned at Miles who put down his knife and fork with a loud clatter.

"What's the matter, Prof? All this straight talk put you off your nosh?" He turned to Vera. "Your boyfriend seems to find my hospitality not exactly to his taste." Vera shrugged and turned away to stare towards the deep mauve horizon.

"Don't get me wrong, Prof. Bernie Prince deals with all sides. Right wing, left wing...all politicians are in hock to people like me. They're jealous of the power we corporate boys have to make our own rules. And believe me, they don't turn their nose up at an invite to party the weekend away on ritzy tubs like this one. I'd work for Old Nick himself if he had a nice fat untraceable offshore account. Done very well with the CIA with those rendition flights. Pity they've taken them back in-house. Very lucrative, they were. Can you believe they wanted to use this yacht as a floating interrogation centre? But they wouldn't cough up the million a week I was charging. Had the nerve to tell me I was fleecing the American people." Bernie burst into guffaws of laughter. He had worked himself up to such an extent that his complexion had turned a deep puce and Miles noticed the veins were standing out on his temples. How on earth, he asked himself, had he been taken in for a second by this gargantuan egomaniac?

Bernie rose and approaching Miles from behind, began to massage his shoulders. The formidable downward pressure of Bernie's hands trapped Miles in his seat.

"Relax, Miles. I'm good at this. You're as stiff as a corpse."

"I'd rather you didn't do that," said Miles through clenched teeth. The tightness of his shoulder muscles meant that the pain was excruciating.

"Suit yourself," said Bernie, releasing his grip. He moved round to sit close to Miles while Vera was now standing by the ship's rail. "Me and Vera have been chewing things over. Haven't we Vera? The upshot is that if I'm to bail you lot out, there's one little extra condition attached. I'm sure you would be more than happy to oblige. You tell him, Vera."

Vera crossed the deck to sit next to Miles who was now

flanked by the two of them. "I wanted to tell you before but somehow..." she started up then paused. "Bernie will pay for a five year research project for me at the Department...your Department. This would be an incredible opportunity. If I bring research money with me, then they can't refuse to hire me, can they?"

"Is this what you discussed with Tony Barstow when you just happened to drop in to see him?" asked Miles, feeling well and truly ambushed.

Vera reddened. "It was only a short meeting. You and me, we talked about me getting a job there, after all."

"I recall mentioning we're having to reduce faculty numbers not add to them."

"Don't you see, Miles? If Bernie makes it a condition, they will have no choice."

"That's not how we do things in Britain. Was this all your idea, Vera?"

"We cooked it up together last night, didn't we?" interjected Bernie. "We'll get our friends in Whitehall to sort out the visa situation. No sweat."

"Of course as Vera's sponsor, I would expect, how shall we put it? ...visiting rights."

"What are you talking about? Visiting rights?" demanded Miles.

"I think you know full well." Bernie tipped his chair back and yawned. "Sharing the goodies can't do anyone any harm. Consenting adults and all that."

Miles glowered at Vera. "Are you really prepared to allow him to treat you in this way?" Vera's expression remained impassive.

"We can all go to Annabel's, just like old times, eh?" interjected Bernie. Pushing back on his chair, Miles started to rise.

"Where are you going?" asked Bernie. "Sit down. You haven't had as much as a flea's fart to eat."

"I want to be put ashore," announced Miles, with as much dignity as he could muster.

"Aren't you forgetting some rather important unfinished business?" said Bernie. "I've given you my word.   Here." Scooping up an envelope from the table, Bernie fished out a cheque which he brandished in Miles' direction. "Bit of a feather in your cap, eh? You can beg at the rich man's table like the best of them."

Miles snatched the cheque and set about tearing it into fragments which were swept away by a sudden breeze.

"Are you crazy?" demanded Vera.

"Hold on a sec, Professor." Bernie had risen to confront him. There was an icy hue to his pale blue eyes. "So you don't like the colour of my money?" Miles began to edge away but Bernie grabbed him by the wrist. "More's the pity."

"Will you please let go of me. You're hurting my wrist," demanded Miles.

"Tell me something," said Bernie, ignoring the appeal. "What turns you on? Maybe you're a secret book sniffer? Talking of books, Vera tells me you have a block. Can't finish your biggie – your great work that's gonna change the world. Rather like not being able to get it up, wouldn't you say?" Bernie erupted in peals of laughter. "Come on. Answer me back! Give me some more of your lip. I expect you to earn your keep, Miles. I invited you on board to keep me entertained."

"I don't have to listen to this. Are you coming?" Miles appealed to Vera. She caught his gaze for a split second then turned away.

"Look at yourself, Miles. You've spent your life trying to keep out of trouble and now trouble's come up and bitten you in the bollocks. And what do you do? You take it on the other cheek." Bernie had begun circling Miles, laughing uproariously as he waved his arms in his face. "Go on!" He pointed to his own chin. "Let me have it. Don't take this shit from an uneducated oaf like me. Hit me!"

The force of the punch knocked Bernie off balance, causing him to sway for a moment before collapsing on to the deck. "Stop!" shrieked Vera, launching herself into the fray in an attempt to pull Miles clear. Miles's response was to push her aside and step up the assault. Dropping on to his knees, he placed his hands firmly around Bernie's neck and began to apply pressure to the windpipe. It was as if a visceral force had punctured his exterior shell, granting him a supernatural strength. Despite the gurgling emanating from his victim's throat Miles tightened his grip still further.

"Miles, leave go, you're killing him!" The hysteria in Vera's voice finally brought him to his senses. Withdrawing his hands from Bernie's neck, Miles stared down at his victim who lay there dazed and ashen, his eyes closed.

"Now look what you've done, he's not breathing," shrieked Vera, staring up at Miles. She had begun slapping Bernie's cheeks in an attempt to revive him.

"Nonsense. Give him a few minutes and he'll be right as rain," said Miles, less sure of his diagnosis than he was prepared to admit. Much to his relief, seconds later Bernie's eyes slowly flickered open. There was a steady trickle of blood flowing from his mouth where the punch had landed and red blotches were visible around his Adam's apple where Miles' fingers had been pressing. Gazing down at the all-powerful man he had laid low, all Miles could see was a vulnerable victim, a reversal in roles he was determined to savour. "Here, clean yourself up. You look like you've been in a playground brawl," he said imperiously, tossing Bernie a linen napkin.

"I'm not going to ask you again, are you coming?" asked Miles, approaching Vera.

Vera shook her head and busied herself with attending to Bernie who was staring up incredulously at his unlikely assailant.

"Well then, if you'll excuse me, I have to pack." Miles turned on his heels and left the deck without a backward glance.

✦

As the launch sped away from La Celestia Miles reflected on the events that had led up to his unscheduled departure. He had been quite sure that he would be forbidden to leave the yacht until some form of retribution had been meted out. In the event, he had no further contact with his host who had apparently given clearance for him to be transferred to dry land at first light. No crew member had witnessed their boss's humiliation and Miles concluded that Bernie would be keen to see him spirited away lest the details of their altercation leaked out.

Miles could not see a reason to censure himself for his actions. Violence had been the only instinctive response possible in the face of such provocation. He had been treated like a freak and a cuckold for Bernie's perverted pleasure. Landing the punch had released a reservoir of rage as with the school bully Entwhistle and more recently, the hapless Tristan. Yet with his assault on Bernie, he knew he had now entered a different league. Had not Vera intervened, who knows if he would have stopped short of actual murder? He, Miles, who had spent a lifetime avoiding confrontation, if Elspeth was to be believed.

This troubling thought was brushed aside by a sense of anguish at Vera's decision to remain on board. He could only imagine that by succumbing to Bernie's lascivious attentions, she believed she would be gaining a cocoon of security that he, Miles, had no prospect of matching. Perhaps she was simply a gold digger after all?

One redeeming thought popped up. If she had been under Russian orders to target him, then surely she would have agreed to jump ship with him? Could the spooks have got it badly wrong? As the coastline grew closer, Miles shivered in the early morning chill. Wherever the truth lay, Vera Petrovna would no longer feature in his life. He would just have to rely on his well-honed talent for sweeping painful realities into a corner of his mental attic.

CHAPTER FIVE

Corsican catenations

Framed by a ring of purple peaks, the tall, shuttered merchants' houses glistened in the morning sun. Miles could see their hazy outlines lying at the apex of the bay. This first glimpse of the island's capital, Ajaccio, had lifted Miles' spirits. It was his good fortune, he told himself, that the nearest point of dry land on which he had been deposited turned out to be somewhere he knew rather well. He had returned to Corsica many times in pursuit of his studies and arrival by sea never failed to give him a sense of excitement and expectation.

Having been put ashore with his suitcase, Miles's priority was to seek some shade. The unseasonable early autumn heat was causing him to sweat profusely and rivulets were running down his neck. He eventually found shelter on the terrace of a sparsely populated café overlooking the water, dabbed his brow and ordered a cooling drink.

As the sun rose to its high point, Miles downed the last of his third beer and wiped the froth from his upper lip. The stretch of quayside was deserted save for two stray dogs engaged in a desultory tug-of-war over a discarded baguette.

Reflecting on this latest example of his inability to form a lasting relationship, he began to feel distinctly morose. He recalled how, awakening from their first night together, Vera had probed him about his former love life. In typical Miles fashion, he had been thoroughly evasive, yet at the cursory mention of his marriage, Vera's eyes had widened.

"How could you lie to me, Miles?"

"I haven't lied. You never asked. One does things when young that one later regrets.

"Why did you get divorced?" she asked.

"We're not. She doesn't believe in it."

"You're not divorced?"

"That's a pure technicality," replied Miles. "We haven't seen each other for years."

"The next thing you're going to tell me is that you're a father."

"No, there were no offspring, you'll be glad to hear."

"What was she like in bed, this wife of yours?"

"To be perfectly honest, I've no idea."

As he sat drinking alone in Ajaccio, details of the sorry saga came tumbling back. If Vera had pressed him, he might have revealed that shortly after she had ensnared Miles on their first day at Oxford, Maureen (known as Mo) had been hooked by the evangelical Christians for whom the notion of sex before marriage was anathema. Her fervour quickly grew in intensity and, throughout their student coupledom, she remained resolutely tight-kneed. In all the time they were engaged Miles had succeeded in spending only a single night between the same sheets. On an archaeological field trip to the Outer Hebrides they had been allotted single rooms above a pub. In the hope that Mo's resolve had been loosened by several whiskies, he was full of eager anticipation and crept into her room, but her guard was still up and the calf-length winceyette nightie had remained unruffled. Thus Mo and he had settled into an 'old sock' relationship throughout their undergraduate years, conjoined by no more than an unspoken mutual affection and a love of delving into dusty volumes. During their ensuing MPhil studies, Mo had refused to countenance the idea of cohabitation. It was not until they had finished that the subject of marriage was broached. For Mo, the notion of a non-church wedding was unthinkable. For Miles, the prospect of a ceremony packed out with Mo's fellow evangelicals - 'the happy clappy' brigade as he insisted on calling them, was anathema. A compromise was eventually reached and the small college chapel was duly booked.

The ceremony itself on a dull November morning was a modest, sparsely attended affair conducted by the lugubrious college chaplain. Miles had decided against inviting his parents, aware of their disapproval of Mo's working class roots, and she was not on speaking terms with her progenitors. Miles' best friend Tristan acted as best man and Mo's only close chum at Oxford, Eileen, as maid of honour. Some musical accompaniment to the nuptials had been planned but the organ scholar, who had agreed to play as a favour, failed to show up and they walked down the aisle as man and wife in abject silence.

The small band of celebrants then retired to the Randolph Hotel for what turned out to be a grisly lunch. Tristan consumed vast quantities of Rioja and became over fresh with the young waitress. She complained to the head waiter and there was a noisy scene with Tristan protesting his innocence in typically expletive manner. As a result, the manager was called and the lunch party was asked to leave without further fuss.

This expulsion proved particularly awkward as, with the legitimacy of their union secured, Miles had gone to considerable pains to plan a luxurious wedding night. The Randolph's bridal suite, complete with four poster, had been reserved at ruinous expense. But as the po-faced functionary made clear, their room booking would not be honoured. After wandering the High, dragging their overnight cases, they headed back to Mo's digs where strong tea was brewed and marshmallows toasted over the gas fire in an attempt to keep their spirits from flagging. A game of rummy proved a mild diversion on what should have been their special day. Miles found it hard to concentrate. His boyish excitement at the night to come was tempered with a growing nervousness.

As the temperature dropped, the glow of the gas fire faded. A desperate search for coins to feed the meter ensued but with no success. Although it was not yet eight o'clock, by mutual consent a move to the bedroom seemed the most sensible way of keeping warm. Miles thought he caught sight of a glint in Mo's eye as she slipped out of her specially procured canary silk dress and lay outstretched in a cruciform position on the shabby Paisley eiderdown. He had begun to strip to his underwear when he realised he would have to pay a visit to the shared lavatory on the half-landing below Mo's rooms. Before he did so, a packet of novelty contraceptives was extracted from his sponge bag and laid ceremoniously on the bedside table. The ancient WC's flush mechanism proved its usual problematic self and it was some minutes before he returned to the bedroom. As he flung open the door to claim his bride, he was met with a stinging blow to the cheek. In her other hand, Mo was wielding the small box which she waved furiously in Miles' face. How, she demanded to know, could her 'celibate' husband explain that in a pack that held five, only four condoms now remained?

He had broken down and confessed all while making it clear that it had all been at Tristan's prompting. He knew full well that Mo had little time for his friend whom she dismissed as a malevolent influence. Since forming an unlikely comradeship in their first term, Miles had soon become weary of the endless boasting about his conquests. For his part, Tristan, finding it hard to accept that the permissive zeitgeist of the seventies had entirely passed his friend by, never tired of challenging Miles' apparent lack of interest in sex. One evening, after they'd downed several pints at the Turf while Mo was at her weekly prayer meeting, Tristan had delivered a stark warning. It was imperative, he argued, that in order to prepare himself for his role in the marital bed, Miles first put in some practice. "Treat it like a driving lesson," he had urged.

After returning with their drinks from the bar, where he'd been in deep conversation with the barmaid, Tristan placed a scrap of paper on the table.

"What's this?" asked Miles peering at what appeared to be a scribbled Oxford address and phone number.

"It's all fixed," said Tristan, nodding in the direction of the barmaid. "Ginette's up for it."

"Up for what?" Miles had replied.

"I've told her you're a complete beginner. She says she's looking forward to the challenge."

"Are you seriously expecting me to sleep with this woman for money?"

"She's doing it as a favour. All she asked for is a contribution to her 'holiday fund' Don't worry, it's on me. Consider it an early wedding present," Tristan replied.

Having taken a swig, Miles stared into the froth. He had little stamina for keg bitter and the cramped saloon was already beginning to revolve. As he gazed abstractedly towards the bar, he thought he saw Ginette deliver a knowing wink. Miles took a further gulp to avoid her gaze.

"Why dilly dally?" said Tristan. "She's got a day off next Tuesday. There's a bus that stops outside. And don't forget the condoms, she has a penchant for peppermint by the way."

"Mo's bound to guess," Miles replied, trembling with nerves at the prospect.

"Tell her you've been consulting a manual. She'll be impressed."

"Perhaps I should. It would be a lot simpler."

"Nonsense," replied Tristan. "There's no substitute for hands-on experience."

"Would she expect me to...go all the way?" asked Miles, who having studied Ginette's shapely upper torso, was beginning to find the assignation marginally more appealing.

"Don't worry Miles. Ginette's got the magic touch. Have a stiff whisky before you go in."

"Should I introduce myself? It only seems polite," said Miles.

Tristan shook his head. "Best be discreet, the landlord doesn't encourage moonlighting. Good, that's agreed then. I'll go and tell her you're up for Tuesday."

✦

Miles had never ventured into the outer regions of Oxford before. Dominated by the vast motor works, Cowley was more as he imagined a Northern industrial town to be. He was early and alighted at a stop some distance from his intended destination. The nondescript grey pebbledash semis grouped around the factory site all looked similar. The further he ventured into the area, the more jelly-like his legs became. Finally, heeding Tristan's advice, Miles dived into a dreary modern pub and downed a large scotch. He emerged suitably fortified.

By the time he'd located the relevant house and summoned the courage to ring the bell, it was well after 2.30. Ginette had taken her time to answer the insistent door chimes and Miles had been aware of net curtains twitching in the adjoining semi. While he waited to gain entry, he buried his face deep in his upturned collar.

"I've been waiting for you, big boy. You're late. My shift starts at five. You can wash in there."

✦

From the fury etched into Mo's face as she hurled the open condom packet across the room, it was obvious to Miles that his candour had only made matters worse. As soon as he had trotted out the excuse that he had been practising for his wedding night, he realised it sounded as far-fetched as it was feeble. He'd never seen Mo angry before. They had pottered through their four-year relationship successfully avoiding any outward displays of emotion. That was not to say that she lacked passion but it was reserved for a higher calling.

Mo now spoke with icy deliberation. "If you did it once, you'll do it again."

"But I won't. That's the whole point," Miles pleaded. "I could have made up any old story about the missing thinga-majig." He glanced awkwardly towards the offending packet which now lay on the threadbare rug having spilled its contents. As if to remove the evidence, Miles attempted to gather up the foil packets. Losing his balance, he ended up on all fours and before he could grasp the items, Mo had kicked them under the settee where he now groped for them amongst the balls of fluff.

"So you would have lied to me?"

"But the point is I didn't. Surely I deserve some credit for that?" suggested Miles, finally hauling himself to his feet.

Mo moved within range of Miles' chest and began pummelling him with her fists. He was forced to back towards the door.

"It's over," she shouted.

"But it hasn't even started. Give me a chance to redeem myself," he pleaded.

"If you don't get out, I'll scream and the whole house will hear."

Raising his hands in the air, Miles could sense that a tactical retreat was advisable. Having been granted five minutes to repack his overnight case, he crept away into the Oxford drizzle.

Settling into his narrow bed, Miles reflected on his misfortune. Accommodation issues would have to be faced. He'd already given notice on his digs. There was the question of how to tell his few friends, yet alone his sister, that he and Mo had separated on their wedding day. Would he have to own up to his misdemeanour? As he curled up under the eiderdown, he permitted himself a glimmer of hope that the morning may bring a softening of her stance.

He rang from the phone box on the corner at nine and again at ten. No reply. Perhaps she had taken an overdose? But he recalled that Mo refused to sully her body with anything stronger than a mild aspirin. There remained the possibility that she had turned the gas on or drowned herself in the bath. By ten thirty he was ringing on the bell of the large

Victorian house in Norham Road. There being no answer, he resorted to repeatedly yelling out her name but to no avail. A stone lobbed towards the window of her first floor bedsit to attract her attention found its mark, shattering a pane. Mo's ashen face appeared for a brief second amongst the jagged shards. She had clearly been close to the window and blood was pouring down her cheek. That stone was to settle matters. Later that morning, Miles received a visit from the Oxford constabulary following up on a complaint. Mo could not be dissuaded from bringing charges and, following a mercifully brief court appearance, Miles pleaded guilty to a breach of the peace. The magistrate let him off with a caution on the understanding that he would go to prison if he harassed his estranged wife again.

Despite this warning, Miles became obsessed with getting back together with Mo. For the last four years, she had just been there as a comforting presence obviating the need to live off Birds Eye dinners-for-one. Now, in his bereft state, he realised he loved her.

Having remained in Oxford to embark on a PhD, Miles took to attending services in St Aldate's in the hope of gaining a glimpse of her. One Sunday evensong, he managed to slip into the pew behind her unnoticed. When the congregation was exhorted to turn to their neighbours on all sides and grasp their hands, Mo was forced to grip Miles' sweaty palm. In retaliation for being trapped in this way, she dug her nails into his flesh causing him to wince in pain. As if in a reflex action, he continued, nonetheless, to wrap her hand in his. A tussle of lower arms ensued before Mo finally shook herself free. Having leapt to her feet and squeezed past her fellow worshippers, she hurried down the aisle towards the door.

Later that month, he spotted her in Broad Street arm-in-arm with Gerald, a rake-thin fellow Christian. Finally, one January night after a solitary curry, he came across her drinking with Tristan. Unable to face his malodorous digs, Miles had dived into the Turf for a swift half and some vicarious human contact. As he was hovering in search of a stool, he spotted them huddled in a corner, apparently sharing a joke. As the laughter subsided, they clinked glasses animatedly. Even in the low light, Miles thought he detected that Mo had taken to wearing make-up and that there was a lascivious gleam in Tristan's eye. The urge to confront the couple became too great to resist.

It wasn't until he was looming over the table that Tristan registered Miles' presence. "Miles, what a surprise! We were just..."

"Just what?" replied Miles with what he trusted would pass for an expression of extreme displeasure .

As Mo craned her head around, Miles found himself gazing into her grey green eyes. Jumping to her feet, Mo grabbed her bag and made for the exit. Miles followed her progress across the crowded bar before turning back to confront his friend. The frothy liquid seemed to fly from Miles' glass of its own volition, drenching Tristan's greasy locks and running onto the dandruff-flecked shoulders of his suede jacket. As his victim spluttered in disbelief, Miles felt a perverse delight.

"Sorry to spoil your evening," said Miles with as much sarcasm as he could muster before turning on his heels. Two weeks later he heard that Mo had left Oxford for good to undertake missionary work in West Africa.

✦

Miles woke from his doze with a start to find the young waiter lightly tapping him on the shoulder.

"Une autre bière, Monsieur?"

Miles shook his head emphatically and settled the bill before wandering off with his suitcase towards the centre of town. Spotting a game of pétanque in progress on a dusty patch under an avenue of plane trees, he paused to watch. He could not help but envy the elderly yet spritely locals' relaxed banter and ease of movement as they focused on the task of eliminating their rivals. He moved on through the cloying late afternoon, eventually finding refuge on a shady bench under the palms in the Place Marèchal Foch. He had retained a fondness for this elegant square dominated by a statue of Napoleon Bonaparte in a toga and flanked by four stone lions spewing water. At school, Miles had become captivated by his studies of the diminutive leader. As he gazed up now at this aggrandised tribute, a pair of pigeons alighted on the great man's head and began what appeared to be an elaborate mating ritual. Miles managed a chuckle. Surely the local feathered population should be trained to respect the island's most famous son?

A selection of postcards depicting Bonaparte in his more familiar bicorn hat caught his eye outside a shop bordering the square. On a whim, Miles purchased one together with a stamp and, returning to the bench, addressed the card to Tony Barstow, care of the Department of Ancient History with the following message: 'Change of plan. No longer aboard yacht. Suggest you contact gift horse yourself. Looked in his mouth and was unhappy with what I saw. Yours as ever, Miles.'

He read the message back to himself with a wry smile. He could imagine his Director's expression on receiving it. Even if Tony were to have him dismissed from the Department, Miles told himself that there was one aspect of his life that could never be taken away, namely the vast body of research he had accumulated over the decades. Although lacking a convincing conclusion, this was, he reminded himself, his whole raison d'être, his gift to posterity, if that was not too pompous a description. Miles turned to gaze up reverentially at Napoleon on his imperial perch and made a solemn resolution. He would resume his archaeological investigations on the island. It would be foolish, after all, to displease Astarte and her fellow Phoenician gods who had led him to these shores. It was not as though there was a shortage of sites crying out to be further explored. All that was needed was a proper plan of action.

His mind turned to more mundane matters. He needed to find shelter for the night. Pressing on towards the old town, he stumbled upon a modestly-priced hotel he recalled that he had stayed at some years before. He was soon installed in a stuffy third floor room with an agreeable view over the jumble of rooftops. Having stripped down to his underwear, Miles pulled back the shabby bedspread and wriggled down between the suspiciously-crumpled sheets for a siesta.

His brain refused to disengage and he lay staring at the ceiling fan that stuttered noisily midway through each revolution. One thought subsumed all others. This new burst of enthusiasm to resume excavation was all well and good but as Miles knew, the painstaking and often gruelling work could not be undertaken without the assistance of those younger and far fitter than himself. His own digging days had come to a painful halt in his late forties after his back had given way and he had ended up supine for six weeks. Since then, he had relied on loyal undergraduate and PhD students to volunteer to spend much of their long vacations on their hands and knees scrabbling in the dust beneath an unforgiving sun. Despite their efforts over the years, nothing of any significance had come to light and no major archaeological activity had been undertaken on Corsica for the past two summers.

Gunther....What about Gunther? Miles separated himself from the clammy pillow and sat bolt upright. The distractions of the last weeks had meant that he had quite forgotten that he had endorsed an independent research trip to the island by his newest PhD student. The young German's somewhat pedantic approach was not to Miles' taste but Gunther was, if anything, over-keen to please. Was he still on the island? There was better than a fifty-fifty chance. Somewhere there must be a note of his mobile phone number. A hunt through the recesses of Miles' over-stuffed wallet drew a blank and neither was it listed on the minimal contact list on his phone. He must have left it at home.

He was on the point of ringing London when the phone trilled into life.

"How are you? It's Jeremy."

"Yes I know who it is," snapped Miles. "I was about to ring your mother."

"I'm here in the flat. She's in the other room. I'll put her on to you in a minute. By the way, we know what happened, on the yacht that is. I haven't told Mother. I'll leave that to you to do in your own time."

"It's no good asking how you know," said Miles. "I'm sure you monitor every move I make. It gives one a queasy feeling."

"Leaving that aside, I've been given the job of giving you some news that might help you relax about things."

"And what would that be?" asked Miles, making sure to maintain a cynical tone.

"Heidi's been taken off your case."

"What do you mean 'off my case'?"

"Just that. Her bosses have realised they got it wrong."

"Do stop talking in riddles, Jeremy."

"Okay. Through our sources, we've found out that they've come to accept that Heidi is barking up the wrong tree if you get my meaning, i.e. she won't get anything out of you worth passing on. It's as simple as that. Mallalieu Mission aborted. Full stop. I've already been assigned to another case."

"I see," said Miles, trying to take it all in. "Am I supposed to feel a sense of relief or disappointment that I've been relegated to the status of a nobody as far as Russian intelligence is concerned?"

"Forget the Russians. The point is Doug and I no longer expect you to report on Heidi's movements or to feed her phony stuff to pass on. I thought you'd be pleased."

"Perhaps it's just as well considering she's still aboard the gin palace and I'm on terra firma with no plans to go back."

"Ah, Mother's just walked in. Hang on, I'll hand you over... if you have any more questions, give me a bell any time."

There was no time to digest Jeremy's news."...Yes Elspeth, I am back on dry land...I'll explain in due course. Listen, I need you to do me a favour. I want you to look on my desk for a note of a student's number I need. His name's Gunther. It's probably somewhere obvious."

"I'm not your secretary," replied Elspeth. "Wait a minute." There was a lengthy pause before she returned to the phone. "Your study is its usual terrible mess. You're in luck though. It was stuffed into your top drawer."

Miles recorded the number in biro on the back of his wrist. "Thank you. Thank you. I'll speak to you later Elspeth. You've been a great help," he added, unable to recall the last occasion on which he had consciously praised his sister.

Miles' head was pounding as he absorbed the ramifications

of Jeremy's call. It would at least explain why Vera had suddenly felt free to devote her efforts to capturing the attentions of the billionaire. She certainly had not wasted much time in finding a new and no doubt more promising partner. It was deeply dispiriting. So much for the theory that she had grown fond of Miles despite her orders to ensnare him. Miles had to get some fresh air. The evening was still thick with the residue of the day's heat and the chattering swallows sounded shrill as they darted in and out from under the eaves. Wandering disconsolately past the strolling couples on the Cours Napoleon did little to improve Miles' mood. He could feel an aching void inside him and, for once, it had nothing to do with physical hunger. To fill that void, he would immerse himself again in completing his research.

CHAPTER SIX

Miracle in the maquis

"Ja? Hallo." The accent was reassuringly familiar.

"Is that Gunther? It's Doctor Mallalieu here."

"Doctor Mallalieu. Yes, yes, it is I. It's so good to hear from you."

"I must apologise, I feel I've rather abandoned you of late," replied Miles.

"It is true I've sent you many emails, Dr Mallalieu but they clearly are not getting through.

"I rather suspect my mailbox is full," said Miles, feeling he had found a reasonable excuse. "I'm sorry to ring you at this hour but I don't suppose you're still on Corsica by any chance?"

"Ja. Absolutely I am on Corsica, Dr Mallalieu. I have been preparing to investigate Site DX1 as we discussed at my last supervision."

"Did we?" replied Miles. "As far as I can recall, nothing of interest has ever been found there. I thought we talked about DX2," replied Miles, attempting to mask his irritation that Gunther had not followed his admittedly vague advice. He would have to choose his words carefully if his student was not to be discouraged.

"Is everything OK, Dr Mallalieu? Are you in London?"

"As it so happens, Gunther, I'm in Ajaccio."

"You are in Ajaccio? Fantastisch!" exclaimed Gunther. "May I ask why you have come? It is an honour to have you here of course," he added.

"Let's just say this is an unscheduled trip," replied Miles.

"If I may be permitted to say so..." said Gunther. "It is fate that has brought you here at this time, Dr Mallalieu. It is for a good reason that I have been trying to contact you urgently."

"And what would that be?" asked Miles.

"I have heard reports about an object that may be of great interest to us, Dr Mallalieu. It is better we do not talk about it on the phone. I am staying in Sartène. Can you maybe come to meet me here tomorrow?"

✦

"You understand Monsieur, it is forbidden to take the car off the main roads?" said the girl at the car rental desk as she rose from the desk and crossed to the door. "It is the red one over there under those trees. Have a nice holiday Monsieur and re-member, in Corsica we drive on the right."

Miles stared at the unfamiliar controls and tried to ad-just the narrow seat to accommodate his bulk. The Fiat 600 proved easier to manoeuvre than Miles had dared imagine and he soon left the outskirts of the capital behind and was purring south towards the ancient town of Sartène. To his re-lief, there was virtually no traffic and the only impediment to progress came from the tarmac which had been turned molten in patches by the heat. Being unfamiliar with air condition-ing controls, he wound down the windows to let in the heady aroma of sage, juniper and myrtle wafting in from the maquis, the dense, sun-baked scrub that covered much of the island. Inhaling deeply, he reflected on the remarkable stroke of luck of having made contact with Gunther. It felt good to be back on Corsica. There was important work to resume which would more than occupy both of them, even if his student's excitement proved to be over-egged.

Sartène loomed up ahead. Perched on a rocky outcrop, this gloomy town had always reminded Miles of a monastery in Lhasa. The ranks of tall shuttered houses which formed its external face glared out over the terrain dotted with olive groves. As Miles returned his attention to the road, a creature darted out from the scrub. He swerved violently to avoid it and in so doing, lost control of the Fiat which veered off the road and ploughed through a shallow gully, before coming to rest within inches of a wide-beamed olive tree.

It was several minutes before Miles could bring himself to move. There was an eerie silence apart from the frenzied chirping of cicadas. He sat staring blankly at the tree ahead as if in disbelief at the narrowness of his escape. Finally, he hauled himself out of the car with some difficulty, holding on to the roof to steady himself. He examined his hands first for signs of injury, cradling one with the other to stop them shaking. His right flank was sore. The seatbelt had dug painfully into his flesh and he was thoroughly winded. Yet a cursory survey of his limbs revealed that he was superficially at least, unharmed. The car may not have fared so well. Miles began his inspection at the front. A veil of blood covered the headlamps. Sandwiched between the car and the tree lay a goat, legs akimbo, its glassy stare confirming its demise.

From previous encounters with the Corsican peasantry while on archaeological digs, Miles knew that their animals were their most precious possessions. Anyone found harming them was likely to face swift and violent retribution. He scanned the low scrub. To his relief, there appeared to be no obvious sign of human habitation nearby, or any traveller visible on the road.

Even with his limited understanding of technology, it was clear that there was no phone signal in this valley. Decisive action was needed with or without Gunther's help. Clambering back into the Fiat, he restarted the engine. Placing the car into reverse gear, he slowly applied the accelerator. Almost at once, there was an overpowering smell of burning rubber as the back wheels began spinning wildly. The further Miles depressed the pedal, the deeper he could feel the car sinking into the soft earth. A thick cloud of dust had enveloped the car causing him to cough violently. Clamping his hand over his nostrils, Miles switched off the engine. Realising that he had made his situation far worse, he rested his forehead on the steering wheel in defeat. There was no other option, he decided, but to abandon the car and complete the final leg of his journey on foot.

Having extracted his suitcase, he set out to trudge up the steeply winding road towards Sartène. As he reached the metalled surface, Miles paused to look back. The car was obscured by the scrub and invisible to any passing motorist. Yet there was no escaping from the fact that the main evidence of the fatal collision had been left in situ and that the owner of the unfortunate animal might soon return. The name of the car rental company was emblazoned on the rear window and if the police became involved, it would no doubt be easy to trace the driver. He had no choice but to turn back.

Using the remaining drinking water he had bought for the journey, Miles drizzled liquid down the front of the car. The blood had congealed and he was forced to use his handkerchief to dab at it fiercely. Miles stood back to review his handiwork. Short of a forensic investigation, he was satisfied that no obvious evidence of the collision was visible on the bodywork of the car. There remained the thorny question of how to dispose of the carcass. Using the shovel for archaeological digs he had acquired from a garage en route, he sunk on to his knees and began digging a grave in a small clearing away from the scene of the accident. After heaving the animal across the stony ground, he used the edge of his shoe to nudge the carcass into its final resting place. He bent down to scoop up earth to sprinkle over the grave. The goat's glassy eye was the last element to be covered and as he showered it with dirt, for a split second Miles imagined he saw it blink. Shaking his head as if to banish the image, he retraced his steps through the undergrowth and once again began the long climb towards Sartène.

A clock was striking some indeterminate hour as Miles dragged himself into the main square which was deserted apart from a posse of skinny cats. He had arranged to meet Gunther in the café bordering the square but the shutters were firmly down.

"Dr Mallalieu." Miles swung round to be confronted with the lanky, bespectacled figure who had appeared from a shady alleyway. "What happened to you? Are you OK?"

"I think so," replied Miles, clutching his chest.

"I am sorry, I didn't mean to shock you. Welcome to Corsica. It is so good to see you," said Gunther, pumping Miles' hand vigorously.

"If you don't mind, I need to find some shade," said Miles, extricating himself as soon as he could. His feet were sore and his ankles like jelly.

"Yes of course. Forgive me. You must be tired after the journey," said Gunther, guiding him to a nearby bench under a large tree. The young German remained standing and cast seemingly anxious looks across the empty square. "May I ask, Herr Doktor, where is your car?"

"Let us just say that I had a little local difficulty. I came off the road."

Gunther crossed to sit beside him and Miles gave him chapter and verse. "Dr Mallalieu. That is very bad news. I hope you are not hurt?" Miles shook his head and shuffled his legs sideways to give himself more space on the narrow bench. "Without a car, we have a big problem." added Gunther.

"I'm rather hoping you haven't brought me all this way on a wild goose chase," said Miles, immediately regretting his cynicism. He was beyond exhaustion and the student's nervy manner was beginning to affect him.

Gunther leant in to whisper in Miles' ear. "It is not a question of a goose, Dr Mallalieu, I believe I have found her!"

Miles' weariness evaporated in a millisecond. He felt he knew at once to whom Gunther was referring.

"How sure are you?" Miles could feel his nerve ends quivering.

"I am ninety seven point five per cent certain. Such a margin of error is very small, would you not say, Dr Mallalieu?"

Miles decided it would be sensible to contain his joy until he had examined the evidence more closely. After all, this was not the first time that a zealous student had announced a breakthrough only to discover that it was nothing of the kind. Yet there was something about Gunther's wild-eyed optimism that kept Miles' expectations intact.

"And where exactly have you found her?" he asked.

"In a church."

"In a church?" repeated Miles incredulously.

Gunther nodded. He produced a dog-eared postcard, its colours well faded. "Well, Dr Mallalieu, what is your opinion? She is well disguised, sure but..." His student looked to Miles as if he was about to explode with excitement.

Miles was on the verge of a Eureka moment as overwhelming as that when he had unearthed a Victorian brooch on his first archaeological excavation in the family garden at the age of ten. "Where did you get this from?" asked Miles, examining the card between quivering fingers.

"Right here in Sartène, in the guest house where I'm staying," replied Gunther. "It was in the pages of an old Bible by my bed."

"She is very beautiful, no?" asked Gunther with a broad smile. Miles could only nod as he pored over the photograph. Broad in the beam, the squat female figurine cradled her swollen breasts.

"Where can we find her?" he demanded feverishly.

"According to my landlady, it is a shrine located in a small church in the middle of an olive grove not far off the road to Bonifacio," replied Gunther. "This statue is only shown twice a year when there is a pilgrimage of some kind. It has some Christian identity now to do with a miracle. This is why it has the appearance of the Madonna. Even her blue cloak. We have great luck, Dr Mallalieu. The next such event is taking place tomorrow. That is why it was so important you came now. Do you not think the gods are on our side?"

"How will we get there?" asked Miles, recalling the abandoned rental car.

"You can trust me, Dr Mallalieu. I will arrange with a garage to rescue your car and we can be at the shrine by eleven. That is when the pilgrims will start to arrive."

There was nothing else to do but to pass what remained of the day in waiting mode. They dined at a local restaurant but Miles could scarcely finish his wild boar casserole washed down with a Patrimonio red, his normally healthy appetite for the rich Corsican cuisine suppressed by a visceral excitement. Neither spoke much during the meal as if to acknowledge the gravity of their impending mission.

"We can do nothing until daylight. First we must get some sleep. Yes?" said Gunther. Miles nodded. The absence of any hotel meant Miles had no option but to accept Gunther's offer to share his room in the widow's guesthouse.

The shuttered house in a narrow side street leading off the main square was in total darkness, the elderly owner having no doubt retired for the night. They crept up the creaking stairs, Gunther carrying Miles' suitcase. As Gunther ushered him into the bedroom, Miles surveyed the low ceilinged interior, noticing with dismay that it contained only one bed. When Gunther offered to sleep on cushions on the floor and donate the bed to Miles, he put up only token opposition.

Battling indigestion, Miles slept fitfully. Among the jumbled dream images he recalled on awakening was a scene of a posse of departmental colleagues led by Tony Barstow, pursuing him down a Corsican country road. He was attempting to escape by breaking into what passed for a run, only to stumble and fall. The mob was on him like a pack of wolves as they prised the genuine representation of Astarte from his hands. As they did so, it was transformed into the cheap replica of the goddess which he concealed in his bedroom cupboard.

✦

Miles was jolted into consciousness by a hesitant prod from Gunther. "Dr Mallalieu! Wake up please. I have been out in the town already and I have found a mechanic who will help us. He will take us to your car in his truck in one hour. Can you be ready?"

Once the abandoned Fiat had been located, a brief inspection showed it to be mercifully unscathed. It took less than five minutes for the elderly breakdown truck to haul it out back onto the road. The garage man hovered, awaiting his recompense. Miles produced a fifty euro note. A more generous sum had clearly been expected and with mumbled curses, the man drove away at high speed leaving Miles and Gunther sheathed in a cloud of blue smoke.

"We must hurry now, Dr Mallalieu. The shrine will be opening in one hour and we must arrive before the crowds," urged Gunther. They were on the point of climbing back into the car when a cacophony of tinkling bells announced the arrival of a goatherd guiding his flock along the road. Miles felt the bile rise in his throat. As he passed them, the herdsman eyed them up suspiciously. Miles gave a studiedly casual wave which was not returned.

It was only after the flock had safely rounded the bend that, to Miles' horror he spotted a small portion of the goat's ear protruding through the dirt.

"It's not far now. The church should be on our left side in approximately two point five kilometres," replied Gunther, poring over the navigational aid on his phone between nervous glances at the road ahead. To their frustration, they found themselves slowed to a crawl by a phalanx of minibuses and cars clogging the road ahead. A row of female heads shrouded in black lace could be seen through the window of the vehicle bringing up the rear of the column.

"This is most unfortunate," said Gunther. "Dr Mallalieu, forgive me but have you thought about how we must behave when we arrive at the church? We are not typical pilgrims. We will look suspicious, no?"

"Perhaps we should try and pass ourselves off as peasant women. How are your acting skills, Gunther?" replied Miles.

"Dr Mallalieu. I no longer know when you are making a joke."

"Well, I'm sure we'll think of something," replied Miles, keen to dispel his student's anxiety.

"Dr Mallalieu. I have one more question," said Gunther, stony-faced.

"Yes, Gunther. What is it now?" replied Miles, maintaining a healthy distance from the convoy. "If this statue is so important as a religious icon, these people will not wish to cooperate with us. Have you maybe thought of this?"

"We can't let a few superstitious locals stand in the way of ground-breaking historical research," replied Miles, whose buoyant mood seemed unassailable.

"Do you mean we will have to steal it?" asked Gunther incredulously.

"The word I would use in this context, Gunther, is 'borrow.' Once the ceremony is over, we have to get it to the lab in Ajaccio to run radiocarbon dating tests. It will only take two days at the most. They may not even notice it's gone."

"Dr Mallalieu, supposing we are discovered?"

"We won't be."

Gunther sighed. "Very well, Dr Mallalieu. You can depend on my cooperation," he replied.

The vehicles in front came to a sudden halt to allow the pilgrims to disembark for the final leg of their journey. Keeping at discreet distance, Miles pulled off the road having taken care to choose a firm piece of ground. Making their way towards a short but steep embankment, Gunther and he peered over the ridge at an arid valley floor shrouded in a blanket of heat haze. In the midst of the valley was a small stone chapel. Once no doubt the focal point of a long-abandoned hamlet, it was all but concealed within a clump of tall holm oaks. A ribbon of black-clad figures was snaking its way towards the chapel, the pilgrims' chatter audible above the tolling of a solitary bell.

Pointing to a steep path leading down through the dense scrub, Miles signalled for his student to follow. Emerging onto the valley floor, they paused to peer out from the cover of a conveniently placed boulder. A swarm of elderly female pilgrims was attempting to funnel through the narrow chapel door. A young, moon-faced priest in a black cassock emerged and began gesticulating in an attempt to slow the onslaught. Yet as the crush became greater, he was swept aside.

As the last of the pilgrims squeezed into the chapel it was clear from the sudden hush that a ceremony was about to begin. Miles and Gunther emerged from behind the boulder and sidled over to the chapel to take up position beneath a small window at the east end. The ledge proved to be a foot or so higher than Miles' eye level. He signalled to Gunther to take his place.

"What can you see? Tell me everything," whispered Miles. A pungent smell of incense wafted out through the window as the intoning of prayers assumed an almost hypnotic intensity.

"I can see nothing, Dr Mallalieu. The glass is not clear enough," replied Gunther, peering inside. "I am sorry."

There was no alternative but to sit it out until the ceremony was over. Miles leant against the rough stone exterior.

Gunther handed him a plastic bottle with barely an inch of water remaining. "Please, Dr Mallalieu. You drink it." Without any pretence of civility, Miles all but snatched the bottle from his student's hand.

The ceremony showed no sign of drawing to a close. Miles and Gunther retreated to a shady spot between the oaks, disturbing a couple of disgruntled billy goats. A further half hour passed before the church bell clanged into life. They watched as the priest emerged and led the supplicants in crocodile formation towards the path leading up to the road. Once the procession was safely out of sight, Miles beckoned to Gunther to make their move. It took a moment for their eyes to penetrate the fog of incense within the chapel. On the simple altar stood the representation of the Phoenician goddess exactly as depicted on Gunther's postcard. Although cloaked in a Madonna's robe, its fecund body mirrored that of his own version of Astarte, a cheap plaster replica bought in a Beirut souvenir shop. On this Corsican Astarte's outstretched palms had been placed a small silver bowl and droplets of a milk-like substance was oozing from her breasts. The sight caused Miles to gasp. His knees grew weak and head bowed, he sank to the stone floor.

"Messieurs, desolé de vous déranger mais il faut fermer l'église." Mile swivelled round to face the priest whose expression was quizzical but not unfriendly. "Vous êtes des touristes... Anglais ou Americain peut-être?"

"I am English and my colleague is German," Miles stuttered in reply.

"Then we shall speak English," said the priest with a smile. "My family is from this region. I escaped to work in the States for a while. I came back here when I received my vocation." He held out his hand. "I am Father Jean-Pierre. Perhaps you would like to introduce yourselves gentlemen?

"Mallalieu? This is a name with a French origin. It could mean bad place, n'est-ce pas? Maybe you had not thought of that?" He chuckled to himself before moving over to the altar and gazing at the statue.

"Are you interested in our little miracle, perhaps?" There was a hint of irony which Miles found unsettling. Should he claim religious fervour as the reason for their presence or come clean as to the true purpose of their mission? Miles decided to take the middle ground.

"I am an historian of the ancient Mediterranean, as is my young colleague. We heard about this event and were curious to find out more. That is all there is to it."

"In that case my new friends, soyez les bienvenus dans ma petite église," said the priest. "It's not often that I have such distingué company. This place is going to bury me alive if I'm not careful. I am hungry for news of the outside world. Tell me everything, and I mean everything. Here. Come with me now please."

He led them from the chapel to a dilapidated outbuilding at the far end of the clearing and unlocked the door. The cobweb-strewn interior was piled high with broken chairs and large candlesticks. "Wait here," said Father Jean-Pierre disappearing into a storeroom before returning with a bottle of wine, corkscrew and three glasses. "This is not the vinegar we give them for communion. This is the finest the island can produce. Help me young man," he said to Gunther, indicating a folding table and three chairs. "Set them up over there."

Miles yearned for the opportunity to scrutinise the statuette yet Gunther and he remained trapped by the priest's liberal dispensing of strong local wine and his insatiable appetite for debate on the issues of the day. It was only when a tasty hard local cheese and a loaf of bread were produced from the cleric's satchel that Miles was temporarily distracted from thoughts of Astarte. After the downing of a second, or possibly third bottle of wine, Father Jean-Pierre rose unsteadily and beckoned to Miles and Gunther to follow.

"Come. Now we know each other a little better, I have something remarkable to show you," said the priest ushering them into the chapel. "Since like me, you are both men of the world, I will share my guilty secret. I cannot resist. But it must remain absolutely between ourselves. That is understood, yes?" Miles dropped his jaw slightly in a gesture that might or might not pass for a nod. By now the priest had reached the statuette. Extending his index finger beneath the still dripping breast he caught a drop of white liquid. "Quel miracle, huh? Yes, even priests must confess. Especially priests who are obliged to keep alive a lie. Here, try. My refrigerator is not working so well. I'm afraid it is not very fresh."

Miles moved forward to sample the liquid. Placing a drop on his tongue, he gave a shudder. The taste reminded him of the half sour milk he had been forced to drink each morning at junior school.

"Every year I must perform this charade," said the priest extracting a white cloth from under his cassock. He began wiping the residue of milk off his hand with a fastidiousness that Miles found mildly disturbing. "To be honest with you, I would like to stop this nonsense but my superior says that even in the twenty first century, these simple people need such a phenomenon to help them through their daily struggles. Naturally, it's good for business too." He pointed to a large collection bowl in the corner piled high with bank notes.

The boldness of this admission took Miles by surprise. He had expected to be circumspect in his approach to the subject of the supposed miracle. The priest's wine-loosened revelation of chicanery was both a puzzle and a huge relief.

"I see you are shocked. Come gentlemen. Since I'm in confessional mood, would you like me to demonstrate how the illusion is created?"

"Perhaps you will allow me?" replied Miles, intervening to point out a barely noticeable indentation in the crown of the statuette's head. "If I am not mistaken the milk is poured through this aperture a few minutes before the appointed time for the miracle. The liquid has to be lukewarm, as if emerging from a maternal breast. That effect is crucial. I imagine you have a stove nearby. Perhaps you would be so kind as to show us?"

The priest stood open-mouthed. "Since you have spoilt my party trick..." He gave a shrug and drew aside a red velvet curtain behind the altar to reveal a small gas cylinder with a burner attached.

"As I thought. Now if I may continue," said Miles indicating the statuette's nipples which were still releasing the odd drop of milk. "Before the liquid is poured into the cavity, wax plugs must be placed on the inside of the breasts. I imagine you can insert them from the base of the statue?" The priest gave a dazed nod. "Then if all goes according to plan," continued Miles, "once the faithful have gathered, the warm liquid melts the wax and hey presto, you have your miracle of maternal succour."

"You are correct in every detail," murmured Father Jean-Pierre, seemingly in thrall to the extent of his visitor's knowledge. "Last year there was a big problem. The wax was too thick and would not melt. I had to send people away for an hour while I prepared it again."

"Didn't they realise then that it was a trick?" asked Gunther, his eyes flashing with excitement.

"You must understand my young friend that these poor people see what they want to see. How..how did you know all this? You must tell me," Father Jean-Pierre demanded.

"All in good time," replied Miles. "But first let me ask you a question; how long has this figure been in this chapel?"

"More than two hundred years. No one knows for sure the exact date."

"Where was it originally found?" asked Miles.

"According to local legend, the figure was discovered by a local farmer, buried in a field. But why...?"

"Where is this field? Please, we must know. There may be other such finds to uncover," interrupted Gunther.

"There are no records. It could be anywhere within a fifty kilometre radius of here. It would be like you say, looking for a needle in a..."

"Haystack?" ventured Gunther.

"Exactly. Now you must answer my question."

Without waiting for a response, Miles carefully peeled away a corner of the faded blue silk fabric of the Madonna's robe and ran his fingertips over the small section of the exposed dull bronze torso beneath. "I'm afraid that Christianity doesn't have a monopoly on such cheap tricks," Miles replied, turning to face the priest. "What if I was to tell you that this effigy dates originally from six centuries before the birth of Christ?"

"I would say you are talking nonsense."

"I know a representation of Astarte when I see her," said Miles authoritatively, resting his palm on the figure's flank.

"Astarte was the goddess of fertility and war. Maybe you have heard of her?" interjected Gunther.

"If I may continue," said Miles. "Around 2,600 years ago, the

Phoenician colonists placed such objects in shrines all over the Mediterranean to keep the local populations in awe of their gods." He pointed to the base. These temple guardian-like creatures, which you agree, have no place in Christianity, are the most important clue. Your predecessors in the Church, Father, have adapted an ancient female idol for their own devotional purposes."

The priest brushed Miles aside to examine the exposed bronze for himself. Miles pressed on. "The ancients knew the value of a miracle. A similar statuette of the goddess with precisely the same mechanism for producing this apparent lactation has been unearthed at a Phoenician settlement excavated on Cyprus, dating from 780 BC." He placed his hand on the idol's head and addressed it directly. "This is the only such example that has come to light on Corsica. If my judgement is correct, it provides irrefutable proof for the first time that that the Phoenicians established a permanent presence here. The ancient history of the Mediterranean would have to be entirely rewritten. You will perhaps understand my excitement." Miles paused to mop his brow.

"And Dr Mallalieu is the best person in the world to rewrite that history," exclaimed Gunther, rushing to fetch a rickety wooden chair on to which Miles sunk gratefully. "This provides the missing evidence for the thesis he has been attempting to prove during his entire academic career."

After a minute or two of silence, Father Jean-Pierre turned to face Miles. "What you suggest is very interesting but what makes you think that I am prepared to help you in any way?"

Miles felt the muscles in his neck stiffen. How could he convince the priest not to stand in the way of this discovery? It would call for powers of persuasion he was not certain he possessed. Although it pained him, he would have to emulate the tactics employed by his more manipulative colleagues in the Department. They, he had observed, were adept at chiselling away at their opponent's weaknesses until they capitulated. Adopting a gesture of familiarity, Miles took the priest gently by the arm and steered him away from the altar before pausing to address him in the least threatening tone he could muster. "It's quite clear to me Father that the whole business of the so-called miracle seems to trouble you a great deal. Why else would you have let us into the secret? I am wondering how you can live with yourself, as an advocate of the truth, that is. You told us yourself you are maintaining a lie."

"Yes, but it is a lie that does no harm to anyone," replied Father Jean-Pierre who had acquired a chilling sobriety.

This first sortie firmly rebuffed, Miles was about to plan his next attack when Gunther intervened: "Forgive me Father, but surely you cannot ask us to deny the existence of such a discovery?"

"You are forgetting one thing, my young friend. So far, this is still all pure supposition. Now if you would please follow me out of the church. I am beginning to regret revealing my secret to you."

"Don't you see? We're offering you the perfect escape route," retorted Miles. "It is quite clear to me you can no longer tolerate maintaining this deception and now, quite by chance, the truth behind the lie has been exposed. You, Father, as we say, are off the hook. All we need to do is to borrow the statuette so that the dating can be confirmed by the university laboratory in Ajaccio. I have no doubt whatsoever that it will be."

Father Jean-Pierre's slender frame appeared to wilt. It was time, Miles decided, to administer the coup de grâce. Manoeuvring himself between the priest and the door, Miles adopted what he hoped would be perceived as an authoritative, even threatening stance. "You should know Father that we intend to reveal the trickery behind this so-called miracle of Sartène whether or not the statuette's real provenance is authenticated now or later. For authenticated it surely will be before long and I am afraid you will be powerless to do anything about it." Miles held his ground and took a deep breath, waiting for his latest salvo to find its mark.

"I misjudged you, Dr Mallalieu," replied the priest after a lengthy pause. "You didn't seem to me to be the kind of man that would destroy the faith and hopes of so many."

"There is such a thing as academic integrity," replied Miles, puffing up his chest before turning to Gunther for affirmation. At this moment, Father Jean-Pierre's eyes began to glaze over and a pallor spread over his features.

"You must excuse me gentleman. I must have some fresh air," he muttered, rushing towards the door.

Gunther was about to follow when Miles motioned to him to remain in the nave. The priest clearly needed time to come to his senses and he would willingly grant him that. Approaching the altar to once again examine their discovery, a delinquent idea flashed though Miles' mind. Could they not take advantage of this hiatus to simply spirit the statuette away? Tempting as it seemed, the plan set off a warning bell in his head and it was dismissed before he could share it with Gunther.

Ten minutes or more passed and Father Jean-Pierre had not returned. The only sound was the occasional screech of a bird of prey against the hubbub of cicadas. Finally, yielding to impatience, he signalled to his student to follow him through the open door. At the edge of the clearing, they could make out a silhouetted figure on his knees, his palms pressed together in prayer.

Seemingly unaware of Miles' and Gunther's presence, the priest continued muttering what sounded like Latin responses. He eventually rose slowly from his knees and tilted his head up to the sky as if appealing directly to the Almighty, remaining in this position for some minutes before erupting into loud sobs of despair.

Signalling to Gunther to stay well back, Miles hovered, unsure as to whether he should intervene. He had always found the faithful of all denominations hard to engage with. The fervour of Elspeth's devotion to her spiritualist church was especially hard to fathom. The present scene was no less perplexing.

A distant bell was heard through the silence, appearing to offer a cue to Father Jean-Pierre. Hauling himself slowly to his feet, he mopped his brow with the sleeve of his cassock. "I appreciate your patience. You are a remarkable man, Dr Mallalieu." His voice now revealed a timbre of freshness. To Miles, it seemed as if the storm that had clearly raged so fiercely within this troubled man had passed on.

"Maybe you can read my soul?" added the priest. "As you can perhaps tell, I have doubts about my vocation, serious doubts. I cannot deny it. Sometimes I feel I'm going completely mad. You have found me in this unhappy state but...." Wiping the residue of tears from his face, he approached Miles and placed a conciliatory hand on his arm before adding: "I have decided that this cannot be your problem. I will not stand in your way. If you are right about this, and something tells me that you are, I am prepared for you to expose it for what it truly is. There is no place for this kind of superstition in the modern world. You have my permission to remove the Virgin for those tests but you must return it within three days. What will happen then to me, who knows?"

Such was his relief that Miles had to restrain himself from grabbing the priest in a bear hug. He turned instead to cast a glance at the newly-found representation of Astarte. For a split second, it seemed to him that her mouth had broken into a half smile.

✦

"Mallalieu here." Jolted into consciousness, Miles had struggled to locate his mobile phone. Despite his efforts to remain alert as he awaited this all-important call at their Ajaccio hotel, the sultry afternoon heat had caused him to doze off.

"Dr Mallalieu. This is Dr Ducasse. I have some news that will please you greatly....."

Miles felt a sudden rush of blood to his head. He had been quite certain that his dating of the statuette would be confirmed by the spectroscopic tests he had commissioned from the laboratory. Yet now that the positive results had come through, he was struggling to absorb the implications. He hurried down the corridor to knock loudly on Gunther's door. The expression of joy on Miles' face caused Gunther to leap up and down, punching the air.

An hour later they were sitting on the terrace of a café gazing at the pleasure boats returning to harbour. The statuette of Astarte, which they had collected from the laboratory, was secreted in a non-descript hold-all on the third chair with Miles keeping constant watch on it. "Who shall we call first?" asked Gunther.

"No one," replied Miles. "What you must understand Gunther, is that some extremely awkward questions are bound to be asked...about how the statue came to be removed for testing in the first place."

"But Dr Mallalieu, the priest allowed us to take it away. Did he not?"

"Perhaps so, but I would remind you that he acted alone and arguably while not in the soundest of minds. The hierarchy of the Church is unlikely to be particularly forgiving."

"If I may say so, you are worrying too much, Dr Mallalieu. I have an idea." Gunther had downed two large beers and appeared to be in frisky mood.

"And what would that be?" asked Miles, conjuring up visions of being hauled before a modern day version of the Inquisition.

"Why don't we just take it back to London before they find out it is missing?"

Miles chuckled. His student's idea was a tempting one. Now that the Phoenician goddess had revealed herself hidden beneath the carapace of Catholicism, Miles found himself feeling increasingly proprietorial towards her. He was however savvy enough to listen to the inner voice that told him the urge to spirit her away must be resisted. He would keep their promise to the priest and let Astarte return to her sanctuary, for the time being at least.

That night Miles was unable to surrender to sleep, his brain still fizzing. Now that evidence of the 'missing link' in his theory had been uncovered, he was gripped by a new surge of energy and purpose as he contemplated the task of completing his magnum opus. Every hour or so, he leapt out of bed to jot down some notes, fearful that his new thoughts would vanish with the first signs of dawn.

He rose late and breakfasted alone as Gunther had left early, duly despatched south, albeit reluctantly, to return the statuette. Miles had given him strict instructions to report to the priest that the laboratory tests were interesting but inconclusive. At best a white lie but it was far wiser, Miles judged, to keep Father Jean-Pierre and his superiors in the dark at this stage. The solid evidence could be revealed at a time of his own choosing, he surmised, no doubt best tied to the publication date of the book. Congratulating himself on this well-considered strategy, Miles summoned the waiter and settled for the comfort of an omelette aux fines herbes topped with boudin noir.

CHAPTER SEVEN

Miles ahead

Fitzrovia London. Eighteen months later.

"Who shall we fire today?" Miles swivelled playfully around in the high-backed leather chair and beamed at Marian across the expanse of mahogany desk.

"Miles, you're outrageous."

"By the way, can we get rid of these? I found them wedged at the back of the bottom drawer." He reached down and held up a crumpled pair of burgundy Y-fronts which he dangled over the desk. Screwing up her nose, Marian disappeared into the outer office to return with a ruler which she used to pick up the undergarment gingerly before depositing it in the waste bin.

"Must have missed them when I was clearing out the desk. After the wife changed the locks, Tony camped in the office, slept on the settee. Stunk the place out. He had the nerve to suggest I might do his washing. I refused of course so he just went out to M &S and bought new underwear."

Miles had yet to extract the full details of his predecessor's sudden departure. The subject clearly remained a touchy one with PA Marian who was clearly delighted to be supporting Miles in his new role as Director. All that Miles had gleaned was that once Marian's official complaint of sexual assault had been upheld but hushed up, a private settlement had been reached. Tony Barstow had been forced to clear his office with immediate effect. Nothing had been heard of him since. There was a rumour he had taken a teaching job in Kazakhstan.

"The BBC crew have arrived by the way. They're downstairs," said Marian. "They want to do the interview in the square. I told them it looks like rain but they won't take no for an answer."

Miles sighed. "What do they want to talk to me about this time? Not Mallalieu's travel tips for the discerning Mediterranean tourist again?"

"What do you think they want to talk about? The book and nothing but the book. You're a publishing phenomenon, Miles. You'd better get used to the idea."

"People will probably end up using it as a doorstop."

"I can think of cheaper doorstops," replied Marian.

"Can't you put the BBC lot off? I've said everything there is to say about it."

"You'll think of something. Besides, doing publicity is part of your contract. You should have read it more carefully."

"Well as long as they don't slap make-up on me again. I had a rash for days after the last filming."

Marian moved round the desk to subject Miles to a close physical inspection. A few flecks of dandruff, imaginary or otherwise, were flicked from his shoulder and his jacket collar was adjusted. "There," she said standing back to admire her handiwork.

"Do I pass muster?"

"Let's just say that I'm less likely than others to see your imperfections," replied Marian.

"Very well but ask them to give me ten minutes, would you? I need to check this press release about the replica statuettes. I don't trust the museum lot when it comes to marketing. I haven't a clue what that term marketing means exactly, but I'm told they're useless at it."

"That's why you've got me to keep an eye on things," replied Marian, with a sparkle in her voice. "Who made sure you got a decent cut of the merchandising revenue?"

"I count myself lucky in that respect. Now leave me to check this drivel, would you?"

Marian gave a mock salute and turned to leave. Miles found himself following her disappearing form. As if sensing this scrutiny, Marian turned to smile before closing the door firmly behind her. Miles turned his attention reluctantly to the draft document.

The success of the book and the attendant public interest had won him new respect amongst the senior echelons of the University, anxious for media approval. This success had clinched his new appointment and saved the Department from the threat of closure once Bernie Prince had withdrawn as benefactor. Applications from prospective international students prepared to pay outrageous sums to study under Miles and his colleagues were flooding in. As for his eligibility for the top job, Miles was only too aware that he lacked a single iota of management experience. As Elspeth was all too fond of reminding him, he had problems enough managing himself.

Much to his surprise, and that of his sister, who masked her pride at his promotion by predicting early failure, he had settled into the role far more effortlessly than he had thought possible. As the weeks passed, he found himself tackling the day-to-day running of the Department with a degree of confidence that astonished himself, and more importantly, his better qualified colleagues who had been passed over for the job. He had made it clear from the start that he had no time for their envious jibes. They would have to accept that Miles' long overdue moment in the sun had come and he intended to savour every moment. Marian guarded his diary like Cerberus. He could rely on her to unravel the tedious internecine issues that junior members of staff insisted on bringing before him.

Having skimmed through the lacklustre press release, Miles gazed abstractedly out of the window at the square below. The handsome plane trees in their emerald spring hues were something of a blur but he could make out a camera crew setting up their equipment on the grass.

Today it was the turn of the BBC. Yesterday it had been The New York Times. The extraordinary success of The Goddess of Love - A Complete History of the Mediterranean in Ancient Times had caught Miles and his publisher entirely off guard. Following the airing of the glossy six-part television series built around the subject, initially modest sales of the hefty tome had accelerated exponentially. It had taken a great deal of convincing to persuade Miles to subject himself to an audition to act as presenter of the series. The prospect of intense public exposure terrified him. His nephew Jeremy, who had somehow inveigled his way into the BBC as an assistant producer after failing to make the grade at MI5, had been assigned the task of encouraging his uncle to undergo this ordeal. At the screen test which took place in a cramped basement studio in Soho, Miles was handed an instruction manual for a washing machine, told to pick a page at random and read it out loud with as much expression and feeling as he could muster.

Much to his relief, Miles' haltering delivery and reluctance to look directly into the camera had at first ruled him out. It was only the intervention of a former PhD student, now Head of BBC History, that swayed the decision. After treating Miles to a fulsome meal on the Corporation at Rules' restaurant where the suckling pig melted in the mouth, the novice presenter's nerves were soothed to the point where he finally agreed to take the leading role. The series was duly given the go-ahead, each episode opening and closing with Miles standing arms outstretched on a lonely outcrop of Corsican coastline as if to receive, or perhaps repel, the next wave of Phoenician invaders. Bolstered by the crew's encouragement on location, he was soon, to borrow a phrase favoured by his nephew, 'having a ball.'

Almost overnight, Miles found himself a palpable if unlikely hit with an audience tiring of more polished interpreters of history. It was never clear to him whether he was regarded as an amiable eccentric able to transmit his deep passion for his subject or simply worth watching for his gaffes. Sensing that these invoked the viewers' sympathy, the producers had elected to leave many in the final version, despite Miles' entreaties.

In short, he was now a celebrity, recognised in his favourite sandwich bar, a sitting target for autograph hunters while he sipped his cappuccino. Interruptions had grown so frequent that he had taken to adopting a disguise consisting of an ancient green felt hat pulled low over his brow and dark glasses worn even on a dull day. As Elspeth pointed out, the effect of this improbable disguise was to make him even more conspicuous.

✦

"Remind me what time I'm supposed to be there," called Miles from behind his desk.

"People are invited for six but if you get there a little late you can make a grand entrance," said Marian, appearing from the outer office.

"You make me sound like royalty. You've clearly made an effort," said Miles, indicating her vivid red cocktail dress. "Where is it again? The Dorchester?"

"Claridges, the ballroom. And thanks for the faint praise."

"It was supposed to be a compliment. Now before you say anything about my appearance, I suppose I'd better go and change," Miles replied, heaving himself out of the Director's chair. "I still can't fathom why they're splashing out on me in this way. I thought the publishing world was on its knees."

"For goodness sake, you've earned it," replied Marian. "Thirty weeks in the top ten, a quarter of a million copies sold. And now to top that, the Samuel Johnson Prize. You might say it's a triple whammy. Now which tie did you bring?"

"You know I loathe wearing a tie. My shirt collars are all too tight."

Marian disappeared, returning after a moment or two with a crisp new blue and white striped shirt which she began to remove from its packaging. Shaking it out, she held it against his chest.

"Well. What do you think?"

"Elspeth says stripes make me look chubbier Marian, why do you spoil me like this?"

✦

The notion of being thrust into a large gathering to make endless small talk would normally have caused Miles to break out in a heavy sweat. Before leaving for the hotel, Marian had seen to it that he had been fortified with a generous gin and tonic, the afterglow of which had left him pleasantly woozy. The nearer their taxi got to Mayfair, the notion of a lavish party in his honour began to seem more agreeable.

"Quite a turn-out, eh?" said Marian, squeezing Miles' arm as they stood at the entrance to the chandelier-lit ballroom, surveying the throng. A glass of champagne and a canapé were offered and accepted.

Cradling his glass, Miles stood transfixed, blinking at the crush of gilded humanity. He was reminded of the vast reception he had been forced to attend at the Foreign Office two years earlier, in the risible attempt by his MI5 puppet masters to make it appear that he, a humble academic, had connections in the highest political circles. It seemed like another life.

"Well we can't stand here all evening," said Marian, gently applying pressure to Miles' back and propelling him forward.

As if on cue, a burst of applause and shouts of 'For he's a jolly good fellow' accompanied his entry into the ballroom. Hands shot out to grasp his from amidst the crowd of florid faced males, their partners masked in elaborate maquillage. Who then were all these people apparently invited by his publisher? Miles was aware that his own guest list had been slender to say the least. Before he could consult Marian, she had been swept away in the melée and he was immediately collared by a fawning junior colleague and his wife. It was some time before Miles was able to seize a minute to himself. He looked around in vain for Elspeth. Surely she had not forgotten? He was distracted by a voice from behind his left ear.

"Well Miles, how are you enjoying yourself?" The familiar accented tones caused him to swivel round, slopping champagne down his shirt front as he did so.

"Vera....what are you doing here?"

"Surprised to see me? Well you shouldn't be. Bernie has just bought your publishers."

"Bernie?" Mention of this name induced a visceral anger. "I suppose he's still on his quest for respectability?"

"You have him to thank for picking up the tab for all this, and for inviting all his friends. Here let me hold your drink while you clean yourself up."

Miles extracted his crumpled handkerchief and dabbed distractedly at his shirt front where an errant prawn had lodged. Snatching his glass back from Vera, he downed a large glug of champagne.

"Bernie is so sorry he couldn't be here," said Vera. "He hates to miss a party. He wanted to congratulate you personally on the book and the new job by the way. You know he's forgiven you... for what happened on the yacht?"

"No I didn't," replied Miles, trying not to choke. "I thought he might press charges. So I take it you're...still together?"

Before Vera could reply, they were approached by a posse of eager guests, clearly intent on buttonholing Miles. Blocking their path, Vera drew Miles to one side. "Aren't you a little bit pleased to see me?" she whispered.

Miles shrugged. His feelings about this unexpected reunion were muddled, to say the least.

"I want to talk to you, to explain things," Vera added.

"What is there to explain?"

"Can I come and see you?"

"You'll have to make an appointment through Marian. She keeps my diary."

"Maybe we could have dinner one evening?"

"Are you sure Bernie would allow it?"

Her expression darkened. "I'm my own woman Miles." She patted him on the arm. "Now I should leave you to circulate amongst your admirers."

"I think you mean Bernie's mob?"

Aware that she was now overheard by fellow guests, Vera whispered: "Here's my new number, call me." She thrust a card into his hand and slipped away into the crowd.

Avoiding the throng, Miles shuffled round the edge of the ballroom to make an overdue visit to the men's room. He was about to make a beeline for the nearest cubicle (standing at urinals made him nervous) when he spotted a familiar figure at the basins.

"Miles, it's great to see you!"

A large moist hand was extended and gripped Miles' tightly. Doug Allardyce fixed him with a warm smile.

"This is quite a bash, huh? Your nephew got me on the list. Now he's in the real world, he seems to have a lot of clout. How about all this? I'd never have known you had it in you, Miles. Once we had no more need of your services, I thought you'd head back into...well let's call it genteel obscurity."

"You'll have to excuse me. Nature calls," said Miles.

"Sure thing. Go ahead. I guess I'm putting you off your stroke." Doug laughed as Miles made a dash for the cubicle and bolted the door.

Eventually he could delay his re-emergence no longer. Doug was still at the basins, splashing himself with eau de cologne and staring intently at Miles in the mirror.

"You're going to have to forgive me for hounding you but I guess it's too good an opportunity to miss." Doug looked around quickly. "The point is Miles, I have something important I want to say to you."

"And would that be an apology perhaps?" ventured Miles who could feel a dam of residual anger about to burst.

"Listen, that business with Vera...we had no choice Miles. One day I'll explain in more detail and maybe you'll see things from our point of view."

"I doubt that," said Miles, focusing on drying his hands.

"The point is I've had it up to here with this spook stuff," Doug continued. "Once an academic always an academic, eh Miles? After that plagiarism business, the CIA had me by the balls. They wanted my brain, I needed a job. It's never too late for a return to academia. How about you give me a job at the Department? We cover the same territory after all. I can help you with the sequel.

"You know what you can do, Doug?" said Miles, turning from the basin. "You can bugger off."

The encounter with Doug Allardyce had left a warm glow of satisfaction. From now on there would be no room for lily-livered politesse. Far better, Miles decided, to dispense harsh words than punches.

The following morning, after a leisurely soak in the bath, he wandered into the kitchen to seek a dose of caffeine before heading for the Department. Elspeth was sitting at the table engrossed in a crossword. She looked up with a startled expression.

"You missed a good party."

"Are you cross with me?"

"It would have been nice to have been able to share my big night with my closest relative."

"I'm sure I told you I had an important meeting at church. I couldn't get out of it."

"God taking precedence over Mammon," Miles replied.

"I hope winning the prize isn't going to go your head, I suspect it already has."

"Aren't you at least going to ask me how it went?"

"How did it go?" asked Elspeth in a desultory way.

Miles could feel sharp words beginning to form but he somehow held himself in check. "If you must know, it was all rather overwhelming," he replied in a studied matter-of-fact tone. A loud clatter emanated from the corridor.

"Did you hear that?" asked Miles.

"What?" asked Elspeth.

"Don't move." Picking up a kitchen knife, Miles braced himself to confront the potential intruder.

"Put it down Miles," said Elspeth, coaxing the knife from his hand. "We have a visitor." Miles detected a blush spreading over his sister's normally ash-white features.

The lavatory door swung open and Tristan emerged adjusting his belt round his spindly waist. On spotting Miles he raised his hands in an attitude of mock surrender.

"Don't hit me....Sorry bad joke," Miles found himself locked in a fierce bear hug. "Long time no see. How are you Miles? Soon to be Sir Miles no doubt."

Having extricated himself from Tristan's clutches, Miles stared fiercely first at him and then at Elspeth. "What in God's name is he doing here?"

"Please don't blaspheme," replied Elspeth.

"I'd sit down if I were you," said Tristan. "You look as if you're about to have a heart attack."

Miles had seen or heard nothing of his erstwhile friend since the fraught attempt to evict him from the Brondesbury house. Tristan had eventually found somewhere else to squat. The house had then been fumigated and professionally cleaned at great expense before being leased to a meticulously tidy Japanese banker. There remained the thorny issue of several Mallalieu family heirlooms that the impecunious Tristan had sold off in order to fund his prodigious consumption of alcohol.

"Didn't Elspeth tell you?" asked Tristan, flopping on to the Chesterfield and grinning at Miles.

"Tell me what?" asked Miles, still flummoxed.

"That she and I are, how shall I say, an item?" Tristan interwove the fingers of both hands to emphasise the point. "Daphnis and Chloe, Abelard and Eloise. Take your pick. We discovered we have a bond you see. You haven't forgotten that it was you Miles who introduced us at Elspeth's 21st?"

"Is this true Elspeth?" demanded Miles.

"You've been so busy with your celebrity career, Miles. It's been happening under your nose. Mind you, this is the first time I've let Trist stay. We normally go to a Premier Inn. They have a special midweek rate."

"How long have you...?"

"We bumped into each other in the street, about three months ago wasn't it,Trist? One thing led to another. We've kept out of your way, until we were sure about it, that is."

Crossing over to Elspeth, Tristan lowered his hands gently on to her shoulders. Miles noticed that at his touch, an aura of calm, even beauty, spread over her angular features. The grey bags which normally looped under her eyes appeared to have faded and there was a skittish schoolgirl feel to the way she twisted her body.

"Can you be happy for us, Miles?" asked Elspeth.

"I think it's best if I leave you two alone to...mull things over," said Tristan, creeping towards the door. He had adopted his familiar hang-dog look designed to evoke sympathy.

"Off you go Trist, you coward. Leaving me to do the dirty work," said Elspeth, smiling.

"There's more," she said, moving closer to Miles once Tristan had left the room.

"Isn't that enough good news for one day?"

"We're going to get married."

Miles swallowed hard. Before he could utter a response, Elspeth added: "I know what you're thinking. Trist's very fond of me and I don't want to face old age alone. Can you understand that, Miles?"

"And why, may I ask did he absent himself for this momentous announcement?"

"His wanted me to raise the subject first...to allow you to get used to the idea."

"To soften me up, you mean."

Elspeth took hold of Miles' hand and placed it gingerly in hers. He could not recall when he had last had physical contact with his sister. It seemed strange and he found himself recoiling from her touch. "Listen to me please, Miles. Trist desperately wants your approval. So do I. It would mean everything to us."

"I don't know what to say Elspeth, I really don't."

"We have a lot of fun together. That's something new in my life. He makes me laugh and that's so important."

Miles nodded abstractedly. Domestic merriment had been conspicuously absent from his life. He felt a pang of envy.

"Of course, we're very different animals," Elspeth continued. "I've made a promise not to try and change him and in return, he'll try not to make too many demands on me. He knows I can't cook to save my life and I'll have to put up with his less than salubrious habits. I have managed to lure him to church."

"That's hard to believe. Tristan's an atheist to his boots," said Miles, conjuring up an unlikely image of this dissolute figure crouched in fervent prayer.

"He did it for me. He quite enjoyed it...all the bells and smells. He says inhaling the incense is better than smoking marijuana, his holy fix as he called it. Can you believe that? Better than marijuana! I told Father Andrew. He thought it was hilarious." Elspeth began tittering. She leaned closer to Miles. "It's high time you found someone. The world is full of single women. You may not be an obvious catch but now you're such a star, they must be throwing themselves at you?"

Miles shrugged. "I've had some offers, it's true. None I would call exactly appealing. There is one woman in Bagshot who sent me..."

"I know you're still smarting from the Russian business but you must get over it Miles. You'll have to learn to drop your defences, just as I did. Open yourself up to Lady Luck. You do know I want you to be happy too?" she added, kissing him lightly on the top of his head, leaving his tonsure pleasantly tingling.

✦

Miles took a lengthier than usual route to the Department in order to reflect on Elspeth's bombshell. The revelation that his sister had been open to romantic entanglement was hard to accept; it was entirely possible that Tristan was less guided by Cupid's arrow than the prospect of self-enrichment. Surely he was not sufficiently deluded to believe that he was bedding some kind of heiress? And yet, it was remotely possible that money might not be the sole draw. Tristan had a penchant for causing mischief for mischief's sake. His friend had admitted as much after attempting to seduce Mo following the uncon-summated marriage. Now Tristan had succeeded in ensnaring Elspeth. Was it merely another round in the game to prove that no significant woman in Miles' life was unbeddable?

Still pondering this unpalatable theory, Miles was hover-ing at the Gower Street traffic lights when ginger-bearded col-league Gavin bobbed into view.

"Quite a triumph last night, eh? All those arse-lickers lin-ing up for an audience with the great man. Sorry I didn't join the queue. Not my style I'm afraid. I retreated to the nearest pub. All that champagne made me puke. You know what I've been thinking?"

"No, what?"asked Miles distractedly.

"Someone with such a great future ahead of them as a scrib-bler and tele pundit shouldn't be wasting their time with all this academic management stuff. You're cut out for loftier things, Miles. Leave the day-to-day shit to the also-rans."

"And would you include yourself in that category?" asked Miles, unable to resist this jibe at his perennially embittered colleague.

Gavin leant in close enough for Miles to smell last night's alcoholic intake. "The point is Miles that I'm up for it," said Gavin, his sky blue Celtic eyes burning fiercely. "...if you ever find it all gets too much. You know something? We think the same way, you and I."

"Do we?" Miles attempted to move ahead but Gavin tugged at his sleeve. "All I'm asking is if you're ever planning to give up the day job, be a pal and tip me off in advance. Just so I can get a head start on all those other losers who fancy themselves running the Department."

"I'm sorry to disappoint you but I've no intention of step-ping down," said Miles. "The fact is I'm rather enjoying myself. I'm afraid you're stuck with me, unless I fall under a bus or am pushed." He smiled finitely at Gavin. "Now if you'll excuse me."

✦

"Aren't you happy for them?" said Marian.

"That's what Elspeth asked me. Yes of course I am."

"You don't sound that enthusiastic."

"I'm coming round to it slowly. Just as long as she realises what she's taking on, warts and all. But she's quite open about it, she doesn't want to be alone."

"I'll drink to that," said Marian raising her glass.

They were sitting at their usual alcove table in the local Italian. The only change in the decor of faded pastoral scenes was the addition of a large signed photograph of Miles in TV presenter mode, precariously perched on a Corsican hillside.

"Where are they going to live?" asked Marian. "You said neither of them have a bean. You can't support them both, Miles and they can hardly co-habit with you."

"You're quite right there. How's your osso bucco?"

"Stop trying to change the subject. Weren't you and Elspeth left a house by your aunt? Why not sign it all over to her?"

"You're talking about the house I let Tristan stay in virtually rent free for years. He wrecked it, I'll have you know. Now I'm getting a decent rental for it."

"Forget all that," said Marian. "Show them you're the generous warm-hearted Miles I know you to be. Do it before they come begging."

"Supposing I find I need somewhere larger of my own? It almost happened before."

"You mean with Vera Petrovna? I saw her collar you at the

do. She's got a nerve showing up like that. Still with her billionaire?" Miles nodded. "She knows when she's on to a good thing," Marian added.

"Are you implying I wasn't a 'good thing'?" said Miles.

"You're not still smitten, are you?"

Miles shook his head and continued chewing on a large mouthful of veal shank.

"Good," said Marian. "Make sure you leave some room for the tiramisu."

When Miles arrived at the pub the following evening, Tristan was already installed, staring into a half empty glass of wine. The bar was crowded and he had sought refuge on a high stool in a corner.

"Saved it for you." Tristan patted the empty stool next to him.

"Thank you all the same but I'll stand," replied Miles.

"The place is full of overpaid yobs. Want to go somewhere else?" said Tristan.

"No. This won't take long. Aren't you going to offer me a drink? I'll have whatever it is you're having."

"Merlot. Pretty rough stuff."

"Fine by me. You might as well get us a bottle. Works out cheaper," said Miles, smiling obliquely. Tristan made a show of extracting his wallet and checking it for ready cash.

"I'm sure they take cards," said Miles as his future brother-in-law heaved himself off the stool and headed for the bar.

On his return with the drinks, Miles looked into Tristan's bloodshot eyes and sensed his nervousness. There was a certain perverse pleasure to be gained in his desperation for approval.

"Come on Miles. Spit it out. Are you with or agin us?"

"I suppose I should be flattered that it matters to you what

I think."

"Course it matters. You're one of my oldest chums and she's your nearest and dearest after all. Go on, put me out of my misery."

"Before we go any further, you'll have to put me out of my misery."

"How do you mean?"

"It's what you might call an historic matter that's been niggling me. I need to clear it up.

"I leave history to you, Miles. Look if you want me to reimburse you for that picture of your aunt's I flogged off..."

"No, it's not that." Miles paused and fixed Tristan with a cold stare. "I'll come to the point. After she and I...went our separate ways, did you or did you not sleep with Mo?

Tristan refilled his glass to the brim. "Fancy you bringing that up. Hadn't thought about her for years."

"I have," said Miles.

"Very well, I did try it on, yes, but as far as I can recall, I got a stop signal."

"As far as you can recall?" Miles repeated the words angrily. "Come on Tristan, you can do better than that."

"Just going with the zeitgeist, wasn't I? Bit of a game really. Women go for shits. Plenty of opportunities in those happy days."

"And plenty of conquests too, no doubt. Tell me straight, was Mo one of them?" As he awaited the reply, Miles could feel the blood rise to fill his skull.

Tristan shook his head. "Put it down to her religious scruples or some misguided sense of loyalty to you Miles, but no, she was not one of my conquests as you insist on calling them."

"Do you expect me to believe that?"

"Yes, for Christ's sake, I do."

An instinct told Miles that for once, Tristan was telling the truth.

"To be brutally honest Miles, I never really fancied your Mo that much and what's more, I'm not sure you did either."

Miles tensed. "What the hell do you know about it?"

"You were shit scared about having to perform on the wedding night."

"Was I indeed?" said Miles. "Perhaps you were hiding behind the curtains?"

"Come on Miles, you were a novice. You can't have forgotten the little arrangement I made for you that night in The Turf, to get some practice in before the big night? Ginette, wasn't it?

Miles grappled with the awkward memory. "If you must know I failed to rise to the occasion, if you get my meaning. I wasn't going to admit it to you though. I would never have heard the end of it."

Tristan's eyes widened. "Welcome to round two of the Truth Game," he added, raising his glass. "My wedding present to you down the drain. I paid Ginette a fiver in advance. You lied to me, Miles. Didn't your Mummy tell you that you'd burn in Hell if you told a Porkie?"

"It was a foolish idea. I should never have agreed to it."

"When we met up the next night you seemed as happy as a pig in shit."

"Did I? I must have been a good actor."

"Why are still so bothered?" asked Tristan.

"I had to know...about you and her. Can you see that?"

"Mo really wasn't your type. Bit of an ice maiden. Just as well it didn't work out."

"Perhaps you're right," said Miles fighting off a maudlin sensation.

"What you must understand Miles is that when it comes to women your chum is always right."

Miles laughed. "Do you know what my old headmaster said to my parents after my dismal O Level results? 'If ignorance is bliss then your son will have a happy future.'"

"Here's to ignorance then!" said Tristan, raising his glass. "And to new beginnings."

CHAPTER EIGHT

Peril in Venice

"I don't 'do' holidays," had been Miles' instinctive response when Marian had suggested that as the Department was in a quiet period, he could surely afford to take a short break. Miles could not recall when he had last considered such an indulgence. Over the years there had been countless summer trips to supervise archaeological digs around the Mediterranean, and more recently to film his television series, but they had presented no possibility of rest and recreation. Not that he would have known what to do with such an opportunity. The prospect of stewing in the sun on a beach surrounded by mewling children had no appeal. Equally abhorrent was the notion of sightseeing in the heat with the camera-clicking hoards.

His reluctance was partly due to the lack of an acceptable companion. Elspeth had made it perfectly clear that she was uninterested in foreign travel and a bleak stay with his sister in a British seaside hotel was out of the question. Her suggestion one year that he might join a group of mature singletons trekking the Samerian Gorge was met with little enthusiasm.

Worn down by Marian's insistence, Venice was selected

as a destination. Sensing this had been her plan all along, he had considered inviting her to accompany him. As someone who tolerated his little foibles Marian, he decided, would provide excellent company. There would be no complications attached, single rooms being the order of the day.

Yet somehow he had failed to issue the invitation and as a result, now found himself drinking in the splendours of La Serenissma alone. As the water taxi from Marco Polo airport nosed into the Grand Canal, Miles marvelled at the hurly burly of waterborne activity. Disembarking at the Pensione Accademia, he felt a surge of child-like excitement. He would make the most of his solitary stay.

It was on his second afternoon, after a postprandial siesta in the pensione's shady garden, that Miles decided on a stroll. On reaching the Riva degli Schiavoni bordering the open water, he paused at the apex of a footbridge spanning the entrance to a side canal. The day trippers heading to and from St Mark's ebbed and flowed around him as he gazed at the imposing campanile of San Giorgio Maggiore. The intensity of the crystalline light striking the water's surface eventually forced him to turn away. Chiding himself for neglecting to pack his prescription sunglasses, Miles tugged in vain at the brim of his elderly Panama which refused to offer his eyes any protection. Squinting, he moved on towards the Arsenale.

✦

It lay there like an upended apartment block, moored directly against the quayside running alongside the Giardini. The yacht's brilliant white superstructure towered over the public gardens and a small crowd had gathered to gape in the hope of catching sight of its over-privileged occupants. Despite an inherent distaste for these gargantuan bath toys, curiosity and a certain sense of déjà vu propelled Miles towards the stern of the vessel to establish its identity.

He had scarcely absorbed the words 'La Celestia' when a female cry greeted him from the open rear deck some twenty feet above him. "Miles, Miles, it's me!" Shielding his eyes from the glare, the unmistakeable figure of Vera Petrovna was leaning over the rail, waving energetically. To Miles, she appeared radiant in a flowing white dress offset by a deep tan.

"What in God's name are you doing here?" she called. "Stay there, don't move. I'm coming down," she added, before disappearing from view.

Miles' first instinct was to make his escape. He had been thoroughly unnerved by Vera's appearance at the Claridges party but had since succeeded in banishing her and the painful memories of their acrimonious parting on board this very vessel from his mind. He was about to slide away when he was collared by a young American couple who had witnessed this exchange. The woman turned to Miles: "Excuse me sir but is she a movie star? Should I know her?"

"I doubt it," replied Miles curtly.

Miles prepared to resume his flight but Vera had hurtled down the gangway and was rushing towards him with open arms.

"It really is you! This is such a coincidence, unless of course you're stalking me?"

Miles felt his shoulder muscles tighten as she threw her arms around him. "I'm not letting you get away," added Vera, attempting to steer him towards the gangway. "You don't have to worry about Bernie. He had to fly off somewhere in a hurry, Tirana I think. I'm all on my own, if you don't count the crew of course." She laughed. "Go on, say something for God's sake!"

Miles' reaction was to turn away from the yacht. With obvious reluctance, Vera let go of his arm and prepared to follow him. "OK, as you wish. We can find somewhere quiet and you can tell me what you are doing here," she said, pointing towards a narrow street leading from the waterfront.

Miles had planned to make his way to La Fenice theatre in the hope of a return for that evening's sold-out performance of Fidelio. If he mentioned this, Vera would no doubt suggest that she might accompany him and he was not prepared for that. Abandoning this idea, he pressed on down the shadowy side street. After a few minutes Vera paused, indicating a table outside a small café.

"How about here?"

"I'd rather walk and talk," replied Miles.

Vera shrugged. "OK, but it's not like the Miles I know to turn down a torta della nonna." She pointed to an alluring example of this local delicacy displayed in the café window.

The closer they came to St Mark's, the more crowded were the alleyways lined with souvenir shops, their windows packed with leering carnival masks. Buffeted by the tourist hoards Vera was struggling to keep up with Miles, who was moving with uncharacteristic alacrity.

"I know you're still angry but just maybe you've been missing me a little bit?" she asked, finally catching up and taking hold of his arm to slow him down.

"My private life's had to take a back seat lately. You shouldn't take it personally," replied Miles, pushing his way onwards.

"Come on, let's get away from these crowds. I want to show you something special. It's not far from here. Just follow me. Relax, Miles, I'm not going to kidnap you. Where are you staying by the way?"

"The Accademia," he blurted out.

"You can always join me on the yacht. There are many spare cabins."

"I rather think I will decline that kind offer," replied Miles.

As he was dragged through the labyrinth of alleyways, Miles berated himself for succumbing to Vera's entreaties. By the time they reached the Campo San Giovanni e Paulo, he was parched. Vera paused at the edge of the piazza and pointed to an imposing bronze statue of a helmeted soldier on a spirited steed.

"That's it, what I want you to see," she said, beckoning Miles on. "Come. Let's take a closer look. Don't you want to know who it is?"

Miles had been gazing longingly at a vacant café table in the shade. He would have given anything to be able to flop down and order a long cold lemonade. As they moved closer to the statue, his view was dominated by the stallion's well-defined genitalia. He moved round to the horse's head and examined the rider more closely.

"Whoever he is, he looks rather menacing," Miles replied, noting the figure's ferocious gaze which seemed focused directly on him.

"You're right. That is Bartolomeo Colleoni. He fascinates me," said Vera. "He was quite a guy, a great military man of the Renaissance. He had no morals at all. He would fight for anybody who would pay him. Do you know that when he was about to die, he called the rulers of Venice together and warned that they should never give any other soldier such power as they had given him? You see, he knew just how easily he could manipulate them."

"You're obviously drawn to powerful men," was all Miles could think to reply.

Vera shrugged. "Does he remind you of anyone alive today?"

"I've no idea," said Miles, taking care not to display any enthusiasm for this enforced cultural stop.

"For me, it's Bernie."

Miles swallowed hard. "You've hauled me across Venice to see a statue that reminds you of your boyfriend?"

Vera pointed up accusingly at Colleoni. "Can't you see? Bernie is exactly like him. I've seen how he operates in business and Miles, it scares me. I needed to come here and look into this guy's eyes to remind myself. He can fool people with all his joking and always picking up the tab."

"I could have told you that and saved us this journey," said Miles with mounting irritation. Turning away, he caught the eye of an elderly woman who had been scrutinising them from her first floor balcony overlooking the piazza. He held her stare.

"Bringing you here to see this statue of this evil man makes it a little easier for me to tell you."

"Tell me what?" asked Miles, mopping his brow.

"I'm leaving him."

Miles took a deep breath and considered his reply. "Does he know?"

"Not yet. You're the first person I've told."

"I imagine that men who know they can buy anything or anybody don't appreciate being rejected. He might make things very difficult for you. Have you thought about that?"

"That's a risk I have to take. Anyway, what exactly are you saying Miles, that he bought me, like a new car?"

"Well that's rather the way it looks."

Vera stared at him, eyes wild. "Bernie doesn't own me, Miles." She prodded his shoulder with a forcefulness that caused Miles to recoil. "OK, you're angry with me still, I understand. Oh Miles, you are so different to him." Vera now placed her palm affectionately on Miles's face and held it there for some seconds. Despite the undeniably pleasurable sensation, he brushed her hand aside.

Miles had been congratulating himself on successfully burying any trace of feeling for Vera. Now those feelings were at risk of being disinterred. He was grateful for the diversion caused by a gaggle of Chinese tourists who had swarmed round them.

"What do you propose to do?" he continued, once the group had moved off. "Would you go back to St Petersburg?"

Vera shook her head. "No chance. I had an email from my boss. I'm seen as a troublemaker. I'm rejected by my own university. You can imagine how that makes me feel. Bernie said he had friends in high places in Moscow who could help me, but of course he's done nothing."

"Do you need money?"

"Please don't insult me. You can't get rid of me that easily," Vera replied with a pallid laugh. "Come!" She clapped her hands as if to disperse the palpable tension. "Let's have a drink. You look as if you need one. I know I do."

Parched and weary, Miles could offer only token resistance as Vera ushered him towards the terrace of the nearby café. For some minutes, they sat in silence, allowing themselves to be diverted by the antics of a group of children kicking a ball around the base of the Colleoni statue. Aperol Spritz was ordered. Vera raised her glass in a toast. Miles felt obliged to clink it in return. The afternoon sun glinted through the bright orange liquid as he all but emptied the contents in one gulp.

Suitably emboldened by the afterglow of the alcohol, Miles

came to a decision. He would procrastinate not a moment longer.

"I have something to ask you. It's been troubling me for quite a while," he said, having observed Vera's instant nervous reaction.

"OK. What is it you want to know?"

"That story about your daughter running away to London, was it just an excuse for you to come knocking on my door?" asked Miles, gazing into his empty glass.

Vera arched her eyebrows. "What can you mean? That was no 'story.' Claudia had run away to meet up with her friend Irena. I was crazy with worry about her. You know that." Vera paused. "Okay. It's true I had no one else in London to contact but after Chicago I wanted to see you again... very much. Why do you ask this?"

"Leaving that aside, how we first met, that was no happy coincidence, was it?"

"In Chicago? You were so sweet and you needed rescuing. I was more than happy to do it."

"Tell me, was it a pile of cash in a Swiss bank account they promised you? Or maybe they expected you to seduce me purely out of loyalty to the Motherland?"

Miles noticed a tremor in Vera's hand. She took a moment before replying. "I have no idea what you're talking about."

"I think you do." He stared hard at her.

"Who gave you these ideas?" Vera's face had emptied of colour.

"Let's just say I had a tip-off from those who keep an eye on Russians like you in London." Vera's eyes remained lowered. "So you don't deny it?"

There was another lengthy pause. "If you think I had a choice, you don't know anything," she cried suddenly, bringing her fist down hard on the table. "If I'd refused they'd have put Claudia in jail on some made-up drugs charge. That's the way they do things there. You don't have children, Miles. There's no way you can understand."

"There's a great deal I don't understand," replied Miles. "But I appreciate your honesty."

"By being honest like this with you I've put myself in real danger. You do realise that if they knew I had told you, the people back in Moscow would have me killed?"

"Well, you can take it that I'm not about to tell them, and I don't imagine you are either," replied Miles, permitting himself a smile.

"For God's sake, how can you make a joke at a time like this?"

"Since you are in confessional mood, answer me one thing: did your people in Moscow really believe I had connections in high places?" Vera nodded. Miles snorted.

Vera's response was to reach out and clutch at Miles hand. "Don't you see? None of this matters." She fixed Miles with a winsome look. "From the first moment in that hotel there was something special between us. Miles, I know you felt it too."

"And yet you abandoned me for Bernie, presumably after they lost interest in me? It doesn't quite fit, does it? "

"I'm not proud of what I did to you. I hurt you very much."

Miles was struggling to recall a line of poetry about 'mankind cannot bear very much reality.' There had been rather too much reality for one afternoon. He knew only that he had to put some distance between himself and Vera. Extracting a twenty euro note, he placed it on the table and raised himself from his chair. "Here, this should cover it."

"Wait! Where are you going? Now all I want to do is to make up for it to you. Miles, I'm not going to let you leave like this."

"If I was in your shoes, Vera, I'd throw my lot in with Bernie and his billions, a far safer bet than me." Miles made as if about to take his leave. He was fully expecting Vera to jump up and plead with him to stay, but instead she slumped down resignedly in her chair.

"Okay, if you are going, go now, see if I care," she said morosely, dismissing Miles with a perfunctory wave . As he turned the corner he reflected on how much simpler matters would have been if he had chosen a different route for his afternoon stroll.

✦

After reaching his hotel room, Miles collapsed on the bed and attempted to stave off the welter of unruly thoughts. However unpalatable, the facts could not be ignored. He had been cynically manipulated, not to mention seduced, by a shrewd operator working for a foreign power. How did he even know that Vera had told the truth about the hold she claimed that the Russians had over her? Was it not just as likely she had agreed to do it for money? Miles pulled the duvet over his head and attempted to seek refuge in an overdue siesta.

When he awoke to the mournful chorus of hooters on the Grand Canal, it was after dusk. Alone in a claustrophobic Venetian hotel room, he now felt an overwhelming sense of loneliness. By way of comfort, he began to conjure up images from the brief period when he and Vera had been at their most intimate. There was no denying the sheer physical pleasure, not to mention the fun, he had enjoyed. Had Vera really been dissembling? If so, Miles reflected, she had shown herself to be a first rate actress. He was disturbed by the shrill ring of the hotel phone.

"Signor Mallalieu? This is reception."

"Yes? What is it?" replied Miles, still disoriented.

"There is a lady here to see you. Will you come down or shall I send her up to your room ?"

CHAPTER NINE

An unforgiving goddess

Four months later

As Marian re-entered, Miles was examining himself in the reflection of a framed print of an explicit Pompeian mural which his predecessor had left behind. He had been meaning to remove it but Marian had reprimanded him for being a prude. The new suit clung limpet-like to his frame. "I'm not so sure I should've gone for the Italian style...your idea as I recall. It makes me look like a spiv."

"Nonsense, Miles. You look as though you've joined the twenty first century. Her Maj will be suitably impressed."

"I doubt it."

"The new svelte you is here to stay. I'm introducing a biscuit ban from now on."

"Take me through that bowing business again. I'm bound to get it all wrong," said Miles, still examining his reflection.

"If you do mess up, you won't be hauled off to the Tower. Rule one: just a short bow from the neck will do, otherwise you'll look like a flunkey."

"What on earth am I going to say to her, Marian?"

"Rule two. Let her do the talking. She's had a few years' experience. By the way, the Palace has been on the phone. They're expecting you to do the guided tour of the exhibition. HM has asked for you especially. Apparently she's a great fan of the series."

Miles felt a stab of pain in his gut. "Are you sure she wants me?"

"Quite sure." Marian moved over to Miles and began brushing some dandruff flakes off his shoulders. She leant into his ear. "Who knows? There could be a CBE in this, or a knighthood maybe. You'd better practise getting down on one knee."

"I'd never be able to get up again."

"Rubbish. Arise, Sir Miles." Marian tapped Miles's shoulder with a ruler she had picked up from his desk. They broke into laughter.

'The Great Phoenician Odyssey,' the British Museum's about-to-open blockbuster, was to explore the influence and material evidence of these ubiquitous seafaring peoples who had preoccupied Miles for decades. In the months since returning from Venice, Miles had been entirely absorbed with the preparations for the exhibition, bouncing back and forth between excitement and apprehension. As the leading academic consultant, every display and artefact in the exhibition would bear the stamp of his scholarship. His elevation to a professorship was also deeply gratifying. Together with his glowingly-reviewed book on the subject, about to be republished in paperback, the show was destined to be the pinnacle of his revived career. In recognition of this, he had been persuaded by Marian that a high level of sartorial elegance was required for the official opening ceremony.

"Here, let's pull that jacket down a bit." As Marian made

the adjustment, Miles ingested her familiar fragrance, a tad too sweet for his taste.

"I'm very proud of you, Miles. We all are. You know that, don't you," she said with a broad smile.

✦

"I'm sorry sir, but I'll have to ask you to leave. You've had extra time already."

Miles was startled out of his reverie by the uniformed custodian who had appeared at his side. After the curatorial team had left that evening having put the final touches to the displays, Miles had spent two hours or more on his own rehearsing the guided tour of the exhibition he was to make with the monarch in tow. He was now standing before the glass case containing the diminutive statue of Astarte. He still could not quite believe she had been safely installed in Bloomsbury. This was to be the first time that this artefact had been allowed to leave Corsica. Once its false identity as a miracle-performing Christian icon had been unmasked, a chastened Church hierarchy had been forced to donate her to the island's museum of archaeology. Miles had spent many months persuading the authorities to release it. Her hollow, featureless eyes seemed to reach out to him, to thank him for rescuing her from oblivion and making her the star of this show. Miles could only stare back with intense devotion.

Miles made his way through the silent galleries to the staff entrance, escorted by the custodian. "Good night sir. I hope you get some sleep. Big day tomorrow, eh?"

As he emerged on to the deserted street, a lanky figure sprung forward to block his path.

"Gunther!" exclaimed Miles, as his student's features

emerged from the shadows. "Are you trying to give me a heart attack? What are you doing here? "

"I'm sorry to give you a shock Professor Mallalieu. I guessed I'd find you at the museum. We have to talk," said Gunther.

"I was hoping to get an early night," replied Miles. His student's normally smooth Teutonic features were stubbled, his eyes ringed with black. "Are you alright?" Miles asked.

"It's not about me. It's about Astarte," said Gunther solemnly.

"What about Astarte? I've just spent a very pleasant few minutes with her."

"I was in Corsica last week... on the new dig, as you know."

Miles had quite forgotten he had sent Gunther back to the island but did not let this show. Gunther now leant in closer to Miles to whisper in his ear even though the street was deserted. "On my last day there, I had a call from the new director of the laboratory we used in Ajaccio to date her. He contacted me at my hotel. His name is Dr Fontanay."

"Fontanay? Never heard of him," replied Miles. "What did he want?"

"He said it was extremely important we meet. I agreed to see him in a bar on my way to the airport. He wanted to buy me a drink but I told him I had no time..."

"Yes, yes, please get on with it," interjected Miles, his sense of alarm growing by the second.

"OK. This is what he told me..." Gunther paused to take a deep breath. "She is not Phoenician."

"Isn't Phoenician? What are you talking about?"

"He said he had just completed a review of his predecessor's test results and he had found fundamental errors in the dating methods used. He showed me the print-outs." Gunther paused. "Professor Mallalieu, it was very clear to me that our goddess is no way as old as we thought her to be."

"And just how old does this Fontanay maintain she is?" asked Miles, sensing a hysterical edge creeping into his voice.

"His review shows that this is a Roman copy, maybe 2nd century AD." Gunther's hangdog expression revealed his utter despondence.

"You cannot be serious!" retorted Miles.

"I can't believe I am having to tell you this, Professor Mallalieu, but we must face the facts. There is now no proof that the Phoenicians ever landed on the island. The whole theory of your book, the TV series and also now of the exhibition is invalid."

"And just supposing that he's wrong?"said Miles. He could sense the bile rising in his stomach.

Gunther paused and stared at the damp pavement. "I wish to God that was so but I have examined every possibility, every calculation ten times or more. Even a non-scientist can see clearly where the original errors were made."

"I want to speak to this Fontanay myself."

"That's no problem, Professor Mallalieu. He has proposed a meeting with you here in London, tonight."

"Tonight?" Miles checked his watch. "Why on earth can't I ring him?"

"He says it is too sensitive to speak about on the phone. Professor Mallalieu, I do not need to remind you your exhibition opens in less than twenty four hours. It's very important that you hear what this man has to tell you, how do you say in English, from the horse's mouth?"

"What I don't understand, Gunther, is why you waited until the eve of the opening to tell me this."

"Professor Mallalieu, I only got the call from Fontanay less than a day ago. I wanted to be quite sure of my facts before I contacted you."

Miles could feel his knees beginning to give way. He had no choice but to lean against the outer wall of the museum to steady himself.

"Let me help you." Gunther attempted to support Miles' elbow but his gesture was rejected. "Are you OK, Professor Mallalieu?"

"If you mean, am I about to have a heart attack, the answer is probably yes. How do I get hold of this man?"

"He's staying at the Hotel Russell, it's only five minutes away." Gunther pointed down the street. "He's expecting you to call him when you arrive at reception. His room number is 305."

"You'll come with me of course? You've met him. You can help me judge what he has to say."

Gunther shook his head. "He insists on meeting you alone Professor. I am so sorry that it has to be like this. It could not have happened at a more inconvenient time."

"That, Gunther, is something of an understatement," replied Miles, attempting to regain his balance as he separated himself from the wall.

"Before you go, Professor Mallalieu, I must mention something...it has been on my mind for some time."

"No more bombshells please Gunther. Are you trying to finish me off?"

"You may think this is unimportant, but to me..." Gunther cleared his throat. "I have not received an invitation to the opening tomorrow."

"Really? I'm sure I saw your name on the list," replied Miles distractedly.

"Maybe I'm being paranoid, Professor Mallalieu, but I am beginning to think you don't want me to be there."

"Don't be ridiculous, Gunther. Why on earth would I not?"

Gunther shifted awkwardly. "We both know that it was I who first made the discovery. It would maybe be difficult for you to accept this now, since you have taken all the attention."

"That's absolute nonsense and you know it," retorted Miles. "There must have been an oversight. But in view of the news you have just delivered, do you really want to witness my public humiliation? Now please, enough of this."

"I have made my point. You must go. And Professor Mallalieu..." Gunther called to Miles who had begun to walk away.

"Yes?"

"Please take care."

Miles gave a dismissive wave before setting off towards Russell Square with a deep sense of foreboding.

✦

"Professor Mallalieu, it is an honour to meet you." The French scientist strode across the lobby to greet Miles with the warmest of smiles. Miles, whose nerves had been further ruffled by being kept waiting, was confronted with a short, slender man with an aquiline nose and alert eyes. "It is very good of you to see me. I am aware that it is late," added Fontanay.

"Before we go any further, Doctor, may I clarify something?" asked Miles, appraising this harbinger of ill news.

"Of course, but please call me Charles."

"Do I take it that you've come to London expressly to see me?" he asked.

Fontanay smiled. "In a way, yes, in a way, no. I'm here to attend the opening of your exhibition at the kind invitation of the Director of the Museum. I am representing my academic colleagues in Corsica. Perhaps you did not see my name on the invitation list?"

"In view of what my young colleague has told me, your presence tomorrow would seem rather ironic, would it not?"

Fontanay appeared put out by this question. "I have not yet decided whether I will attend. That depends on our discussions tonight. Come, let us go to my room and I will explain in detail how the unfortunate mistakes were made."

✦

"You must forgive the chaos," said Fontanay, holding the door open for Miles and indicating a bed strewn with sheaves of papers. "Take a seat Professor, and I will guide you through the comparative data, the old and the new."

It was almost eleven thirty before Fontanay had completed his presentation, by which time Miles' brain had become clogged with detail. It was all too clear however from the re-analysis of the data that there was indeed an indisputable discrepancy of many hundreds of years.

The scientist crossed to a side table and poured a large whisky. He carried it over to Miles who accepted it without a word. "For the sake of scientific integrity, you understand I could not remain silent?" Fontanay said, pouring himself a drink and raising his glass. "Here's to the truth, however painful it may be. A votre santé."

Miles did not reciprocate. "And what, if I may ask, has happened to your predecessor? I presume he has lost his job," he replied, feeling the liquor take effect.

"I regret to tell you, Professor, that he died suddenly earlier this year, shortly after he retired. Heart attack." Fontanay moved across the room to perch on the edge of the bed close to the chair in which Miles was sitting. "So far your student and you are the only other people to know of these unfortunate new conclusions. That means we still have some choices." The Frenchman spoke quietly and in a measured tone.

"And what would those be?" asked Miles still flailing about in disbelief.

"We could arrange to lose these new findings?"

Miles stared at Fontanay. "What exactly are you suggesting?"

"You see, Professor, my lab is struggling to survive. Our budget has been cut in half. If we were to say two hundred and fifty thousand euro? It would not be for me personally you understand. This would allow us to continue our operation for another year. It could be in the form of an anonymous donation."

"What you are proposing is outright blackmail. I should inform the police," replied Miles, gripping the arms of his chair.

"That would not be very sensible, Professor. It would be very embarrassing for you if the media were informed of these results just as Her Majesty was about to arrive at the British Museum." Fontanay rose and began pacing the room. "I am not proud to have to make this demand. You must put the blame on our philistine politicians who have no understanding of science. They have taken us down to their level."

A sudden wave of anger overtook Miles, the intensity of which he had not felt since the incident with Bernie. He was on the point of lunging at Fontanay when he somehow found the strength to restrain himself. Instead, he rose without speaking and headed for the door.

"Of course, you will need time to think about it," Fontanay called out after him. "I will give you until ten o'clock tomorrow morning. If I don't hear from you, I shall have no choice but to go to the media and sell my story. There is nothing my countrymen like to read about more than an embarrassment for the British Establishment."

Emerging onto the steps leading from the hotel's entrance, Miles paused to take a deep gulp of the damp night air. Having buttoned up his coat against the chill, he skirted the perimeter of the square heading in the direction of his flat.

The light on the communal stairs was not working and he was forced to grope his way up to the third floor, using the glow from his mobile phone. The flat itself was also in darkness and, fumbling for the light switch inside the door, he narrowly avoided toppling the coat stand in the hall.

"Elspeth, wake up. I need to speak to you. Are you alone?" he called through her bedroom door.

"Of course I'm alone. What's the matter?"

"I thought Tristan might be..."

"Well you were wrong.. Wait a second, will you? You woke me from a deep sleep."

Elspeth finally emerged, bleary-eyed and fastening the belt of her chenille dressing gown.

"I've nobody else to turn to," said Miles, noticing that his hands were shaking.

"Well, what is it? You look terrible."

They moved to sit together on the Chesterfield and the saga poured out. From the moment when he was accosted by Gunther outside the museum, Miles spared no detail.

Elspeth sat quietly throughout, showing no signs of either disapproval or shock. Eventually she said: "So tomorrow's off then? I'll have you know I bought my dress especially. It cost me a small fortune and I gave Tristan £300 to buy himself a suit."

"Is that all you can think about?" demanded Miles. His sister's solipsistic response was infuriatingly predictable. "If Fontanay goes to the press, I might as well curl up and die."

"None of this defeatist talk. I won't have it!" cried Elspeth, bringing her fist down on the antimacassar. "Just because some foreign laboratory got the dating wrong doesn't mean your theories are rubbish."

"I'm afraid that's exactly what it does mean," he replied mournfully.

"Spare me your rescue dog look, Miles."

"Elspeth, this man means what he says." Miles let out a deep sigh. "There's nothing for it. Brondesbury will have to be sold to pay him off."

"How can you even consider such a thing? You've promised the house to Trist and me and that is that."

"What else do you suggest I do?"asked Miles, expelling a groan of despair. "I don't have that kind of money lying around."

"Call his bluff. Let this Frenchman stew in his own juice. He may not have the guts to carry out his threat. In any case giving in to him would be completely immoral."

"What's more immoral in your eyes?" demanded Miles. "Going back on my word to you about Brondesbury or covering up these new findings? I think I know the answer,"

"Oh do you now? How on earth do you manage to get yourself into these scrapes?"

They were interrupted by a ping from Miles' phone announcing the arrival of a text. Miles peered myopically at the screen. "It's him. He'll give me more time to come up with the total but he wants a down payment before eight in the morning. A mere ten thousand in ready money, which of course I haven't got." Miles scrolled further through the text.

"Apparently, he'll settle for a precious object in lieu of cash. Nothing bulky."

"How very gracious of him!" exclaimed Elspeth. "This just confirms my view that you academic lot are all out and out rogues."

"Elspeth, don't you see? It would at least silence him until after the opening. What happens after that God knows," said Miles, his eyes straying to the mantelpiece.

"Miles, don't even think about it," cried Elspeth who had followed his gaze. "I absolutely forbid it!"

Miles had moved to the mantel shelf with the intention of seizing the valuable Meissen figurine which his parents had left to his sister. Elspeth rose and made an attempt to restrain him. Taking a sideways step to avoid her, Miles succeeded in gaining a purchase on the slender object and clutched it to his chest, intending to seek sanctuary in his bedroom. Elspeth made a crab movement to block his escape route, her eyes narrowed in anger.

"That's not leaving this flat!" cried Elspeth, attempting to wrestle it away from Miles and a fierce tug-of-war began. Suddenly Miles felt the pressure slacken. He staggered backwards, almost losing his balance.

Miles stared at the decapitated figurine. Elspeth was left holding the head. "See what you've done!" cried Miles, aggressively.

Miles took a deep breath. "Have the lot, for what it's worth," he replied quietly, tossing the torso towards his sister. Heading for the hallway, Miles grabbed his overcoat and slammed the front door behind him.

Turning south, he wandered distractedly through the West End. No progress had been made: he still needed a plan. He knew only that Fontanay's deadline was drawing ever closer and that lack of sleep had robbed him of clarity of thought. Caffeine was now a necessity. Bar Italia was exactly as he remembered, its walls hung with faded black and white signed photographs of sporting heroes and celebrities who had frequented this timeless Soho institution. Miles found it heaving with the flotsam and jetsam of the London night clamouring for their cappuccinos and arguing over football. Having ordered a coffee, he found a seat at a small table towards the rear. The air of normality had a palliative effect on his anxiety. A sallow-faced younger man at the next table, dressed in a dinner jacket with bow tie askew, turned to him with an engaging smile. Miles' customary defensiveness melted.

"Busy in here. Lucky to get a seat, eh?" Miles nodded. "Haven't seen you in here before. So what's your line of work then?"

"I'm an historian," replied Miles, taken aback by his directness.

"Me croupier. Hate it. Hate the hours. But I totally love history. Can't get enough of it." The young man peered closely at Miles. "Haven't I seen you on telly?"

"Quite possibly."

"I know what it was!" the croupier exclaimed. "Those pirates who terrorised folk round the Med. You really got me hooked. Binge-watched the whole series."

"They weren't strictly pirates, they were more like traders," replied Miles.

"Well you're the expert..." The young man laughed. "You know what I really love...?"

Miles shook his head, warming to their exchange.

"...the way you're lost in your subject, like you're on another planet. It must be so great doing something you're passionate about, and getting paid megabucks for it. You don't know how lucky you are."

Miles toyed with the froth on his coffee. He wished he felt lucky. The croupier's tired eyes were alight now. "Finding the statue of that goddess by chance must have blown your mind," he added. He grinned at Miles. "By the way, my big sister's got a thing for you."

"Really?" Miles felt his cheeks redden.

The croupier winked. "She thinks you're cuddly. That's a compliment by the way." He drained his coffee and stood up. "Got to go. Break over. Great talking to you Professor. Can't wait for the next series." He leant over to shake Miles' hand vigorously.

With sleep now an impossibility, a strange compulsion propelled Miles in the direction of Buckingham Palace. He had reached the foot of the Duke of York steps when a troop of mounted artillerymen thundered past him in tight formation along the otherwise deserted Mall. The metallic clatter of hooves reverberated around his skull. He placed his hands over his ears to block out the sound. As the troop cantered past, one of the steeds emitted a stream of ordure which lay steaming close to his feet. Symbolism or what? he reflected.

Miles moved quickly on, his gaze drawn magnetically to the Royal Standard fluttering above the Palace. He peered down at his watch. In a matter of hours he was due to stand before what was to have been the star exhibit, with the monarch in tow. The prospect caused him to shudder. A reviving gust of air brushed his face. He turned into the wind. Almost at once he felt his exhaustion lift and a new resolve emerge. It was now all perfectly clear. How could he consider letting down the croupier and the thousands more like him who had put their faith in his scholarship?

✦

It took several buzzes before he heard Marian's startled voice over the intercom. "Who is it?"

"It's me."

"Miles? You're keeping very odd hours these days. What the heck are you doing out this early?"

She opened the door of her flat in a kimono-styled dressing gown, flicking aside unruly strands of her normally coiffured hair. She stared anxiously at him. "You look terrible... like you've been pounding the pavements all night."

"I have," he replied, virtually falling through the door. "I need to sit down." He indicated the armchair visible through the doorway leading to the sitting room.

"Didn't I tell you to get a good night's sleep?" said Marian ushering him in. "How on earth are you going to get through today?"

"With great difficulty," replied Miles, flopping down in the chair.

"We need you to be on peak form. You'd better have some coffee."

"Never mind that, Marian, we haven't got long. Come and sit down. Hear me out..."

After he had recounted the events of the night including the spat with Elspeth, Marian took a deep breath before replying. "I want you to listen to me very carefully Miles," she said, adopting a chillingly solemn tone. "Appalling as it may seem, you've no choice but to pay this man off."

For a moment, Miles was unable to believe what he had heard. "What do you mean 'no choice?'" he finally replied. "You of all people, Marian. If I go to the media first and tell the truth then at least I'll hang on to some shreds of what passes for integrity."

"Integrity my....You have to get real, Miles. Once they get their hands on this, you'll be crucified, however much you protest your innocence."

"I am getting real, as you put it. If I get in there first then I've more chance of a fair hearing. I'll give one interview and that's it. I'll be relying on you to fend off the hoards of calls."

"You'll do no such thing." Marian stooped down to unplug the landline phone on a side table. Having done so, she approached Miles.

"Now give me your mobile!" she demanded, extending her spare hand.

"I thought I could trust you, Marian, as my friend!" exclaimed Miles.

"As your friend, I'm telling you that you'll be hung out to dry...the job, the book deal, the TV sequel, snatched away just like that," said Marian with an emphatic flick of the hand.

"Then that would be the price I'd pay for being able to live with myself. Do you really expect me to maintain this lie?"

"Don't you see, it's not only Number One you should be thinking about? What about the Department? Me? You'll take us all down with you, Miles. How does that make you feel?"

"For God's sake, Marian, stop being so over-dramatic."

"You know as well as I do the scandal would be exactly what they've been waiting for."

"Who's they?"

"The bean counters the Vice-Chancellor's brought in, of course. They'll seize on this fiasco as an excuse to close us down. They've been wanting to do it for years. For Christ's sake Miles, you can't be that naive?"

"Call me naive, but I rather thought I had brought the University some favourable publicity," Miles replied.

"Don't kid yourself. Your high profile's given us a couple of year's grace, no more. All those academic also-rans are dead jealous of your TV exposure. They'll be rubbing their hands at the thought of your being found out."

"I have not been 'found out,' as you put it," replied Miles indignantly. "We've been badly let down by the science and now I've got to face the consequences. I expected you of all people, Marian, to tell me to do the right thing."

"Miles, for once in your precious bubble-like life, think of others for a change."

"So that it? I'm damned if I do and damned if I don't," said Miles, burying his head in his hands. "Elspeth took the exact opposite approach, whatever her reasons may be."

"Well, I'm not your sister, I can be more objective. People always say I'm married to the Department. Well, here's my chance to show what a loyal spouse I am." Without a further word, Marian swept out of the room. She returned immediately with a small casket which she placed on the coffee table in front of Miles.

"Open it."

"What is it?"

"Just do what I say."

Inside lay a diamond studded bracelet of considerable beauty. The early morning light caught the highly polished surfaces, dazzling Miles with their brilliance. Marian handed him a sheet of headed paper.

"See there. Valued at nearly fifteen grand." She picked up the bracelet and dangled it before him before replacing it in the box. "It was my grandmother's. I never wear it. Don't go anywhere posh enough. Go on, give it to this Frenchman. It'll show him you're prepared to do his dirty business," she added, attempting to thrust the box into his hand.

"You can keep your precious jewels." Pushing it away, Miles rose and headed for the door. He was just stepping onto the street when he heard Marian's voice. He looked up to see her at her first floor window. She was dangling the bracelet as if about to drop it at his feet.

"Take it! Don't be a fool!" she shouted. But Miles kept on going.

✦

Miles was distracted by a persistent throbbing in his pocket. Somehow his mobile had been switched to 'vibrate.' He paused to scrutinise the smeared screen. There were six missed calls from Gunther. He had failed to give him a report of the meeting but his student would find out sooner rather than later that his mentor had taken the honourable course of action.

Miles turned into the forecourt of Broadcasting House with a newly honed decisiveness. As he approached the main entrance, he was overcome with dizziness and was forced to clutch onto a bollard until the sensation eased. He had not slept, he realised, for thirty or more hours. A security man was scrutinising him with obvious suspicion. Miles made a token attempt to smooth his ruffled hair and straighten his collar before plunging into the revolving doors.

"Can I help you, sir? Do you have an appointment?"asked the receptionist who took a moment or two to recognise him.

"I'd like to speak to my nephew. His name is Jeremy Folgate. As far as I recall, he's in the News department.

"I'm sorry Professor but they're all in the early morning editorial meeting."

"You'll have to interrupt him. You can tell him that I have a story for him that will be of considerable interest," replied Miles.

"Perhaps you could tell me a little more of what it's about?" asked the receptionist.

"Perhaps you would prefer it if I took it to your competitors?" said Miles.

"Folgate, you say? Wait a minute please while I try and locate him....Bear with me...Is that Jeremy? I have your...uncle here in reception. He says he has a story for you."

Placing her hand over the mouthpiece, she glanced up at Miles. "He asks, can it wait an hour? He has a heavy deadline for the lunchtime news."

"Here, let me speak to him," replied Miles, leaning over the desk to grasp the receiver. Having hesitated, the receptionist allowed it to slip from her grasp to avoid an unseemly tug-of-war.

"Yes, yes, yes, it's me.... Let's dispense with the pleasantries...get down here this minute and bring a notebook. I'd rather you hear this sorry story from me before someone else tries to peddle it to you."

✦

Miles opened his eyes slowly to be faced with his nephew's lugubrious features. "Where am I?" he demanded.

"UCH. You had a collapse...just as we had finished interviewing you. They thought you might have had a heart attack. False alarm you'll be pleased to hear but they've kept you in for observation." Jeremy produced a bag of grapes and offered them to Miles who waved them away.

"I can't remember a thing."

"That's because you're concussed. We got it all in the can though. It went out on the midday news. Now there's a Twitter storm. It's gone viral on Facebook too." Jeremy fished out his phone and dangled it in front of Miles' face. "Look at this one: 'TV Prof confesses star exhibit is a fake hours before Queen due to open blockbuster exhibition.'"

Miles sat bolt upright and pushed the phone aside. "It's not a fake! It's simply not Phoenician. How dare they distort the facts!"

"That's social media for you. I owe you one by the way...got loads of Brownie points," said Jeremy, clearly unable to prevent himself from beaming with satisfaction.

"And the Palace?" asked Miles.

"Don't worry, they won't put you in the Tower," chortled Jeremy. "They reacted pretty smartish...issued a statement saying the Queen was suddenly indisposed. The opening was called off at the last moment. The BM Director's gone ape shit and there was even a question asked in the House about public subsidy for incompetent museums."

"And the Frenchman?"

"He's obviously gone to ground. Ducking interviews. Can't stay long but look who's here." Elspeth's angular face loomed into view, replacing Jeremy's in Miles' blurred field of vision.

"I'm proud of you Miles. You did the right thing. I've forgiven you about the Meissen. Never liked it much anyway." She stroked her brother's forehead. "Does that hurt? Apparently you hit your head on a Dalek on display in the foyer. The BBC are probably worried you're going to sue them."

Elspeth now leant over and whispered into Miles' ear, close enough for him to catch the inevitable whiff of Fisherman's Friend. "Don't get me wrong. It was good of you to think of Jeremy, Miles, but why on earth didn't you give the story to Tristan? You know perfectly well he's trying to resurrect his journalistic career. It would have been his big breakthrough. He's very miffed."

Miles stared at Elspeth in disbelief. "Is that all you can think about?"

No doubt sensing a sibling row brewing, Jeremy stuffed the bag of grapes back in his pocket and leapt to his feet. "Sorry. Gotta go. Look after yourself. Thanks again for the scoop." He gave Miles a sheepish look before loping off down the ward.

Miles turned to his sister. "Never mind Tristan, whatever's going to become of me? I'm finished."

"Plenty of time for navel gazing. You need to get your strength back. I'm sorry I didn't bring you anything by the way."

They were interrupted by the appearance of the ward sister who, having ensured that Miles swallowed a cupful of pills, hovered with intent by the bedside. "Are you his next of kin?" Elspeth nodded. "Well he needs to get some rest. He'll have more tests tomorrow. We'll ring you when the doctor has discharged him."

Elspeth seemed more than willing to take this cue to retreat. "Get some sleep. I'll come and fetch you home," she said, puckering her lips and aiming them at his forehead. Alerted to her intentions, Miles rolled over just in time to avoid contact. "Better go, I'm no good with hospitals. They make me queasy," she added, backing away from the bed with an over-cheery wave. Miles closed his eyes and was soon drifting gratefully into a sedative-induced fug.

✦

"What are you doing here?" Miles asked, startled out of his doze by the thump of what transpired to be a large bouquet being deposited on the bed.

"You'll need a big vase. You should be in a private room.

Not among..." Vera indicated the serried ranks of the sick. "Poor, poor Miles. I came to find out how you are...."

"We're not allowed flowers. Didn't they tell you? Apparently they suck the oxygen out of the air." Miles nudged aside the bouquet which slid on to the floor.

"You don't seem very pleased to see me, Miles," replied Vera, bending down to retrieve it.

"You startled me, that's all. I thought visiting hours were over."

"I told them I was a relative who had come all the way from Russia," replied Vera perching on the bed. She smiled.

"How on earth did you find out where I was?" asked Miles, shifting awkwardly in the bed.

"I called Elspeth. She told me everything. I saw the News... Poor, poor you...I wanted to come and say I'm so sorry about Astarte. The whole thing is a nightmare."

"You're not as sorry as I am," said Miles expelling a deep sigh. Vera placed her palm on Miles' forehead. "Enough. We can talk about that another time. You're very hot. Maybe you have a fever. What do the doctors say?"

"They say I'll live. Not that there's much to live for. I'm about to become a non-person, Vera, My career's over. I won't be worth knowing."

"What do I care about any of that? Why do you never call me?"

It was true that since the Venice encounter, Miles had toyed with ringing Vera on several occasions but had some-how stopped himself. After all, had he not been hurt enough?

"We had such a lovely time in Venice. Such a coincidence," added Vera, pausing to check for a reaction. "Well, didn't we?" Avoiding her gaze, Miles felt his cheeks reddening. "You don't need to be embarrassed," added Vera with an impish grin. "It was fun. We both know that."

Miles' short term memory might have been wiped clean by his recent collapse, but his recall of the second Venetian encounter Vera alluded to remained pin sharp. He had been about to find a back route out of the hotel to avoid seeing her when Vera spotted him emerging from the stairwell. Reluctant to make a scene in front of the receptionist, Miles had been persuaded to join her on a stroll down to the Zattere 'for a quick aperitif'. The sunset promised to be spectacular and Miles had found himself at a smart alfresco restaurant where, to his surprise, the maitre d' appeared to have been expecting them. They were ushered towards the best table overlooking the water, now shot through with streaks of crimson and gold. Bathed in the silky, fading light, Vera had appeared at her most beguiling. Miles had been unable to maintain his sangfroid beyond the antipasti.

After devouring an elaborate seafood feast washed down with the best Borgo Del Tiglio, they had tottered back to the hotel. Echoing their first encounter in Chicago, she was adamant that she should see Miles safely to his room. After much fiddling with an intransigent lock, they had virtually fallen into the room and collapsed together in a mirthful heap on the bed. Miles had awoken before dawn to find a scribbled note informing him that she had returned to the yacht as Bernie was expected within hours. Miles, meanwhile, had been left in a more confused and conflicted state than ever.

He was distracted by Vera gently dabbing his forehead with a tissue. "What were you thinking about?"

"Nothing much."

Vera now edged closer to him on the narrow hospital bed and whispered in his ear. "I have some big news. Maybe it will cheer you up and help you to recover."

"What sort of news?"

"I'm pregnant."

"You're what?" he exclaimed loudly enough to attract a stare from a neighbouring sick bed.

"You heard me. I am expecting a child. I know I'm technically old to be a mother but...."

Miles swallowed hard. "I see...I'm pleased for you, Vera. Bernie clearly hasn't wasted time extending his dynasty."

"Bernie had nothing to do with it."

The hairs on the backs of Miles's hands began to tingle. "What are you saying?"

"That the expected date, due date or whatever you call it, doesn't work out. The baby was made...how do you say?... conceived before Bernie flew back from his trip to the Far East. That can only mean one thing, Miles."

"Are you trying to finish me off?" Miles asked, his heart rate accelerating.

"I thought it would make you happy. Becoming a dad, I mean." Vera appeared crestfallen.

"How can you be so sure?" Miles demanded.

"Take a paternity test by all means but I know it's yours, Miles. I must have forgotten to take my pill that day."

"Is it money you want...for an abortion, I mean?" demanded Miles angrily. "Did you do it on purpose?"

Vera stiffened. "Why do you always think the worst of me? Of course not. There is no question of an abortion. It would be against all my principles."

"But...but... what have you told Bernie?" stammered Miles.

"Bernie thinks it's his. He's crazy about the idea of becoming a father again, particularly as his own kids won't speak to him after the divorce. He's already calling the child 'my little

Russian bastard'."

"I suppose that's his idea of humour," said Miles.

"You don't know Bernie as well as I do, Miles. If I tell him he's not the father, he's quite capable of having me...well, eliminated. He is insanely jealous. He'd make it look like an accident of course."

"Does this mean you've dropped any notion of leaving him?"

Vera's eyes came alive. "Miles, what are you saying here?" She took Miles' hand and guided it on to her belly. Miles pulled it away sharply.

"Be realistic, Vera. What could I offer this child or any child for that matter? A disgraced, middle-aged academic with no prospects."

Vera sighed and shifted away from Miles. "Ok. Have it your own way." Vera hugged herself defensively. "It looks like I have no choice. Bernie's even started talking about names. If it's a boy, I've told him my favourite is Selim."

"Rather archaic, isn't it? Naming him after an Ottoman sultan."

Vera nodded. "Exactly. I told Bernie that he was a distant ancestor of mine and he believed me. He quite likes the name. He hasn't got it. S..e..l..i..m?" Miles' mind was still fuzzy. "Come on," added Vera. "You're being slow. What is Selim backwards?"

"Good God! What kind of sick joke is that?" Miles demanded. "If Bernie has even the slightest suspicion that the child might be mine, he's quite likely to have me disembowelled."

Vera placed her fingers on Miles' lips. "You don't need to worry. This will be our little secret."

"Why did you tell me? You could have so easily kept me in the dark."

Vera shrugged. "I don't know....I just knew it would not have been right not to...tell you, I mean. You are the biological parent after all."

"Strange at it may seem to you, I had not planned on becoming a father, particularly at my age."

Vera smiled. "OK. Now you will have the satisfaction of becoming a parent without any of the responsibility. The perfect arrangement for you, yes?"

"I think I'm going to pass out. Hand me that water."

"Calm down, Miles. You are in shock. But whatever happens, it, he, she... is yours. This is something that can never be taken away from us."

"I'd like you to go now," said Miles.

Rising calmly from the bedside, Vera picked up the bouquet. "Well then it's goodbye, Miles. At least wish me luck." She bent over to kiss him on the forehead before withdrawing.

CHAPTER TEN

Miles apart

"Tray's outside. Eat before it gets cold." Elspeth's voice bored through the bedroom door. Miles could anticipate word for word what would come next: "You can't stay in your room all day every day. It's been goodness knows how many weeks now. It's just not healthy. Do you hear me?"

Miles expelled a non-committal grunt from the safety of his cocoon. He was in no hurry to retrieve his supper of what was likely to be an over-boiled egg with curled-up soldiers. If Elspeth was feeling generous, there might be browned apple quarters and a Kit Kat bar.

"Tristan's coming round later. He wants to know if you'd like to play Gin Rummy."

"How many times do I have to tell you? I hate card games."

"You're behaving like some stroppy adolescent. It's time you snapped out of it. Open up now. I can't keep yelling through a door!" Miles kept watch as the handle was rattled but the flimsy lock held firm.

"Just leave me alone, Elspeth...please." Miles could hear heavy sniffing, which he guessed to be the prelude to a full-blown sob.

"Please, Miles. Just because it all went wrong with ....you can't hide away forever."

"How many times do I have to tell you Elspeth? I don't need a nurse maid."

"If I wasn't here, you'd die of starvation."

The intercom buzzer sounded. "I don't feel like seeing anybody. If it's for me, tell them to go away."

"Nonsense. You need some company," Elspeth retorted.

His wishes were ignored. A murmured conversation was followed by a tentative knock at his bedroom door.

"It's me, Marian."

"I thought you weren't speaking to me. What are you doing here?"

"I need to see you, Miles."

"I'm not decent."

"I can cope. Aren't you going to let me in?"

During his hermit-like existence, Miles had missed Marian's reassuring presence more than he cared to admit. He adjusted his pyjamas bottoms and edged open the door.

"God, you look terrible. When did you last shave? Where shall I put this?" asked Marian holding out the supper tray.

"Anywhere. I'm not hungry. I'm afraid you must take me as you find me," he indicated the near impenetrable clutter.

"You need to get some air into here," said Marian, wrinkling up her nose. Crossing to the window, she prised it open before turning to examine Miles more closely. "You've certainly lost a lot of weight."

"Well that's something positive at least. You were always nagging me about my diet. Let's dispense with the niceties, Marian. What brings you here? I thought you were still angry with me for sacrificing the Department's future for my dubious principles as you put it so eloquently."

"I realise now you did the right thing, going public about the dodgy statue I mean. I came to say I'm sorry and to find out how you are. There's no crime in that, is there?" Marian glanced around at the chaos. "This is no way to live, Miles."

"You mean in my cave? It has its plus points, believe me."

"May I?" Marian pointed to the only chair which was piled high with papers. Miles nodded. Marian picked up a bundle and placed it on the floor. Miles remained standing with arms folded as if guarding his territory.

"Can't you see you're beating yourself up unnecessarily? The whole thing has been a vast over reaction on your part."

"How can you call thirty years of painstaking research down the drain, an over-reaction?" Miles hunted around and fishing a letter from a nearby heap, waved it in Marian's direction. "I'll save you the bother of reading it. The second edition of the book's been cancelled and the remaining copies of the first have been pulped. You can't possibly know what that feels like."

"Maybe I can, maybe I can't. I'm just a simple soul. I think you appreciate that in me."

"So why have you come, Marian? Let me guess. You've come to tell me I'm officially history?"

"Sit," replied Marian. "You're making me nervous." Miles complied by perching awkwardly on a corner of the bed. It was clear that Marian was on the verge of tears.

"There's a letter from the VC on the way. I'm so sorry Miles but there was just too much reputational damage to keep you in post. That's their excuse anyway."

Miles brought his fist down hard on the bed. "Reputational damage! It's a department of Ancient History for God's sake, you make it sound like a multinational oil company."

"Education is a business these days and we all have to get used to it." Marian gazed sympathetically at Miles.

"It was those stories on social media, they were the final straw."

"What stories?"

"You know perfectly well what I'm talking about...those allegations that you tried to cover up the mistakes in dating the statue and only came clean when you had no choice."

"That's a complete lie, Marian and you know it," fumed Miles.

"I know, but that kind of fake news has a habit of sticking these days. Besides, you didn't really expect them to allow you to stay on gardening leave forever?"

"In case you hadn't noticed, I don't have a garden."

Marian rose from the chair and sat next to Miles, her expression one of deep concern. She appeared to be on the point of taking his hand but pulled back. "Listen to me, Miles. They may have forced you to stand down as Director but you're still a member of the Department. They can't take that away from you."

"I can't face going near the place. It's doomed and I have to accept my part in its downfall."

"It was...doomed, that is." Marian paused.

"How do you mean?"

"They were about to announce they were axing us when...

"When what?"

"In he rode, on his white charger...or should I say helicopter?"

"Who for goodness sake?"

"Bernie Prince. He's finally coughed up a tidy sixteen million. Changed his mind. That's a lot more than we were hoping for when you were schmoozing him on the yacht."

"I was not 'schmoozing' him, Marian. I was grovelling under duress."

"Anyway, the Vice-Chancellor sat next to him at some do or other on Monday night. Apparently they got on like a house on fire and the next thing Bernie was pulling out his chequebook. There was a meeting to announce it today. We're all in shock."

"How could they? Take his money. The man's an out-and-out crook." Miles extracted a pill from a box on his cluttered bedside table. He gulped it down, hands visibly shaking. He lay back on his pillow staring at the ceiling. "I refuse to believe it."

"None of us saw it coming. Particularly after what you did to him, the assault I mean. All we can say is that it's better than closure," replied Marian. "Please don't get too worked up. We don't want you to have another episode."

"Knowing Bernie, he'll want something in return."

Marian hesitated. "There is one major condition..."

"Don't tell me? His name on every sheet of loo paper? I promised him that already."

Marian averted her eyes to the floor. "Vera Petrovna as Director. Your Vera. The University Council rubber stamped it right away. Needless to say none of us were consulted."

A sharp pain seared through Miles' chest. Sensing his obvious distress, Marian rose to her feet and hovered anxiously.

"Vera? But... but she's had no experience of running anything," Miles stuttered.

"Neither had you. She's been foisted on us and we can do nothing about it. They've even got the Home Secretary to waive the normal visa requirements."

Miles surprised himself by breaking into a smile. "Actually, the more I think about, there's something utterly predictable about this, a sort of natural symmetry. I'd have given anything to have been a fly on the wall when Gavin and his Trotskyite cabal found out that capitalism had saved their bacon."

Marian remained stony-faced. "If you can be serious for a moment, Miles. I'm thinking of handing in my notice. I couldn't work with her. Something tells me she'll be a nightmare. But then you probably know more about that."

He rose from the bed and walked towards the window as if to catch the crack of air. "I'm not sure you should do anything in a hurry, Marian. She may not be free to take up the post for a while."

"What do you mean?"

"Just take my word for it." Miles approached Marian. "Anyway, what will you do after...?"

Marian shrugged and smiled weakly. "Maybe become your carer? The way things are going, it looks like you need one. Must go now, but before I do, Elspeth asked me to mention something."

"What's Elspeth been saying?"

"She wants to make the move to Brondesbury you promised her, but she feels she can't leave you in this state. She's torn in two, Miles. I said I'd be willing to give her a break." Marian hesitated. "Why not come and stay for a while? I'm between lodgers. It's not a bad room, nice and sunny and space for a few books."

"No point. I can't read anymore. I can't concentrate. It's those bloody pills, I'm sure of it. Mind you, without them I might have topped myself by now.

"Don't say that Miles, please."

"I thank you for your offer Marian but I'm quite snug here. Now if you'll forgive me, I need to get back to bed."

Marian looked at her watch. "It's not even tea time!"

Miles gave a watery look before crossing to the bed and

climbing in. As Marian closed the door behind her, he lay staring at the cobwebs which glistened in the few streaks of early evening sun that penetrated his lair.

Miles tried to calm himself by reflecting on the fact that Vera had had no hand in his downfall but had merely capitalised on it. After all, she was an ambitious woman whose talents had clearly not been fully recognised. Could she be blamed for seizing this opportunity?

This placatory thought was quickly dismissed. Had Vera for a moment considered how he would feel on hearing at second hand of her takeover? Could she really be that insensitive? And what about the child, how would she cope?

As the day drew to a close, he dialled Vera's number on the hour every hour. On each occasion he left an identical message in a carefully neutral tone of voice. Ten o'clock arrived and still she had still not responded. After that, he gave up and fell into a fitful sleep.

✦

"You're up early," said Elspeth, staring at Miles incredulously as he prepared to leave the flat for the first time in what seemed like weeks. "Don't tell me you've decided to rejoin the world. Wonders will never cease."

"You might want to see this, but then again you might not," said Elspeth, attempting to hand Miles a page from what he took to be a celebrity photo magazine. "I've been meaning to give it to you. I tore it out in the dentist's waiting room when no one was looking."

Miles brushed it aside. "Why on earth do you think I would be interested in that kind of tittle tattle?"

"Because it involves a friend of yours, or should I say former friend?"

Miles took the page from Elspeth and glanced at it. A bullet headed middle-aged man and his female companion were beaming out below a headline reading: 'Billionaire Bernie to become dad for fourth time.'

"Thought you'd be interested!" said Elspeth.

Miles thrust the page back into Elspeth's hands. She screwed it into a ball and took aim at the wastepaper basket but overshot her target.

Once Elspeth had left the room, Miles retrieved the page and tucked it in his pocket.

✦

"I'm not allowed to speak to the press," the concierge growled. The friendly young Russian who had been on duty during his first visit to the Brook Street apartments in search of Claudia had been replaced by an older man of sterner ilk.

"Do I look like a journalist?" replied Miles.

The concierge shrugged. "They come in all shapes and sizes. Mr Prince has given strict instructions that he is not to be disturbed by callers of any kind."

"As it happens, it's not Mr Prince I wish to see, it's Dr Petrovna," said Miles, holding in his irritation. "Please tell her that there is an old friend to see her in the lobby."

The concierge rose and crossed round to the front of his desk. "I must ask you to leave." There was an implied menace in the concierge's body language which persuaded Miles to make a strategic withdrawal. He had at least established that the Prince entourage was in residence. He would just have to bide his time.

Propping himself up against a railing on the opposite side of the street, he prepared for a long wait. What would he do if Vera were to emerge with Bernie? It was best not to give it too much thought. He pulled the collar of his overcoat up round his neck to fend off the chill.

The wait was mercifully short. Within a quarter of an hour, an empty limousine drew up outside the building. The personalised number plate, BP 1, confirmed the ownership. Miles was on the point of crossing the street when Vera slipped out of the entrance. Much to his relief, she was without an escort. As the Prince chauffeur snapped to attention by the rear car door, Miles negotiated a passage through the traffic in time to place himself between Vera and her driver.

"Miles! What are doing here? I'm late for a meeting. Please let me pass." It was clear that the chauffeur doubled as security guard and was about to intervene. "It's OK Georg, he's a friend," added Vera, indicating that they should be left to talk in private. Having returned obediently to the driving seat, Miles noticed that Georg kept glancing at them in the rear view mirror.

Caught in an awkward silence, Miles and Vera stood facing each other.

"Why don't you answer my calls?"

"I am sorry Miles. There's so much going on," Vera replied.

"That's something of an understatement. Well....is it true?"

"Is what true?"

"You know perfectly well what...."

"If you're talking about what I think you are, the answer is yes."

"I see," is all Miles could find to reply. His pent-up anger had given way to a feeling of numbness.

"Why not me as Director?" said Vera, folding her arms

tightly. "I'm not exactly unqualified, you know. I had meant to tell you myself before you found out. But Miles, if it wasn't me, it would be someone else you wouldn't approve of for sure. Anyway, it wasn't my idea. It was Bernie's and I could hardly refuse."

"You, you ...planned this all along, didn't you? Using Bernie's ill-gotten gains to push your way to the top," Miles spluttered.

"That's crazy. How can you say that? It wasn't easy to persuade him to rescue your precious Department after that little incident on the yacht."

"He deserved worse. I let him off lightly," said Miles, still seething.

"Listen to me. You know something? I did this to help you. Sure you're not the boss any more but you can have all the time you need now to carry on your researches. Have you thought of that?" She touched him lightly on the arm. "You have so much more to contribute, Miles."

"I'd rather sweep the streets than take your boyfriend's dirty money, and the way things are going, it may come to that," replied Miles.

"Well, that's your decision. Whatever you think I've taken away from your career, just remember I will be giving you a very special gift that only you and I know about." She took Miles' hand and for the second time, placed it gently on her belly. "Did you feel it move? Now I have to go," she added, kissing him lightly on the cheek before opening the rear door and climbing in.

Miles peered into the limousine as it purred past him but Vera was only a dim shadow behind the darkened glass.

✦

"Is that Mr Mallalieu?"

"It's Professor Mallaliieu. Who is this?"

"It's Kate from the Marylebone Clinic. Can you come in later this afternoon for your results? We like to give them out in person."

✦

Miles emerged from the discreet side entrance tucked down a mews off Wimpole Street. It had taken him many weeks to make the decision to submit his DNA. Tucking the test results safely away, he set out in the direction of his flat.

"Well Miles, wonders will never cease."

As he entered the flat Miles was confronted by the shambolic figure of Tristan about to put on his greasy raincoat.

"What on earth are you talking about?" asked Miles.

"Well A, you've left your lair for the first time in weeks and B, you're looking oddly cheerful," replied Tristan. "This needs further investigation. We need to absent ourselves rather speedily. Elspeth's got the spiritualist lot round. I haven't got the heart to tell her I think it's a load of old tosh."

Before Miles could take off his coat Tristan had steered him through the front door. "We've got something to celebrate, your re-entry to the world, casting off your sackcloth and ashes. You've been such a miserable bugger recently."

"Chin chin," announced Tristan, returning to their perch in the saloon bar with two large glasses of red. "Let's face it Miles," he continued. "You've had every reason to be depressed: lost your dream job, lifetime's research been rubbished, your book pulped, and you're still unattached. Elspeth's been driving me mad. Worried you're going to top yourself. She'll be mighty relieved to see you emerge from your hermit's cave." He leant in towards Miles. "Earth calling Miles. Did you hear what I said?" Miles nodded. He was content to let Tristan prattle on in his usual acerbic way. He could use the time to gather his thoughts. The test result was burning a hole in his pocket but he determined to say nothing, knowing it would be most unwise to broadcast the news, particularly to Tristan of all people.

"Bet you were gobsmacked when we two got together, eh? You were far too tactful to say so though. To be honest, it wasn't in my game plan. Can't blame you for suspecting my motives. Do you know it was thirty years ago we first fancied each other? Before she met that dumb arse stockbroker who banged her up. Could call it unrequited love, or lust. Your sis was a handsome woman Miles, still is in a horsey sort of way. Have you noticed how perky she is nowadays?"

"That's not a word I would associate with Elspeth."

"Well, she's still got the spark in her. Know what I mean? Let's just say I've been pleasantly surprised in that department."

"You're trying to shock me Tristan but you're not going to succeed," said Miles, fighting back his irritation. "If you do the dirty on Elspeth, you'll have me to contend with."

"Ah, majestic Miles defending the females of his tribe. I'd better watch it, that violent streak may emerge again. You can be quite scary, do you know that?"

"You'd better not provoke me then," replied Miles with a sardonic smile.

"My intentions towards your sister are strictly honourable," replied Tristan. "Besides you promised us Brondesbury. You haven't gone back on your word, have you?"

"Why would I do that?" recalling Marian's advice to continue to rent the house out to the Japanese bankers for large sums of money.

"You've been very good to your old chum, don't get me wrong. I blew it, I know. Turned the place into a pigsty. I'm a waste of space. Rather think Elspeth's taken me on out of pity. It's good of you not to stand in her way."

"It's her life."

"I know what you're thinking, she made a lousy choice with Ian and now she's made another one."

"I didn't say that. Anyway, how do you know what I'm thinking?"

"Touché. Let's face it, you're completely unfathomable, Miles, always have been."

As Tristan leant in closer to eyeball him, Miles recoiled from his bloodshot pupils and liverish pallor.

"What I want to know is who the fuck are you?" demanded Tristan. "Are you just some kind of alien existing in a parallel universe? A zombie even? Is there blood flowing in those flabby veins? All that library dust clogging up your arteries? And what about the primitive urges that afflict us mere mortals? Don't you ever pass a woman in the street and feel something stir? Take your Russian piece. Never understood why you let her get away. Super bright, a real looker, young, well a lot younger than you. Christ knows what she saw in you. Let's face it, you're not exactly a prime physical specimen... Maybe it was that that finally blew it? Your Vera couldn't find any sign of life between the flab. Bernie what's his name clearly had no such problems." Tristan was leaning in close enough now for Miles to smell his winey breath. "Do you know what your problem is Miles? Has been all your life. It's commitment with a capital bloody C."

"Have you quite finished? In case you've conveniently forgotten, it was Vera who left me," replied Miles curtly. "And I don't appreciate the pot calling the kettle black. I don't have to listen to this." He stood up and made as to leave.

"Stay. What about the ever-faithful divorcee, Marian? All those cosy little tête-a-têtes after work. Does she invite you in for a liqueur after you gallantly escort her to her door? Now you're out of the big job, there'll be no mixing of business with pleasure."

"Marian and I are just friends and you know it."

"Balls. She's always had the hots for you. She knows far too much about your habits but that doesn't seem to have put her off. She's dying to become your nursemaid, Miles. Spank you when you're naughty. Your round. Mine's the Merlot. Drink up then," said Tristan draining the last dregs of his glass.

Riled now beyond breaking point, Miles could feel his chest about to burst open. The words came tumbling out unchecked: "What if I told you I'm going to be a father?"

"You?" Tristan erupted into laughter. "Immaculate conception, was it?"

"Just got the result of the test an hour ago. You caught me on my way back."

"What test?"

"DNA match. These days they can do it before the child is born. It's all very easy."

Tristan looked as if he was about to choke. "Christ Miles... you're kidding me? You haven't paid a surrogate, have you?"

"What do you mean?" replied Miles blankly.

"Forget it, clearly not. So you and Marian got carried away behind the filing cabinets."

"That's an utterly offensive suggestion." Miles was by now deeply regretting loosening his tongue. "I really must go." He began to rise from his chair.

"Sit. I've got it! Your fickle little Russian minx. You sly beast. So there's lead in your pencil after all?"

Miles felt his face flush. He stared down into his glass and avoided catching Tristan's eye.

"Are you sure she's not lying?" added Tristan. "Another of her little traps. Let's face it, from what I hear she's played you like a gypsy's fiddle."

"You're talking about the mother of my child-to-be. I would ask you to show more respect."

"A mini-Miles maybe. Elspeth will be over the moon if it's a boy. You'd doing your bit to keep the illustrious family name from dying out."

Miles bit down hard on his lip. "I've no idea of the gender. I should never have told you." He turned and grasped Tristan by the arm. "I need you to swear you'll never reveal it, even to Elspeth. Do I have your word?"

"OK, OK. Swear on my old grandmother's corsets, hope to die and all that. How on earth did you do it, Miles? I thought Bernie the billionaire kept her trapped in her golden cage. How did you penetrate....?" Tristan guffawed at his pun. "He's not going to be a happy bunny if he finds out. I wouldn't like to be in her shoes when he does."

"He's not going to find out. Is he?" Miles' icy stare caused Tristan's smirk to vanish.

"Well, well, Miles, you must've pressed all the right buttons. You always thought of me as a Lothario but let's face it, I'm not in your league. You may be over the hill but you've got two women after your body and one's giving you a child. You've done the manly thing Miles, sowing your seed. I'm dead jealous..." Tristan rattled on, burying his head in his hands. "You don't know how lucky you are, leaving something, someone behind you. You're not just a scrap of useless cosmic dust like me." As Tristan withdrew his hands, Miles could see tears welling up. "Sorry. It's the wine talking. You think I'm a hopeless drunk. You're dead right. It's just that I can't function without it...in any department, "he added, pointing downwards. "You Miles are a stud, a fucking stud."

Tristan's raised voice was beginning to turn heads. "I need some fresh air," said Miles rising from his seat. "And remember what I said about not breathing a word of this upon pain of..."

"OK, OK" said Tristan, making an attempt to rally himself. "Mum's the word." He eyed his empty glass. "Think I'll just hang on for a bit."

✦

Miles emerged into the dreary West End late afternoon, far from steady on his feet. He had been far more affected by Tristan's lachrymose expression of envy than he had at first realised. It went deeper than that; he had been profoundly moved. Had he not received unequivocal evidence of new life with his imprimatur on it, his genes? Was that not something to celebrate, to shout from the rooftops even? Miles sauntered off down the street, his head clearer now. Seeming to float as he took each step, he began whistling some half-remembered tune. He had not whistled consciously for as long as he could recall. A traffic warden glanced up from issuing a ticket as Miles passed by. They exchanged smiles.

A curtain of rain swept down the street as if prefiguring his sudden change in mood. Reality struck home with the force of a fist between the eyes. As matters stood, the child would grow up to be a complete stranger to him. Bernie Prince would have no cause to question his paternity and Vera's progeny would be raised with no knowledge of its biological father. It had been true, as he acknowledged, that he had never taken any interest in 'ankle biters', a term he ascribed to his tiresome nephews when young. Yet the prospect of now being denied a role in the formative years of his own flesh and blood was, Miles now realised, unthinkable.

As he strode on, Miles' thoughts turned to practical matters. To rectify this situation would mean physically extricating Vera from Bernie's clutches. This would be no easy task and, even assuming she would agree to desert her billionaire, it would mean casting aside the doubts he Miles, harboured about Vera's true feelings for him.

The rain clouds parted allowing a milky sun to filter through. Miles paused and, tilting his chin upwards felt the comforting suggestion of warmth on his face. All remaining doubts and anxieties must be set aside. He knew now what he had to do.

✦

"I've just had the results. I have to see you." Miles could hear the palpable excitement in his voice as he spoke into the phone.

"I can't speak now. Bernie's close by. I have to go. But Miles..." Vera's voice had dropped to a barely audible whisper.

"Yes?"

"I couldn't be sure how you would react. Now I think I know. I'll call you later, I promise."

✦

"Miles? I need to speak to you."

"Can't it wait?" There was nothing he disliked more than being disturbed during his ablutions. He was balanced precariously with one foot in the bathtub and the other hovering above the slippery tiled floor as Elspeth began tapping frantically on the door.

"Jeremy's just rung. Apparently, it's all over social media."

"You know I don't look at that stuff," Miles called out.

"Well you'd better start looking now. They haven't named you yet but, according to Jeremy, it's glaringly obvious. It's only a question of time before it all comes out in the wash."

"Wait one minute, will you?" Still dripping wet, Miles bundled himself into his dressing gown and, slipping the latch, peered angrily round the door. Elspeth greeted him with a broad smile.

"What are you talking about? What's obvious?"

"That...that you're the real father ....of Bernie Prince's babe." Elspeth's excitement was rising fast.

"I can't tell you what this means to me, Miles. If it's a boy, the Mallalieu name will live on after all!"

✦

It had taken three hours and countless unanswered messages before Miles finally reached Tristan. According to Elspeth, he had left the flat at nine without saying where he was going.

"I know, I know...you're hopping mad, Miles. You've every right to be. I don't know what to say, it just slipped out. After you left me, I had another couple of drinks. Just about to call it a night when who should walk in but Charlie Elmwood...knew each other from Torygraph days. Usually try to avoid him. As creepy as ever but he offered to buy me a drink and you know how it is, one thing led to another. Opened my big mouth. Turned out Charlie's on his uppers. Got me feeling sorry for him. He's always looking for leads to flog. Said the bloke he knows at Mail Online pays a monkey for really juicy stuff. I'm sorry Miles. Mea culpa, mea maxima culpa. You're not going to slug me again, are you? God knows I deserve it."

✦

"I wanted you to hear it from me first, Marian. The press will be sniffing about. It was that low-life seducer of Elspeth's who tipped them off...I could murder him. You need to hear my side of things."

"What are you trying to tell me, Miles? It's not just some fake social media tittle-tattle? Anyway, what proof do you have, that it's yours?"

"I just got the lab result today. DNA. No margin of error." Miles paused. "It wasn't planned. I can assure you of that."

"Oh come on Miles, you know me well enough by now. I'm no prude. I got through two husbands for Christ's sake."

"I appreciate you not judging me, Marian, thank you."

"It's obvious though, isn't it? She's just trying to trap you, but there again, I would say that, wouldn't I?"

"You must think what you like. I was a fool to think that Tristan would keep his..."

"Stop beating yourself up, Miles. At least, you're off the hook as far as nappy changing goes. I can think of worse starts in life than having a billionaire for a dad. That is assuming she's going to keep it of course."

"Of course she'll keep it," snapped Miles, unnerved by this suggestion.

"He may make her have an abortion. Have you thought of that?

"He can't force her. It's her body."

"Am I reading you correctly here? Something in my water

tells me you seem quite keen on the idea of becoming a dad."

✦

"Was it you who told them?" There was fear and fury in Vera's voice when she called.

"No, of course not. It was Tristan."

"But you must have told him? Why in God's name Miles, do you trust that man?"

"Believe me, Vera, I regret it bitterly, but what's done is done. Where are you speaking from? Where's Bernie?"

"I'm back on the yacht. Bernie flew off to Moscow this morning."

"When's he due back?"

"Not for forty eight hours but he's seen the media stories for sure. So far I've heard nothing. I know him, he's punishing me with his silence." There was a pause. "Miles, whatever happens, I must not be here when he gets back. I'm scared of what he'll do."

"Hold on...are you in a harbour?"

"No. Damn it. Then it would be much easier to get away."

"Where's the nearest land?"

"Corsica. I can actually see the coast. But Miles, I'm a prisoner. I know the crew have been told to watch me."

"Haven't you got any friends on board? Anyone you can trust? What about that steward who looked after us ?"

"He got fired months ago." Vera paused. "There is one young guy. He's from St Petersburg and I know for sure he's come to hate Bernie."

"In that case, listen very carefully, Vera..." Now there was a need for decisive action, Miles had discovered an inner steeliness that kept the panic at bay. "You'll need his help to get off the ship without being detected. It must be done tonight. Do you hear me? Bernie may change his plans and come back early. What's the weather doing? Is there a full moon?"

"You sound like some navy commander, Miles. Not like you at all."

"Don't you see, Vera? We have to treat this exactly like a military operation. There can be no slip ups."

"OK, OK. Actually it's quite cloudy and I didn't see the moon last night. It's asking a hell of a lot of this guy."

"Just turn on the charm, Vera. It's not as though you haven't done it before."

"You make me sound like some bimbo, Miles."

"This Russian of yours is our only hope. We'll find out just how much he hates Bernie."

"He'd have to use the motor boat," replied Vera. "It'll be noisy."

"Tell him not to start the engine until he's well clear of the ship. Have you got that? Here is what you have to do now..."

✦

Having slipped out before dawn, Miles had hailed a cab in the street to take him to Victoria Station where he caught the Gatwick Express in time for an early flight. Shortly before take-off, he had received a text from Vera to say that, remarkably, the nocturnal escape had gone without incident and that she was now safely ashore in Porto-Vecchio. She urged him to contact her the moment he landed.

Crossing the tarmac at Ajaccio airport, Miles could feel his heart beating like a steam hammer. The plane had been only half full and he was through into the arrivals hall within a matter of minutes. The woman on the rental car desk remembered him from previous visits and enquired casually why he had come out of season. Miles made up some story about visiting old friends.

The roads from Ajaccio to Porto-Vecchio through the rugged interior were virtually traffic free and Miles made good time, despite the precarious hairpin bends which he negotiated at excessive speed. A little more than two hours later he drew to a halt by the harbour. To his relief, Vera answered his call immediately.

"I'm on my own, Miles. I'm very frightened. Bernie's going to send the crew to look for me, if he hasn't already, that is. Can you hear that sound? I'm pretty sure it's the helicopter from the yacht. I'm being hunted down. You have to come now!"

"They can't kidnap you in broad daylight."

"Don't kid yourself. Bernie thinks he's above the law. He's not going to just let me disappear out of his life without getting his revenge."

"Well, we're not going to let it happen, are we?" said Miles, impressed by his defiant tone. "You need to keep very calm and tell me exactly where you are now."

"Pensione Syracusa. It's in the back streets, hidden away. That's why I chose it. I'll text you the address. Come quickly now. I am getting some bad pains. The baby's been moving a lot in the night, like it knows something bad is happening to me. Miles, I need you here now."

Having given up the attempt to decipher a faded town map displayed by the quayside, Miles plunged the small Fiat through a maze of narrow, one way streets in what he took to be the direction of Vera's hotel. More than once he was forced to reverse his way out of an impasse, at one point scraping the wing mirror against a stone wall.

At the point of despair, he finally spotted a sign with an arrow indicating the Syracusa was fifty metres ahead. Leaving the engine running, he hurried into the lobby to find Vera huddled on a low chair in a corner with only her shoulder bag for luggage. Visibly shaking, she was clutching her belly. The young receptionist was staring at her concernedly, clearly unsure as to what to do.

"Thank God," said Vera. "What took you so long?"

"Map reading was never my strong point." As he held out his arms to help Vera to her feet, he was surprised by her unsteadiness.

Vera gave the receptionist a wan smile. "I'll be OK, now my partner's here."

Checking first that the street was clear, Miles ushered Vera out into the car. The clatter of a helicopter's rotor blades could still be heard over the town.

"Where we are we going?" asked Vera as the Fiat 600 hurtled over the cobbles, narrowly avoiding an oncoming scooter.

"We'll work something out," replied Miles. "The important thing is to get away from the coast. Put your seat belt on, you're carrying a precious cargo."

✦

After passing the outskirts of Sartène, the arid landscape, punctuated by clusters of holm oaks and granite outcrops, grew more familiar. Miles even recognised the spot where the fatal collision with the goat had taken place. He gave a shudder and drove on at high speed. Having reached the brow of a low hill, he applied the brakes and swerved off the tarmac in a cloud of dust. The car came to a sudden halt behind a screen of dense scrub.

"What the hell are you doing, Miles?" Vera was clutching the door handle, the other hand spread protectively over her bump. "Why are we stopping here?"

"This is the place I was looking for. Nearly missed it. We'll wait until it gets dark before moving on. Come on. I'll show you. There's somewhere we can shelter. Have faith in me, I beg of you."

Vera turned to Miles with a weary but affectionate look. "Don't think I am not grateful for what you are doing for me... and our baby."

Miles broke into a smile. "We need to leave the car here and walk. It's not far."

"Wait. There is something you must have. I meant to give it to you before." Vera delved into her bag and extracted a small envelope which she opened to reveal a memory stick.

"What's on it?" asked Miles, impatient to move on.

"You don't need to know for now. Just keep it very safe. If anything happens to me, then you must use it as you will. You could say I risked everything, my life even, to get it."

"Yet another mystery. Nothing about you Vera would surprise me anymore. Come on, we need to get going," replied Miles, sliding the envelope into his inner jacket pocket. Easing herself out of the car, Vera took Miles' arm as he guided her gingerly down the steep slope strewn with loose rocks.

"Be careful...it's slippery," he warned. A bird of prey which had been circling, nose-dived to the ground. They paused to watch as its rodent victim was lifted skyward, emitting a high-pitched squeal. The door to the chapel was unlocked. Dust-filled sunbeams filtered in from the high windows as Miles guided Vera towards the altar. He stood still, gazing at the statuette of the Madonna which had been returned to this place of pilgrimage after its Phoenician provenance had been debunked. Before he could reflect on this re-encounter, Miles was distracted by a cry from Vera. She was pointing to a trickle of clear liquid running down her left calf.

"My waters...they've broken."

"What...what does that mean?" asked Miles. His knowledge of the preliminary stages of childbirth was beyond rudimentary. Could Vera be about to miscarry?

"It means, Miles, that labour can start anytime now. We need to think what the hell we're going to do, unless of course you're going to deliver the baby yourself?"

"Here, you'd better take this." Miles could think of nothing else but to hand Vera his handkerchief.

"Right now Miles I haven't got the strength to walk even ten metres. Find me somewhere to rest. Not in this church, it spooks me out." She pointed to the Madonna.

Doing his utmost to keep a semblance of calm, Miles led Vera out of the chapel and into the small outbuilding at the edge of the clearing where the drinking session with the troubled priest had taken place. The gloomy, spore-filled interior looked as though it had not been visited for some time. Miles guided Vera over to the one battered but serviceable armchair. His attempt to first plump up the cushions released a cloud of dust which caused them both to break into a violent cough.

Collapsing into the chair, Vera closed her eyes and appeared to sink into an uneasy doze. Miles found himself a rickety chair which he positioned near the door to afford a view of the chapel and its approaches through the murky window panes. As far as he could tell, they had not been followed from Porto-Vecchio but it would be wise, he decided, to stay vigilant.

He was disturbed by a low moaning. Doubled up in pain, Vera was clutching her belly.

"It hurts so bad now. It looks like my contractions have

started. It can happen. The baby's two weeks early but it may be very quick, the second child.... Oh Miles, I'm so scared." Vera held out her hand which he grasped tightly. Her skin was strangely cool.

"Let's not panic. What's the emergency number in France? I can't for the life of me remember?"

Still immersed in the pain, Vera shook her head. "Try 911."

Miles extracted his phone. One glance at the screen had told him that his battery was dead. He discarded the phone in disgust. "Where's yours? She pointed to her bag and Miles began rummaging in it. "It's not here."

"Look harder."

Miles searched again. "I'm telling you it's not here," he snapped.

"I must have dropped it then. God knows where." Vera clutched at Miles' arm, her eyes flickering as another contraction engulfed her. "What are we going to do? I can't move. The baby may come any time now!"

Miles took a deep breath and expelled it slowly. He grasped her hands in his. "I'll have to drive back to Sartène and get help."

Vera looked aghast. "But... you can't leave me here alone?"

"Do we have a choice?"

"How long will you be?"

"An hour, maybe less." A cloud obscured the weak sun, causing Miles to shiver. He glanced through the window. A breeze had sprung up, creating snake-like eddies in the dust.

At first he thought it must be a mirage. The stooped figure of an elderly woman dressed in black could be seen heading slowly towards the chapel.

Miles attempted a friendly wave as he emerged. The woman let out a startled cry at the unexpected presence of an interloper in this holy place. She was on the point of vanishing into the chapel when Miles caught up with her.

"Madame, je m'excuse de vous déranger mais c'est ma femme..." He gesticulated frantically towards the outbuilding "Elle est enceinte et sur le point d'accoucher. Aidez-nous, je vous en supplie." The emotional appeal appeared to find its mark. After examining him quizzically, the woman was apparently satisfied enough to follow Miles. She gave a gasp on seeing Vera's condition and began probing the bump with her fingers.

"Who is this woman?" Vera sat upright with shock. "Where did she come from? Tell her not to do that, Miles." The woman was muttering in broad Corsican dialect which Miles could barely follow. "What is she saying? Tell me!"

"As far as I can tell, she says it's a bad idea to move you. Your labour's too far advanced. If the baby comes early, there could be complications. She has had five children herself. We're in luck though. It turns out her eldest daughter is the local midwife. She's at home now. Call it a miracle if you will."

Miles paused to decipher the next stream of verbiage. "There's a slight complication. Would you believe she has no phone? I explained that ours......anyhow, she's agreed to stay with you. I'm to ask at the café in the main square and they'll fetch her daughter right away."

"You can't leave me with this stranger!" Miles squeezed Vera's hands tightly. His gaze fixed on the contours of her belly. He leant over her and kissed her on the lips. "I'll be as quick as I can, I promise."

"You'd better go then," replied Vera resignedly. "The pain's gone for now but it will be back. Whatever happens, I love you, Miles, you know that, don't you? Go now."

✦

On his arrival in Sartène, it had taken no more than a few minutes to make contact with the midwife. She was clutching at the door handle as Miles threw the car round the tight bends oblivious to the possibility of oncoming traffic. The midwife kept repeating that she had urged her mother to carry a mobile with her at all times, adding: "But then the old are obstinate, are they not? Please, Monsieur, slow down a little or you will kill us both. And what good would that do your wife?"

The piercing wails of a newborn were carried by the breeze as they reached the edge of the clearing. Miles froze. The midwife tugged at his sleeve to urge him on. As they entered the outbuilding, her mother hurried towards them, blocking their view of the interior. She was clutching the blotchy, bloodstained creature to her chest, its tiny form swaddled in the folds of her black lace scarf. Her face was etched with grief as she tried to comfort the child.

It was only then that Miles' eyes adjusted to the gloom. The dark red stain was spreading slowly over the rough stone floor. Vera lay motionless, her skin porcelain white, her head slumped back in the chair, blank eyes focused on the ceiling. Miles dropped to his knees and held his palm to her cheek. The midwife meanwhile felt her pulse as if going through the motions. Guiding the arm slowly back to lie on Vera's chest, she turned to face Miles: "Ma mère a fait tout ce qu'elle pouvait, mais c'était trop tard Monsieur, hélas trop tard." Gazing towards the chapel, she crossed herself and muttered a prayer.

✦

The approaching sirens stabbed at the silence. It had taken less than twenty minutes for the local police and paramedic crew to arrive. A string of uniformed figures could be seen running past the chapel. As they entered the outbuilding, a stretcher was unfurled but after a brief assessment, there was little apparent sense of urgency. A policewoman took the baby from the midwife's arms and turned to display it to Miles."Vous avez un petit garcon, Monsieur. C'est bien, n'est-ce pas?"

The newly-minted pupils seemed to acknowledge his presence. It was uncanny to think that he had played any part in the creation of this perfect creature.

Locking his gaze with the child, Miles felt his despair supplanted by a surge of unadulterated joy, jolting him like an electric charge. It was as if his son's acknowledgment of their bond had freed Miles from the laws of gravity and he was empowered to soar effortlessly above the earth. This brief moment of euphoria was interrupted by the policewoman who led him gently aside."Je suis vraiment desolé pour vous Monsieur, mais Dieu merci, le bébé paraît en bonne santé, malgré le fait d'être prématuré. C'est vous le mari de cette femme malheureuse?"

Miles shook his head."Non. Mais c'est mon enfant."

The officer exchanged some muttered words with her colleague and turned again to Miles. "En tout cas, il faut emmener le petit tout de suite à l'hôpital a Propriano, Monsieur, pour un examen médical. En suite il sera pris en charge par la municipalité. Je vous donnerai leur numéro de téléphone au bureau. Maintenant vos papiers..."

"That's my child. You're not taking him anywhere!" shouted Miles, interposing himself between the officer and the door.

Miles made a sudden move to prise the baby from the policewoman's arms but she took two steps back and her male colleague blocked Miles' attempt, allowing her to break away.

"You've no right to do this!" he yelled."Je suis son père! Je peux le prouver!" Miles' anger was all-consuming. Yet, in the presence of new life, he succeeded in reining it in. He let the policewoman and child pass by without further incident.

The policeman turned to Miles with an unyielding expression. "C'est la santé de l'enfant qui est notre priorité avant tout, n'est-ce pas, Monsieur? Vous auriez certainement l'occasion de le visiter, j'en suis certain." Ignoring him, Miles turned slowly towards Vera's body. "Et je vous assure Monsieur que vous auriez la possibilité de voir votre amie après l'autopsie. Voila les numéros de téléphone pour nous contacter" He held out a printed card. Making no attempt to accept it, Miles allowed it to flutter to the floor. The policeman retrieved it."-Prenez-le Monsieur...s'il vous plait." Snatching it from him, Miles stuffed it in his pocket. He approached Vera's body, now shrouded in a green blanket.

CHAPTER ELEVEN

The making of Miles

"It's Miles...Miles Mallalieu."

"Miles, good God! I haven't heard a rat's fart from you ... since you joined the ranks of the academic rejects like me. How does it feel to be a non-person?" Miles was about to remind Doug Allardyce that he had gone public on his discredited research of his own volition but decided to let the provocation pass.

"Don't tell me you're after a career change?" added Doug. I can put in a good word for you, no problem."

"It's nothing like that. We need to meet, and it can't wait."

Miles' gravity in tone appeared to have the intended effect. "Sure. Why not?" replied Doug. " No point asking what it's about, I guess?".

"Tomorrow morning at nine at my health club. I'll text you the address."

"Your health club? Don't tell me you're on a fitness kick, Miles? Never too late, I guess."

Although riled again, Miles failed to react. "We can talk there without being disturbed. I've got something to show you, something you should see. I can't say any more than that."

"OK, man of mystery, your health club it is, just as long as I'm not expected to torture myself on all that masochistic equipment."

✦

Miles arrived early and had been keeping watch on the entrance from the members' café. He emerged to meet Doug who had appeared at the appointed time in formal office attire. Miles handed him a card.

"Day pass. You're my guest."

"Good God man, what's that?" Doug asked, indicating the maroon tracksuit which was slightly too large for Miles' now reduced frame. "Looks like unemployment suits you. You've certainly lost...."

"I'm here most days, it's become a bit of an adrenalin fix, you could say." replied Miles after they had settled in a corner of the café.

"I need to follow your example," replied Doug patting his belly. "How are things?

Vera Petrovna...Bad business that. It must've been a total nightmare."

"You could say that," replied Miles coolly. He had no appetite for Doug's commiserations.

"And what with you turning out to be the father of the child and all." Doug reached over to pat Miles consolingly on the back but Miles withdrew from range. "To be honest, I didn't know you had it in you," added Doug. "I guess Bernie's washed his hands of the kid. If it's any consolation, you do know why she left you for that bastard?

"She was seduced by the high life, I couldn't compete.

Simple as that," replied Miles dismissively.

Doug shook his head. "Wrong, my friend. That's what you were supposed to believe. Now she's no longer with us I can tell all. The truth is our counterparts in Moscow changed her orders. Having told her to drop you like a sack of potatoes, she was ordered to focus her charms on Bernie the Billionaire. They'd have used her daughter as a bargaining chip just like they did with her assignment to win you over. Threatened to throw the girl into a mental institution for the rest of her life. You look shocked. Does any of this surprise you?"

Miles shrugged. He had expected to command the agenda for this meeting from the outset and he was determined not to be deflected despite this revelation.

"You gotta see it from Vera's point of view," Doug continued. "She had no choice but to play the doting girlfriend and provide Moscow with updates on Bernie's nefarious activities, or at least what she could gather from pillow talk. I don't need to tell you that he's got his greasy fingers in every lucrative international pie from Azerbaijan to Zanzibar. You've been quiet so far. What do you think?"

Miles played with his coffee spoon. "Are you telling me that things had become so unbearable with Bernie that she was prepared to defy her orders from Moscow?"

"It sure looks that way. There is of course another explanation: that her feelings for you got the better of her, shall we say? Looks like she couldn't bear to be without you, especially in view of the baby. Messy business, emotions."

Miles rose suddenly from the table. "Are you OK?" asked Doug.

"Yes, yes...Call of nature," he called out as he hurried away.

Miles stood staring into the men's room mirror. He scarcely recognised his own reflection. The effects of the strenuous exercise regime he had undertaken since returning from Corsica had lent him a gaunt, haunted look. He needed space and time to absorb Doug's revelations. Vera, it now appeared, had cogent reasons for rejecting him which she could not reveal for fear of compromising Claudia. Perhaps he had suspected this all along but had failed to give her the benefit of the doubt? If only she had given the merest hint of her mission to entrap Bernie, any lingering suspicions about her commitment to him might have melted away. Fighting off self-pity, he strode out to rejoin Doug in the café.

"Before we go any further, let me get one thing straight," said Miles purposefully as he sat down. "I presume you're still doing the same job, protecting the interests of our two great nations?"

Doug nodded. "OK, Miles, I don't blame you for being cynical. The Agency's been good to me. Had a promotion as a matter of fact ... Assistant London Bureau Chief... great perks... beats academia hands down."

By now the café was beginning to fill up with other gym users who were rewarding themselves with sticky pastries after their early morning exercise regimes. "We'll have to find a quieter spot," said Miles, indicating to Doug that he should follow.

To Miles' relief, the changing area was deserted. He ushered Doug towards the lockers.

"Hold on, Miles. I told you, I've got gym phobia. What the

heck do you expect me to do?" asked Doug.

"Just read this." Miles had opened his own locker and extracted a foolscap envelope containing the print-out of the material Vera had handed him in Corsica.

"What is it? Is that what you've dragged me here for? Why all this cloak and dagger stuff?"

"You of all people Doug, should appreciate why," replied Miles. "When you've read it carefully, replace it in my locker and bring me back the key. I'll be waiting for you in the steam room. It's hardly ever used at this time of day. Now get undressed. You don't want to spoil that nice suit," added Miles, handing Doug the locker key and a towel.

"You do realise this is not in my job description, Miles? It had better be juicy."

Miles thrust the envelope into his hand. "I think you'll find it is."

✦

"Where the hell are you, Miles? I can't see a darn thing."

"Over here, in the corner. Give it a moment. Your eyes will adjust."

"I'm sweating like a hog on heat."

"You're supposed to. Stop hovering. Sit down."

"Are we alone?"

"Yes, Doug, we're alone."

"Okay, where did you get that stuff? Or can I guess?"

Miles nodded. "It took her months to cobble it together. She left it in my safe-keeping, in case anything should happen to her. She wasn't going to let them, or should I say you all, get away with it."

"Jesus, Miles, you do realise what this would mean if it all got out, assuming it's genuine of course?"

"It's genuine alright, it's easily checked. Vera made sure of that. And as to whether or not it reaches the public domain, well that rather depends..."

"On what?"

"On whether or not you agree to my modest request."

"Stop playing games, Miles, damn you!"

"If I am, I learnt the rules from you and your shady fraternity of dirty dealers, upholders of patriotic duty, call them what you will. And by the way, there's a copy deposited with my lawyer. She'll forward it to the press should I just happen to disappear without trace." Miles gave Doug an acidic smile. Doug's look of utter dismay was just visible through the clouds of vapour.

"Jesus, Miles! Can't we talk somewhere else? I've to get out of here. I've just been diagnosed with high blood pressure. This could finish me off. What is it you exactly want from me?"

"A meeting with your superiors...in the next twenty four hours. And when I say superiors, I mean the top of the pile."

✦

"You've got fifteen minutes." The brisk young special adviser who led them along the corridor gave Doug a look as if to say: 'This had better be as important as you maintain it is.'

The Home Secretary looked up from studying the Petrovna Papers. Her drawn, angular features reminded Miles of his mother at that age. As he took in the surroundings, Miles could not help noticing that his desk at the Department had been equally large. This comparison served to increase his bullish mood and he was now more determined than ever to force her hand.

"Well Professor, your late Russian friend was clearly very busy in her spare time. I'm surprised Prince didn't get wind of her activities." Pushing aside the papers, the Home Secretary rose and walked round her desk to confront Doug. "If it's any consolation Mr Allardyce, I think we can agree that Washington and Paris come out of this as badly as we appear to do."

"You should be aware, Home Secretary, that this is only a sample of what Dr Petrovna unearthed. There is more, much more," said Miles.

"Mr Allardyce tells me you're threatening to go to the media with this. I imagine there's little point in appealing to your sense of loyalty to your country, to the stability of the world order even?"

"None whatsoever," replied Miles.

"If you don't mind me saying so, Professor, you seem to be an unlikely blackmailer. Unless of course you have political motives?" She gazed at him over the top of her pince-nez spectacles.

"I hardly need to remind you, Home Secretary, that your security services were happy to blackmail me. This has absolutely nothing to do with my politics, such as they are. But if you press me, I would tell you that I have nothing but disdain for the current so-called world order. Even to an ivory tower relic like me, it's clear that it's built purely on self-aggrandisement and greed."

The Home Secretary raised her eyes. "Please spare me your lectures, Professor. Leaving your tenuous analysis aside, it might be more useful if I attempt to summarise my understanding of where we stand, and correct me Professor if I get anything wrong."

"By all means," replied Miles, exchanging glances with Doug who had the look of someone desperate to vanish through the floor.

"You would have us believe that this collection of financial information and emails demonstrates Mr Prince's success at buying of services and influence via kickbacks, bribes, call them what you will. In exchange for access to government contracts, it would seem that senior British government ministers both condoned and personally benefited from these deals to the tune of many millions of dollars. I seem to be the only member of the inner Cabinet who hasn't allegedly been the beneficiary of Mr Prince's largesse. Am I correct so far?"

Doug nodded, his expression darkening further. "There are also documents relating to sanction-breaking arms shipments to Syria, Iran and North Korea," he interjected.

"Let me continue," said the Home Secretary. "And sitting at the centre of this web is a loud-mouthed British-born billionaire who considers himself untouchable, who is as welcome in the Oval Office as he is in Downing Street or the Kremlin for that matter."

"I couldn't have summarised it better myself," said Miles with a wry smile.

"The Professor is worldly enough to know that if it comes to light, this material's toxic enough to bring down Western governments, including you British of course," interjected Doug. "Our enemies will think all their Christmas's have come at once."

"If it's cash he wants, then that's no problem," said the Home Secretary. Ignoring Miles, she turned to Doug who nodded in agreement. "He can name his price. I can assure you that Washington would chip in."

"But perhaps we're misjudging the Professor," she replied.

"Perhaps it's not money but rather his old job he's after?" She addressed Miles directly again. Her expression had changed to one approaching sympathy. "I imagine you feel hard done by, after all those marvellous programmes and all that painstaking research. You were badly treated. No question about it. That might be hard to fix, but not impossible. As it happens, the Vice-Chancellor's a good friend."

Unfazed by her conciliatory tone, Miles placed his palms on the leather surface of the desk as if laying out his cards. "You're wrong on both counts. It's neither money nor ambition that interests me. Let's just say that I'm someone who believes in fulfilling his personal duty, not to some abstract notion of national pride but to those who follow us."

"You're talking in riddles. I have limited time." She turned angrily to Doug. "Are you aware of what the Professor is demanding exactly, Mr Allardyce?

He shook his head. "He wouldn't say. He insisted on putting his terms to you himself ma'am."

"And put them I will," said Miles. "As you may be aware from the newspapers from which your government receives so much support, I am the biological father of the child Mr Prince had assumed to be his. After Dr Petrovna's untimely death, the boy, whose name is Selim by the way, has been taken into care by the French authorities. I fully intend to adopt Selim and raise him as my own son and nothing will be allowed to stand in my way."

"I see," replied the Home Secretary after a deep intake of breath. "I would not have thought that someone of your age...."

"My demand is simple," interjected Miles, "that you intervene with your French counterparts to ensure that the adoption process proceeds smoothly and quickly. Until it is complete, the incriminating documents will remain in my possession. Do I make myself absolutely clear?"

"You're asking a great deal, Professor. Our relations with the French these days are not what..."

Miles rose to his feet to indicate that, as far as he was concerned, the meeting was at an end. "I have every confidence in your abilities."

The Home Secretary sat silently for a moment, twisting her pen between her fingers. She then rose from behind her desk and approached Miles. "Tell me, Professor, are you seriously considering full-time fatherhood? Have you thought this through? Do you have a permanent partner? I imagine that will have a bearing on our case."

"I can fix that," replied Miles with a broad smile.

✦

"When I said I'd be prepared to take you on Miles, this is not exactly what I had in mind," said Marian with a knowing smile. They were distracted by the steady grizzling from the buggy. Selim had awoken prematurely from his afternoon sleep. They had reached the southern edge of Regent's Park where they strolled most days before stopping for tea at the café where mothers, and the occasional house father, gathered with their outsized buggies and pampered offspring.

"Bottle time," said Miles. Having extricated the formula milk from the giant baby product holdall, Marian wiped the teat before handing it to Miles. "Your turn. He needs to get used to you. Those specs of yours still scare him."

"Nonsense. Just you watch this," said Miles. Stooping down to Selim's level, Miles dangled the milk in front of him, while humming a snatch of the only nursery rhyme he recalled from his infancy.

Selim's sleep-filled eyes flared into life, connecting with Miles' briefly before the bawling began at full strength. Unfazed by this setback, Miles extracted a knotted red hand-kerchief from his top pocket and swung it back and forth in Selim's eyeline. Captivated by the movement, the pupils followed the handkerchief's arc. The crying ceased.

Miles gazed up at Marian with a self-satisfied smile. "The master's touch. Never fails to do the trick."

AFTERWORD

Twelve years later

"This is really cool," said Selim. "How long have you had driverless cars in St Petersburg?"

"We were one of the first to get one. This is a new model. You could say we've been very well looked after since Mum died," said Claudia. "Unless you're tired after the flight, maybe you want to go straight to the cemetery?"

Claudia parked the Mercedes by the gilded iron gates. "This way," she said, pointing into the heart of the small cemetery in the leafy suburb.

"This is not a grave, it's more like a mausoleum," said Miles, studying the Cyrillic inscription on the impressive polished marble edifice. "Who paid for it may I ask?"

"The Russian state of course. They forgave Mum for running away from Bernie. She had already passed them a lot. Not that she had a choice. She died on active duty as far as they were concerned and the SVR looks after its own." Claudia indicated the receding rows of immaculately tended graves fringed by closely-mown grass. "Everyone here is a hero of Mother Russia. They have special privileges, in the afterlife too."

"So it would seem," said Miles, impressed with the fluent English Claudia had acquired in her digital marketing role, as she described it. Miles turned round to look back at Selim who was dawdling. Miles was about to remonstrate with him when Claudia intervened. "Leave him. This is hard for him, you know. You've waited a long time to bring him here," she added.

"He wanted to come. He's still young but he senses it's important," Miles replied.

Claudia took Miles' arm. The punk look of her teenage years had been replaced by a well-tailored woollen suit and designer handbag. "To say Mum was a reluctant spy would be a massive understatement. Thanks to you, I know now she did it to save me and I have to thank her for that. They would have let me rot in an institution for years on some excuse that I was crazy after doing so many drugs."

"She talked about you a lot, you know. She worried about you but you made her laugh too," replied Miles.

"Now she's gone I have to live with the fact that I enjoy a good life paid for by a criminal regime," said Claudia.

"Why don't you leave?" asked Selim who had caught up with the adults and was listening in.

"It's not that simple. If we go, they will seize our possessions and all our money. As far as they are concerned, we have propaganda value as the children of a Russian hero. Our apartment's in the best part of town and the rent is pretty cheap. It's got a great view too. So you see, my husband and I are trapped like butterflies in a jar."

"What has always puzzled me is how did your mother come to the attention of the SVR in the first place?" asked Miles.

"That's easy. They look for people with a weakness. I was

that weakness. I got in with a bad crowd and got arrested more than once. She was always having to bail me out."

Claudia had not exaggerated the beauty of the twilight view from their 10th floor apartment along the Neva towards the Alexander Nevsky bridge. Over dinner on the terrace, Miles turned to Selim who was wolfing down his steak. "Go on, ask her. I know you're dying to," Miles whispered.

Selim gazed uncertainly at Miles, finished his mouthful and then turned to Claudia. "What was my mother...our mother like?"

"I thought you had a mother in England, Selim. How is Marian by the way?"

Selim scowled. "She's fine. I meant my birth mother of course."

Claudia shrugged. "She was not a hands-on mother. But I know now she would have done anything, anything at all to protect me." Claudia turned to indicate Miles. "Anyway, maybe you should ask your father?"

About the author

Martin Thompson began his writing career scripting original drama, drama documentaries and literary adaptations for BBC Television and ITV. As Associate Producer on Granada TV's *Brideshead Revisited*, he had a major hand in adapting Evelyn Waugh's book as an award-winning television series. His co-adaptation of Brian Moore's novel *The Temptation of Eileen Hughes* gained one of the largest audiences for a BBC single drama ever recorded. As a print journalist, he has contributed feature articles to the national newspapers and magazines over many years. *The Vera Conundrum* is his first venture into full-length fiction.

Printed in Great Britain
by Amazon

77703483R00161